STONEHILL
BOOK TWO

friends
without benefits

Cover design by Okay Creations
Book layout by Lori Colbeck

ISBN-13: 978-1-950348-03-9

Printed in the United States
29244LVS00002B/199-297

STONEHILL
BOOK TWO

friends
without benefits

MARCI
BOLDEN

PINK SAND
PRESS

So many people have helped me along the way, but none as much as my husband who has shown unwavering support, even in the toughest times. Thank you.

CHAPTER ONE

"You bastard," Dianna seethed, sending a coffee mug sailing across the kitchen. The ceramic shattered into several large pieces, and dark liquid streaked across the floor. She scoffed. The mess perfectly represented her life—broken and wasted.

Still queasy from spending the morning sitting in front of a judge, Dianna forced back the urge to vomit. She swallowed hard against the saliva forming in her mouth. The questions wouldn't stop echoing through her head, and she was forced to relive the unfortunate moment when she walked in on her husband screwing some overly tanned blonde on Mitch's desk. The hearing to decide the split of their marital property had stirred the anger and humiliation she had worked so hard to bury.

She clenched her jaw and dug her nails into her palms to stay in the here and now, but the memory of Mitch thrusting into another woman filled her mind.

"Stop it," she hissed, recalling Mitch's smug smile as the judge made his ruling.

In yet another blow to her once perfectly constructed life, Dianna had been awarded the house along with a suffocating mortgage, bills, and a pathetic amount of child support. The judge opted out of giving her alimony. Since their children were all but grown, he hadn't seen a need for Mitch to support the woman whose only job for the last twenty-two years had been raising kids and keeping a home. When Sam turned eighteen in seven months, any financial obligation Mitch had to his family would end.

And that was it. Case closed. Mitch could move on. He was free.

She inhaled deeply and ran her hands over her cheeks, dragging her tears away as she breathed again, this time more slowly.

Her best friend, Kara, was trying to help Dianna meditate into a healthier mental outlook, one that was less bitter and homicidal. She wasn't convinced she wanted to kill Mitch any less, but she had to admit learning how to take a moment to calm down had helped tremendously since he'd left her.

In with the good energy, out with the bad. Inhale peace and serenity, exhale anger and frustration.

She was nearly relaxed when the doorbell moaned out a deep bass tone, filling the house with a mournful sound that echoed the misery that now filled it. The bell used to ring a happier, high-pitched tune, but like her marriage, she had ignored it for too long and the chime was slowly and pathetically dying. Whoever was at her door—Kara, she suspected—was about to get an earful about showing up when she'd been clear she wanted to be left alone.

Dianna slowed her angry stride as she neared her glass-paned front door. A man she didn't recognize stood bundled in an expensive-looking tan overcoat with a cobalt blue scarf wrapped neatly around his neck. He gave her a friendly smile, and crow's feet wrinkled the smooth skin around his light-colored eyes.

"Mrs. Friedman?" he asked as she cracked open the door.

Mrs. Friedman? Not for much longer. "Yes?"

His smile faltered. "I'm sorry to bother you. My name is Paul O'Connell," he offered hesitantly.

Her heart squeezed tight in her chest, and her breath rushed from her lungs as surprise punched her hard in the gut. "O'Connell?"

"Michelle was...*is*...my wife."

Michelle. Better known as *that home-wrecking-husband-stealing slut.*

"Oh."

Dread settled heavy on her chest, and the bile she'd just barely managed to contain started churning in her gut. She still hadn't made sense of what had happened in the courtroom. She'd gotten stuck with so much debt and no way to pay for it. Seeing her husband's mistress's husband standing at her door only added to her sense of confusion, and she couldn't quite think of anything else to say.

She stared at the stranger for longer than what could be considered polite, trapped by some kind of morbid fascination, taking in the man who had been replaced by her husband. He wasn't as tall as Mitch, and instead of thinning hair, Paul O'Connell had a head full of silver strands. His face was long and thin. His straight nose came to a slight point, but not so much that it was unattractive. If anything, it drew attention to his full lips.

Paul's gaze skimmed over her as well, and Dianna suspected he was making the same assessment—comparing her to his wife. His young, skinny, overly made-up wife. Dianna had already accepted that she failed miserably compared to Michelle. Dianna was still thin by most standards, but she wasn't fit like Michelle. Years of running kids to games and events while stuffing cheeseburgers and fries down her throat hadn't done her body any good. She had curves, and not all of them were as subtle as they used to be.

She hadn't stepped a foot inside a salon since before Mitch had left, and she cringed thinking of the gray strands that had crept into her long chestnut mane. Months of sleepless nights had made the bags under her eyes dark, and her near-constant frown had deepened the lines around her mouth and between her brows.

So, no. Compared to Michelle, Dianna wasn't beautiful. She probably wasn't even that pretty anymore. But at least she was wearing the slacks and blouse she'd put on for her divorce hearing instead of the oversized T-shirt and yoga pants that had become staples of her wardrobe. If nothing else, at least Paul O'Connell's initial comparison between her and his wife was of Dianna dressed nicely instead of the depressed bum she'd turned into. Maybe, just maybe, his first thought wouldn't be acknowledgement of why Mitch went looking for another woman.

She forced herself to slowly exhale the breath she'd been holding. *Out with the bad.*

"May I come in for a moment?" he asked.

Startled from her thoughts, she looked into eyes that were similar in color to his hair—silver with flecks of black.

"Please?"

Dianna stepped aside and gestured toward the hooks on the wall. He shrugged out of his coat and hung it and his scarf next to hers.

"Would you like some coffee?"

"That'd be great. Thank you." He tugged the sleeves of his suit coat down one at a time, a gesture that made her think he must be anxious.

She swallowed as her own nerves started to feel frazzled. "It's decaf."

"That's perfect. I'm trying to cut my caffeine intake. I haven't been sleeping well."

"I'm sure that has less to do with coffee than other things."

He pointed to the broken cup and spilled coffee on the kitchen floor as they entered. "Did that help?"

Dianna's cheeks warmed with embarrassment. "No. Now I'm just pissed that I'm down a mug and have to clean up the mess."

Paul's quiet laugh was a nice sound, even if it wasn't heartfelt. She couldn't recall the last time someone had laughed in her kitchen.

She opened a cabinet and pulled out two mugs. "How do you take your coffee?"

"Cream, if you have any."

"It's caramel-flavored."

"That's okay." He kneeled down and gathered chunks of broken mug.

"Don't. I'll clean that up."

"I don't mind. I've broken a few dishes myself. Although, I usually empty them first."

She laughed as her cheeks warmed again. "I'll remember that next time."

He dropped the pieces into the stainless steel trash can next to the counter. While she filled their mugs, he wadded up several paper towels and wiped the coffee from the floor. "I'm afraid that's all the cleaning I'm good for."

"That's plenty. Thank you."

Paul washed his hands as the silence in the room pressed down on Dianna. She still had no idea why he was in her kitchen. He finally quit fussing and sat across from her at the table, adding creamer to his coffee. He stirred the liquids together much longer than needed. Each passing of the spoon added tension to the knot in Dianna's stomach.

Finally, the quiet overwhelmed her. "Mr. O'Connell?"

He stopped stirring and met her gaze. "Paul. Please."

"Paul, why are you here?"

He tapped the spoon on the edge of his mug before deliberately setting the utensil on a napkin. "I feel like I should—" He drew a deep breath and let it out loudly. "I'm sorry. For what she did."

Dianna creased her brow. She didn't know what she'd thought he was going to say, but that certainly wasn't what she'd expected. "Why?"

"*Why?*"

"Why are you apologizing for your wife sleeping with my husband? Didn't she cheat on you as much as he cheated on me?"

"Yes, she did."

"So, why are *you* apologizing?"

"Well, someone should. Don't you think?"

His question caused her heart to sink. Her eyes, which were still irritated from her last bout of tears, began to sting anew. Yes, she did deserve an apology. Too bad the two people who should be sorry for what she was going through hadn't offered it, though.

"Yes." She swallowed in an attempt to tame her emotions. "I think someone should. But I don't think that someone should be you."

"Maybe, maybe not. Michelle sure seemed to think her affair was my fault."

"Oh, yes. I didn't understand his needs anymore."

"I smothered her. I needed her too much, put too much pressure on her to make me happy." Paul looked far more than miserable. He looked guilty, as if he were to blame for being on the receiving end of his wife's adultery.

Dianna wanted to assure him he wasn't, but she didn't have the conviction. She'd failed to buy that line too many times to try to sell it to him.

Instead, she looked into her mug so she couldn't see the pain in his eyes. "Do you know... Do you know what today is? Is that why you're here?"

"No. I've been meaning to stop by. I just hadn't worked up the courage."

"Oh."

"What is today?"

Her lip quivered. "My divorce hearing was today. I just got home not too long ago, actually."

"Jesus," he whispered. "I'm sorry. May I ask how it went?"

The stress of the judge's decision hit her again. "Um...not well, actually. I don't know how I'm going to..." She gestured lamely at the room around her. "Our oldest son, Jason, is away at college and Sam is a high school senior, so the judge didn't feel that Mitch owed me anything. I've been a housewife since we got married. I'm not sure how I'm going to...you know..." She pushed herself up from her seat when a sob started building in her. "When I get stressed, I bake. Would you like some cookies?" She didn't wait for him to respond. She grabbed a container off the counter. "I made oatmeal and chocolate chip. Sam ate most of the chocolate chip ones as soon as they were out of the oven, but there's plenty of oatmeal left." She put the container on the table and sat down. "Please. I don't need to eat all those myself."

He hesitated for a moment but then grabbed a cookie. The silence returned as he took small, measured bites. She watched until she noticed the light glimmering off his wedding band.

"He wasn't wearing his ring," she said before she could stop herself.

Paul lifted his brow in question. "I'm sorry?"

"This morning. At the hearing. It's the first time since we were married that I've seen Mitch without his wedding ring."

Paul nodded, as if he understood exactly how much that had hurt her. He took the last bite from his cookie and carefully brushed the crumbs from his hands onto a napkin, which he folded and used to wipe the table clean. He chased the bite with a sip of coffee. "Look, there's never going to be a good time for me to ask this, but I was wondering…"

"What?"

"I, um, I'm so sorry, but… When Michelle told me she was leaving me, I asked her what she was going to do when this *great guy* she was seeing decided he didn't want to leave his wife. She said that wasn't going to be a problem because you had caught them together. Is that true?"

Her mind again flashed to the night she'd walked in on Mitch and Michelle having sex in his office. He had her bent over his desk as he gripped her hips and thrust into her. Those sounds returned—skin smacking against skin, soft moans. Michelle's black skirt was hiked up onto her back as she clung to the edge of Mitch's desk, and his face was tense as he neared release—a look Dianna knew all too well.

She winced. The painful memory still struck her like a slap across the face. "Yes, it's true."

Paul's cheeks lost a few shades of color, as if she'd confirmed something he was trying to deny. "Well, now she's trying to say that her relationship with your husband wasn't sexual."

Dianna laughed bitterly. "Oh, it was sexual, all right."

The muscles in his jaw tightened, and she had the sudden urge to reach out and stroke his face to help ease his tension. Her hand was several inches off the table before she realized what she was doing and stopped herself.

"I know it can't be easy for you," he said quietly, "especially having just gone through your hearing, and I swear to you I wouldn't ask if there were any other way, but would you be willing to testify on my behalf? About when you caught them together."

Dianna exhaled slowly. She'd give anything not to have to think about her husband's affair ever again. She didn't want to remember how completely unexpected catching Mitch cheating had been. Or how she'd walked into the room, as she'd done a hundred times before, carrying his still-warm dinner. How the Tupperware container fell to the floor. How the sound of plastic crashing onto the tiles pulled the lovers from their passion as shock rolled through her, numbing her mind and freezing her body. She didn't want to remember how Mitch gasped out *her* name or how the woman he was screwing lifted her face off his desk to smirk.

Dianna closed her eyes, and hot tears slid down her cheeks. She didn't try to hide them. Her pain overpowered her dignity, as it had so many times in the last six months. How could she care that this stranger was seeing her cry when her heart hurt so much?

"Please, Mrs. Friedman—"

"Dianna," she spat. "I *really* hate the Friedman part right now."

"Please, Dianna. She doesn't deserve alimony."

She scoffed. "God. Wouldn't that be something? I was informed that *I* don't deserve alimony because I am capable of work. Yet you think *she'll* get alimony when she's got my husband to support her."

"I think she's got a hell of a better attorney than you had."

"Yeah, well, I couldn't afford to pay the bills, support our children, *and* pay for a top-notch attorney, could I?"

He didn't respond.

"Sorry," she whispered as her angry words lingered between them. "That wasn't directed at you."

"I know. I have no right to ask you to go through this again, but she will get alimony if I don't stop her."

"Well, that hardly seems fair. To either of us."

"So, you'll testify?"

Those damned memories flashed through her mind again, bringing with them the familiar stinging and crushing of her soul. She reached into the container sitting between them and grabbed a cookie. She'd likely eaten a dozen the night before, but that didn't stop her from biting into another as she debated.

"Yes," she said, finding a conviction that she hadn't felt for a long time. "Yes, I will testify."

CHAPTER TWO

*P*aul admired Dianna. Though she was very clearly hurting, she maintained her composure as the judge presiding over the dissolution of Paul and Michelle's marriage asked deeply personal questions. Dianna's voice quivered from time to time, but she sat, straight as a rod, explaining how the events unfolded that night. Sniffing occasionally, she described walking in on Michelle bent over Mitch's desk. Paul's gut twisted as details he really didn't want to hear came to light.

The judge sighed audibly when Dianna testified that while Mitch buttoned his slacks and fastened his belt, Michelle took it upon herself to let Dianna know they had already found a new place and were all but living together. All that was left was getting rid of their respective spouses.

Paul should have been thrilled at the disgusted look the judge cast toward his soon-to-be-ex-wife, but he was hurting too much. Not just for his betrayal but for Dianna's. She looked so vulnerable and small. He wanted to wrap her in his arms and promise she was going to be better off in the long run. Maybe not today, maybe not tomorrow, but someday she'd look back and realize she deserved so much better than that lying bastard she'd married.

Michelle glared at Dianna as she left the chair next to the judge, but Dianna didn't pay any attention. She walked, eyes straight ahead, to a plastic chair a row behind the table where Paul sat with his lawyer. Paul noticed, however, and when Michelle looked at him, he cocked a brow, silently daring her to act like she didn't deserve to be called out for her behavior. She smirked at him, and Paul wondered what he had ever seen in the cold-hearted bitch.

He turned in his seat and waited for Dianna to meet his gaze. When she did, he looked into her bloodshot blue eyes and offered her a supportive smile, which she returned. United in their misery. Solidarity in their heartache and humiliation.

Relief washed through Paul when the judge announced that Michelle wouldn't get a single penny in the divorce settlement. What had been Paul's, namely the house and bank account, would remain Paul's. Once the courtroom was dismissed, Dianna slid her arms into her coat and stood. She had just moved into the aisle between the rows of hardback chairs when Michelle stepped in front of her, blocking her exit.

Paul ground his teeth together as he pushed past his attorney. Michelle had already put Dianna through enough, and

Paul had done his share by asking her to relive her husband's betrayal. He'd be damned if he'd stand by while Michelle rubbed her nose in the mess all over again. Luckily, Michelle's lawyer reached the women first and gently but firmly pulled Michelle away.

"I'm sorry," Paul said as he approached Dianna. "For whatever she said."

"She didn't say anything. She just glared at me like the petulant child she is."

Paul's lip twitched, but he couldn't quite bring himself to smile. He lowered his face and ran his hand through his hair. Suddenly exhausted, his breath left him in a rush and his shoulders sagged.

Dianna put her hand to his upper arm and squeezed it gently. "Are you okay?"

He nodded before meeting her sympathetic stare. "I am so sorry. I know testifying wasn't easy on you."

"Couldn't have been any easier for you to hear than it was for me to talk about."

"Probably not. But at least I didn't have to actually live through catching them. I always knew she could be callous, but the way she acted toward you that night... I'm sorry."

Dianna's focus drifted to the chair where she'd testified as she dropped her hand from his arm. "Well, congratulations. On not having to pay alimony. I guess that's what I should say, right? Congratulations?"

"Yeah, I guess that's what you'd say. Thanks. I mean it. *Thank* you."

"You're welcome."

"If there's anything I can do for you…"

Dianna was shaking her head before he even finished. "There isn't. Thanks, though."

Paul's attorney approached them and patted Paul on the shoulder. "I'm heading out. If you need anything else, give me a call. Mrs. Friedman." He nodded in her direction.

Paul looked at her when they were alone. She appeared stronger, more confident now, but pain still reflected in her eyes. He wished he could say something to make it better for her, but his experience told him reassurances and sympathy didn't offer much comfort. Instead, he gestured toward the exit. "May I walk you out?"

"Sure."

She waited where she stood while he gathered his coat.

As they left the small hearing room, he asked, "Is your divorce final?"

"Not yet. Any day now, my lawyer says."

Paul scoffed. "Happy holidays, huh?"

A sad smile tugged at the corner of her mouth. "This will be the first Thanksgiving in a very long time that I won't be hosting a houseful of in-laws."

"Well, maybe there are one or two perks to this situation, huh?" He smiled when she laughed. "I want to thank you again," he said a few moments later. "I know you didn't want to testify."

"Actually, I was happy to do it. Just to stick it to her. That sounds cruel, but..."

Paul came to an abrupt stop. One of the things Michelle excelled at was making other people feel guilty for her wrongdoing. She'd stay out late, not call, not respond to his text messages, and then twist things around until Paul felt he was in the wrong for expecting her to check in with him. She was like a teenager testing her boundaries instead of a grown woman with a husband to consider. The fact that Dianna would feel an ounce of remorse for telling the truth about Michelle pissed him off.

"She deserves everything that happens to her," he snapped. "If she hadn't been so damned full of herself, neither one of us would be here right now. Neither one of us would have had to tell the judge what a selfish bitch she is."

Dianna stared for a moment before tilting her head and giving him that damned sympathetic look again. "The rage sneaks up sometimes, doesn't it? I thought I'd be beyond that by now, but just last night I screamed at a telemarketer for a good three minutes before slamming the phone down. The poor bastard asked to speak to my husband and had to listen to me tell him where they all could go."

"I don't want you to feel bad for being here today, okay? She deserved the consequences for what she did. She *more* than deserved the consequences."

Dianna nodded. "Yes, she did. I wish I could have taken a picture of her face when she realized she wasn't getting alimony. That was fantastic."

"Not nearly as fantastic as my face when I realized I wasn't going to be *paying* alimony." He pushed the heavy glass door open, and they stepped out into the cold autumn day.

She pulled her coat more tightly around her and glanced up at the heavy gray clouds that were threatening rain. "Well, it was a good day for both of us, then."

"Better than anticipated. Where are you parked?"

She nodded toward the north end of the street. Paul gestured to the south.

"Well." She sighed. "I guess I'll see you around."

"Right. I hope, despite everything, that you have a good Thanksgiving, Dianna."

"You, too, Paul."

He started to thank her again, but he stopped the words. He'd said that already. And he'd wished her well. There was nothing left to say. She tilted her head slightly, patiently waiting. He couldn't seem to figure out what he wanted to say.

Finally, she saved him by gesturing behind her. "There's this café a few blocks away. It's a little rundown, but the coffee's good. Care to join me?"

He hesitated. He could say no and go back to work, where he'd likely bark at anyone who tried to talk to him. He could go home, look around his empty house, and replay Dianna's testimony over and over in his mind. Maybe he could go visit his sister and hear how she'd told him so. Or his brother and hear how he'd be better off.

He nodded after a moment. "My treat. I owe you."

She opened her mouth as he put his hand on her elbow and turned her toward the direction she had pointed moments before.

"Don't argue," he insisted.

She pressed her lips together and shoved her hands in her pockets. They walked nearly a block in silence before he glanced down at her.

"Are you okay?"

She laughed softly, but the sound was hollow. "I just thinking about..."

"What?"

"Nothing. It's...embarrassing."

He nodded, not wanting to push her, and silence fell between them again.

After a few moments, she said, "The last time I sat in a restaurant to have coffee with a virtual stranger was my first date with Mitch. We talked about everything from sports to art. I was *so* enamored by him. I couldn't believe he was interested in me." She looked up at Paul, and her wistful smile faded as her eyes grew wide. "Not that having coffee with you is a date. Nothing even close to that."

He grinned at the way her stumbling admission made her blush.

"I just... It made me think... I'm going to shut up now."

Paul chuckled. "I know what you're saying. The smallest thing can trip a memory. There's a woman at work who wears a perfume similar to Michelle's. I have grown to detest that woman for absolutely no logical reason other than that she smells like my ex. I met Michelle at a bar. I was there with some co-workers celebrating a win on a case. A bunch of men in suits and ties drinking too much. I'm sure she felt like a fox in a henhouse. Just pick one, any one, and go for the kill."

"Do you really think that's all you were to her? A target?"

"Honestly? Yes. A target with the money to give her what she wanted. And when I started to get wise to her, she moved on to her next target. Unfortunately, that was your husband. For that, I'm sorry."

"Please. I'm smart enough to realize a person can only be led astray if he chooses to be. He's as much to blame as she is."

Dianna pointed to a hand-painted wooden sign that read *Stonehill Café*. He pulled the door open, and they stepped inside. The small restaurant was rundown, as she'd said, but the dining area was cozy, and he wondered why he hadn't visited the place before. They sat at a table by the big window overlooking the street. Pumpkin-spiced something filled the air, and Paul inhaled deeply as they slid into a booth. Within moments, they'd ordered two coffees and uneasiness fell between them again.

Finally, after taking a sip of the brew that had just been set before her, Dianna said, "I feel like we need to just get this out of the way."

He lifted his brow. "What?"

"How long were you married?"

"Ah." He sat back but left his drink on the table. "Three years. You?"

"Twenty-two."

He winced as sympathy stabbed at his heart. "Ouch."

"I've stopped thinking about how much time I wasted being married to him and have started thinking about getting the most out of the time I have left. He hated the theater and concerts and all those things that I loved doing, so eventually I just stopped asking to go. I'm hoping to get season tickets to the community theater next year. And I keep checking the concert lineup in the city. Mitch hated the noise and the crowds, but I love the excitement. I can't afford to get tickets yet, but one of these days I will." She bit her lip, as if embarrassed by what she'd blurted out. "I'm rambling. I'm sorry. I do that sometimes."

"No, you're excited. That's good. Post-marital bucket lists are good. It gives you something fun to think about. I remember doing that after my first divorce." He grinned when she stopped lifting her coffee cup to her lips. "I'm two for two now."

"I can't imagine going through this twice," she said quietly. "I don't think there's enough of my heart left to survive it."

Paul leaned forward and toyed with his silverware. "You heal over time. Forget how much this part hurts."

"Like childbirth, right? If you remembered how much it hurt, you'd never do it again."

He smiled. "I've heard that."

"So, how much did you get marked off your list before getting remarried?"

"Not nearly enough. I think I'll revisit it."

The light mood faded a bit.

"I didn't mean to upset you," she said quietly.

"You didn't."

"I did. I can see it on your face."

He shook his head. "It's just that...when I married her, I thought I had things figured out. I thought I had *her* figured out. I knew she was self-centered and narcissistic, but when I was with her, I felt like I was part of something that had been missing in my last marriage. I thought, even though she was always more about herself, that we were partners in our marriage. I took care of her and convinced myself that she took care of me as well. I can see more clearly now. Everything between us was as one-sided as my family kept telling me it was. I loved her. But I don't know if she ever actually loved me. When I think of the things I gave up to be with her...I feel so stupid."

"Love has a way of blinding people, Paul. That doesn't make you stupid any more than my contentment made me stupid. I trusted my husband. That's what I was supposed to do, right? Believe him. Support him. Trust him. We weren't stupid. We were betrayed. It's hard to remember that sometimes, but *that* is the truth."

Paul looked out the window, but he wasn't seeing the world around him. "How are you doing, Dianna? Really?"

"Really? I don't know. Mitch is gone. My boys are grown. All of a sudden, I'm alone. I go to work, I come home, and there's so much quiet I want to scream, but I can't seem to bring myself to do anything else." She stared into her coffee cup. "It feels like too much work to try to find a new place in the world."

"Your friends and family—do they still look at you like someone died?"

"Yeah. The ones who still talk to me anyway. An amazing number of people have simply disappeared from my life. But those who have stuck around have more pity than I care to see."

"The disappearing friends thing happens every time a relationship fails. People either feel like they have to choose sides, or they don't know what to say so they simply avoid you. Don't take it personally. At least you know who you can count on."

She nodded. "So how are you? *Really?*"

Paul turned his mug in his hands. He wasn't quite sure when coffee cups had become so damned fascinating, but somehow that was easier than looking at Dianna. The way she gazed at him, with so much understanding, made him want to talk about things he'd rather not.

"I'm still pissed as hell," he admitted. "I gave that woman everything she wanted. *Everything*. I did everything I was supposed to do. I sent her flowers, took her out, took her on vacations. She called it smothering. She said I expected too much out of her. The only expectation I ever had was for her to keep her goddamned legs closed when I wasn't around." He raked his fingers through his hair and exhaled harshly as he realized what he'd said. "Sorry. I shouldn't have said that."

"That's okay." Her voice was soft. Supportive. "You have every right to be furious. It sounds like you were a wonderful husband."

He shook his head. "My first wife left me because I was a stranger to her and our kids. I thought my job was to provide for them, and that's what I did. I worked day and night to give them security. But I was wrong. They needed more than that. I swore I was going to do better with Michelle, so I paid as much attention to her as I could. And guess what? That was wrong, too."

Dianna frowned. "For a long time I thought all the anger I felt was because I caught them. But now I realize it's not what I saw. It's what I felt. It's how he made me feel for so long, how I *let* him make me feel. Like he was doing me a favor by being married to me. Like I had to give up everything *I* wanted because I owed him the perfect wife and children and home."

Something in the way she said the words, the way her voice was so melancholy, made the need to protect her from something unseen rise in Paul's chest. "Was he bad to you?"

She lifted her gaze to his and shook her head slowly. "No. He was just...*indifferent*. He'd been so indifferent for so long that I didn't even realize it anymore. I was his maid and his chef and his errand girl, but I stopped being his wife a long time ago."

"You deserve better than that."

"Well, so do you."

"You know what? They did us a favor. I mean, sure we're miserable as hell right now, but at least they gave us the opportunity to move on and find someone who wants to be with us. Now that I think about it, I'm lucky to be getting out before the facelifts, implants, and liposuction begin. You better believe in the next five years, her lips and chest will be as fake as her veneered teeth."

Dianna's mouth widened with obvious shock at his bitter assessment, and then she grinned. "Oh, Mitch can't handle high maintenance."

"Well, he's getting high maintenance. I mean like...bow-before-me-and-blow-smoke-up-my-ass-every-day maintenance."

A laugh erupted from her, despite the hand she put to her lips. Her amusement tickled his, and for the first time in months, a genuine laugh escaped him. She dropped her hand to her chest as she rolled her head back and the musical sound coming from her grew louder.

"I can't..." She inhaled and shook her head as she met his gaze. "Oh, he has no idea what he's getting into, does he?"

"Probably not. She kind of springs it on her victims when they least expect it." He was breathless, his words coming out between gasps.

She chuckled harder. "He's going to be so miserable."

"Good. Maybe he can share his misery with her." He shook his head as he regained control of himself. "God, I haven't laughed that hard in months."

"Me either." Leaning forward, she put her elbow on the table and supported her chin in her palm.

Her smile, her *real* smile, eased the crease between her brows, making her look much younger. Her eyes lost the haunted shadows, and the parentheses around her mouth creased upward instead of falling into a scowl. She was quite beautiful when she wasn't looking so damned sorrowful. Not that she hadn't been attractive when she was throwing coffee mugs in her kitchen. He hadn't missed the graceful way she moved or the soft curve of her face that day. But he certainly hadn't noticed it as strongly as he was with her grinning at him.

He must have stared too long. She averted her gaze as she cleared her throat.

"So what are you going to do now?" she asked.

"Well. I'm going to finish my coffee. Then I'm going to go home."

"And?"

He swirled his drink as the momentary lapse in his misery ended. "Hide in my office, probably. There's too much of her in that house. I can't escape her. I keep thinking I should just sell it and get the hell out while I'm still sane."

Sadness returned to her eyes. "I'd love to stay in my house. My boys grew up there, but I can't afford to keep it. However, with the holidays coming up, there is no point in putting it on the market right now. And my SUV. The payments are outrageous, at least for my budget. I have to trade down, but I don't even know if that's possible."

Paul ignored the voices in his head—his sister telling him Dianna's problems weren't his concern and his brother warning him not to be the hero to yet another damsel in distress—and asked, "Did you get possession of the car at your hearing?"

"Yeah. The car, the house...the bills." She looked down. This time when she blushed, it clearly didn't have anything to do with him staring at her. "I'm sorry. It's just that I've never had to worry about money before, and now it's all I do. Mitch got a great job right out of college, and I had babies. That doesn't pay well." She laughed softly.

"Not to impede your newfound independence or anything, but call me when you're ready to trade in the SUV. My brother has a dealership. He'll take good care of you." He reached into his suit pocket.

She took the business card he extended toward her. "Paul O'Connell. Attorney at Law." She lifted her brows. "A lawyer? Wow. You seem so human."

His mouth opened, but he couldn't quite find the right comeback. She threw her head back and laughed.

"I'm sorry," she said after a moment, but the smile on her face said otherwise. "That wasn't nice of me. I...sincerely. I apologize."

"I can tell by the way you're still grinning."

She pulled her lips between her teeth, but her smirk remained. Paul couldn't help but be amused right along with her.

"Thank you," she said. "I mean it. I appreciate it."

"You're welcome. And my sister is a real estate agent, so, you know. Let me know about the house, too. I bet she can sell it for you in no time."

Her grin faltered at the mention of selling her home, and guilt kicked him in the gut. Before he could apologize, she grabbed a handful of her long red-brown hair and made a show of looking down at the strands.

"I would kill for a makeover. Do you have a sibling for that?"

"No. But if you're ever in need of a fancy dress, my cousin does own a boutique on the square."

"What? *Really?*"

He warmed at the way she scrunched up her nose. "We're a diverse bunch."

"I guess so. Well," she said thoughtfully after a moment, "I'm a fantastic cook, so if you need help feeding yourself, let me know. I'm also very good at decorating, party planning, and raising money for the booster club."

"Good to know."

A young couple entered the café and shared a kiss as they slid into a booth. Paul's good mood faded at the reminder of what he'd lost. That was how it seemed to go. For a moment he'd forget how miserable and alone he was, but there was always something to remind him. He shook the sting away and focused on Dianna again.

"This has been really nice," she said.

"It has been. Thank you. I didn't think my afternoon would go this way."

She finished her drink and turned her empty cup from side to side a few times. Paul watched, almost as mesmerized by her turning cup as he'd been by his.

"He left me almost six months ago now," she said quietly, "and I'm still in this tailspin. I can't seem to get my footing. It's just...a constant up and down of emotions. It's going to get better. Right? It'll even out?"

He sighed when she lifted her gaze and the sadness had returned to her eyes. "Yes. It will get better."

She hesitated before reaching into her purse and pulling out a pen and a scrap of paper. She scribbled on the paper and held it out to him. "This is going to sound like I'm trying to pick you up, but I'm not. You're one of the few people who doesn't make me feel like my life is completely ruined because Mitch left me. I don't want to feel like that, so call me if you need to talk or just want to grab a coffee."

He took the paper and then reached for the business card she'd set on the table. He flipped it over and wrote on it. "That's my cell phone." He slid the card back to her. "Anytime, anything you need. Okay?"

"Okay."

She tucked the card into her purse and zipped it while he put her number into his pocket. Standing, she slipped her arms in her coat sleeves and buttoned up the front while he dropped some cash onto the table. He walked with her to her SUV and held the door as she climbed in.

She looked at him and smiled slightly. "Thanks again, Paul."

"Thank you, Dianna." He closed the door and walked away. Looking up at the sun trying to break through the clouds, he tried to figure out how his day had gone from horrid to not so bad in less than an hour.

CHAPTER THREE

*D*ianna held the mouse of her computer so the pointer hovered over the button she needed to click to accept Paul's social media friendship request. They'd already traded numbers. It wasn't like Facebook was some kind of personal commitment, but even so, she wasn't sure they were at that level. Whatever *that* level was.

She stared at the button for at least a minute, debating the pros and cons, before she slammed her finger into the mouse and clicked to accept. Divorce certainly made social media an awkward place to be. She hadn't changed her relationship status from married to single. She'd just hidden that bit of personal information.

What had Mitch said about the end of their marriage? Had he simply changed his relationship status from *married to Dianna Friedman* to *in a relationship with Michelle O'Connell* without comment or explanation? Now the site would be announcing to the world that she was *friends with Paul O'Connell.*

"What the hell?" she asked, speaking to no one since she was the only one home.

She was about to log off the computer and find something else to do other than dwell on what the online community would think of her new friend, when another friend called her cell phone.

Dianna put the phone to her ear. "What's up, Kara?"

"Who's the hottie?"

"What hottie?"

"The silver fox you just friended on Facebook."

It was almost as if Dianna had foreseen this very conversation just a few moments ago. "He's my husband's girlfriend's husband."

"*What?*"

"Exactly."

"Wait. Back the hell up. He's the husband of the woman who stole your husband?"

Dianna closed the window on her computer. "Yes."

"Why are you friends with him?"

"I told you I was testifying at his divorce hearing today."

"That explains nothing."

Dianna pushed herself up from the kitchen table to get a glass of water. "We had coffee after the hearing and offered to be each other's support system."

"Are you...you know...*interested* in him?"

"Kara, I'm not even divorced yet. I'm not *interested* in anyone."

"Well, before you decide you are, know that he still has a lot of pictures of that slut on his page."

She imagined Kara, strawberry blond hair twisted in a messy braid, squinting at her computer as her reading glasses sat unused atop her head. Kara had been on social media for all of three months—thanks to Dianna's insistence—and already had learned the finer art of snooping. "You're stalking him? Already? I just friended him five minutes ago."

"I'm creeping his page as we speak. His privacy settings won't let me read his status updates, but I can see all his pictures. He's handsome, isn't he? Why the hell would she leave him for Mitch?"

Dianna shook her head. Kara had known Mitch in high school, and they hadn't exactly been friends. The first time she'd met Kara, Dianna could sense her distrust of Mitch. In a strange way, it was what had drawn Dianna to Kara. Everyone else, it seemed—even Dianna if she were honest—had been fooled by Mitch's charming smile and soothing laugh. It was nice to meet someone who looked at him with suspicious eyes.

Right now, however, Dianna didn't want her friend's perspective on things. "I have to go, Kare."

"Want to come to yoga with me in the morning?"

Saturday classes were free, so Dianna had no excuse not to go. "Yes," she said, even though she knew she would probably sleep in. "No. Maybe."

"You have commitment issues. That's okay right now. But you should work on that before you guys get serious."

Dianna opened her mouth to argue, but Kara's laugh cut off as her friend ended the call. "Jerk," Dianna muttered as she dropped her phone.

She looked at her beckoning laptop as she took a long drink from her glass. Finally, she set her water down and went back to the computer.

"Don't do it," she whispered to herself. The words had barely left her before she reconnected to the Internet. She opened Facebook, clicked on Paul's name, and looked at his page.

His profile said he was married, though it didn't specify to whom. She clicked on his friends and searched for Michelle's name. When she didn't find it, relief washed over her. Had he still, by some sick twisted need for torture, been friends with his wife, Dianna would have had an undeniable urge to look at her page. She maneuvered back to Paul's wall and scrolled through his status updates. There hadn't been many in the last few months. The ones that had been posted were mostly commentary on the weather, sports, or saying he was somewhere with someone he'd tagged in the status.

Nothing he said was very revealing. The pictures, however, told of what appeared to be a happy marriage. Photos of him with his wife seemed endless—parties, barbeques, on vacation someplace with palm trees, and holiday after holiday.

Looking at Michelle's smiling face, even if she wasn't standing next to Mitch, made Dianna's hands shake and her heart race. She felt like she was breaking Paul's trust somehow, and even though she felt guilty and didn't want to see how happy Michelle had pretended to be, she couldn't stop. She flipped through his photos, her heart pounding harder and her stomach tightening more and more until she had seen every one, including their beach wedding.

Michelle seemed to have played the part of doting wife well, at least in public. Paul must have been completely blindsided when she told him she was leaving.

"Poor guy," she whispered to herself.

Dianna navigated away from Paul's photos and into her own, just to see what he would see if he chose to snoop through her social media profile—which she assumed he would. Her status updates, much like his, had been sporadic in the last few months. Where his few had been about weather, hers were about Sam and Jason.

While Mitch was in a few, her photos were mostly her smiling next to her sons or her friends. She hadn't even realized how much of her life she had been living without her husband. Where was he? Had they really been that far apart for so long?

Dianna frowned as she closed the window again. She texted Sam to see if he was going to be home for dinner. When he responded that he wouldn't, she pushed herself up and grabbed a container of leftovers from the fridge to eat while watching a movie. Alone.

Paul stared out the window of his front room. The house was too quiet. It hadn't bothered him the last six months since Michelle had gone. He had no idea why it was bothering him now. He hadn't missed her loud music, with the thumping bass and lyrics he supposed were intended to be clever. Perhaps if he were a drunk twenty-something in a club, he would have thought they were.

He chuckled to himself and took another pull of his brandy. Michelle had told him he'd been fun when they'd gotten married but he'd become such a bore. He wasn't a bore. He'd finally just accepted that she was never going to grow up, and he was tired of spending all day every day at work listening to excuses and whining from his clients and coming home and listening to excuses and whining from his wife. So what if he wasn't up for dinner with half a dozen of her friends after being in court all day? So what if he didn't want to spend every single weekend tailgating or going to bars like a damned college student?

That's what he got for marrying someone so much younger, he supposed. That's what Matt and Annie had told him. His siblings certainly didn't hold any punches.

He looked at his computer when it made a noise. Setting his glass on the coffee table, Paul swiped the mouse until the screen lit. Dianna had accepted his friend request. He wondered if she'd debated accepting as long as he'd debated sending. He wasn't much for social media. He signed up for Facebook mainly to keep up with his kids. They were both in college, and other than texting, this seemed to be the only way to be sure they were still alive. He had, however, felt compelled to friend Dianna to get a voyeuristic look into her life.

After clicking on her name, he looked at her page. He scrolled through, noting that six months ago, there was a significant drop in the number of people on her wall. She hadn't been exaggerating when she'd said her friends had abandoned ship as soon as Mitch left her.

He couldn't help but smile, though. Her life, even after Mitch, seemed so much more together than his. It was clear from the photos that her sons adored her. Her friend—Kara, according to the photo tags—looked like a modern-day hippie, whereas Dianna looked more like the soccer mom type. A mixed pair, but it apparently worked for them. They were laughing in most of the photos.

In just a few minutes of snooping through Dianna's social media, he thought he had more in common with her than he ever had with Michelle. The irony that he'd altered his entire life to suit a woman who left him because he wasn't what she wanted wasn't lost on him. She didn't want kids—she was too much of a kid herself—so he'd lost what little ground he'd gained with his sons when he'd married Michelle. He saw them occasionally but not nearly as much as a father should.

He'd put distance between himself and his siblings because even when they weren't telling him what a mistake he'd made, he could see their disapproval in their eyes. Friends? He'd never really had many of those. Most of the people he knew were through Michelle, and much like Dianna, they'd picked sides when things had gone to hell—and most hadn't chosen his.

Who the hell needed them anyway? He didn't. His life was much quieter without the parties his wife felt compelled to throw. He looked at a photo of Dianna with her boys and wondered what kind of get-together she'd host. Somehow, he doubted it would be like a frat party gone wrong.

Paul closed the page and leaned back with his drink, wondering why it even mattered.

♪

Dianna winced, her hamstrings screaming in protest as she leaned forward to try to touch her toes. Why had she done this? Why hadn't she just stayed in bed like she'd wanted to?

"So, what's he like?" Kara whispered from the yoga mat beside her.

"Who?"

"The husband."

"Paul?"

"Yes, Paul."

Dianna exhaled slowly per the instructor's direction and frowned at her friend, who was effortlessly leaning over her bent and twisted legs. Dianna kind of hated her at the moment. "How did you get so flexible?"

"Don't change the subject."

The woman on the other side of Kara wasn't exactly glaring,

but she didn't have the serene look that was supposed to go along with doing yoga.

"Shh," Dianna hushed. "We'll talk later."

She was relieved when the class was told to go into *savasana*. Lying flat on her back taking deep breaths? Yes, *that* she could do. She tried to clear her mind, but Kara was relentless.

"Is he as cute in person as he is in his pictures?"

Dianna exhaled much faster than would be considered relaxing. She imagined Paul smiling, that real smile he flashed when they'd shared a few laughs. "Yes."

Kara grinned as if she'd learned some great truth.

Dianna rolled onto her sit bones and crossed her legs as she put her hands into prayer. Several more deep breaths, a well-wish spoken, and the class ended.

"Do you like him?" Kara asked.

"We spent twenty minutes drinking coffee and talking about how horrible our spouses are. I don't think that qualifies as *liking* him." She started rolling up her mat. "Besides, I am not the least bit interested in having a man in my life." Slipping her shoes on, Dianna did her best to ignore Kara's concerned stare.

"He's been gone six months, Di."

"Six months is nothing compared to twenty-two years. When I'm ready, I'll be ready, but it isn't going to be with *her* husband."

"I'm just tired of seeing you so down on yourself," Kara said as they walked out of Stonehill Community Center.

"I'm fine."

They stopped in front of Kara's car.

"Come to lunch with me."

"I can't. I have a ton of stuff to do before Thanksgiving."

"Do you and the boys want to come to our house for dinner?"

Dianna chuckled, imagining the chaos that would be a holiday at Kara's. She had a way of taking in strays who had nowhere else to go. Dianna's amusement faded when she realized that she'd become one of those wayward souls with no family of her own to share the holiday. "No. I can manage."

"I know you can, but you don't have to."

"This is my life now. I have to face it sometime."

"I'm proud of you. You're doing great." Kara brushed a strand of hair from Dianna's face.

It was that kind of maternal touch from Kara that Dianna needed and hated at the same time. Kara had become an emotional rock for Dianna, but Dianna was determined to make her way through her divorce on her own. She had to prove to herself that she wasn't as weak and co-dependent as Mitch had made her feel. Even so, she couldn't help but smile at her friend. "Then stop trying to fix me."

Kara hugged her. "I'm a fixer. It's what I do."

"I know, but..."

"You want to find your own way. I get that. I really do. Don't forget to drink lots of water. You'll be stiff as a board tomorrow if you don't."

Dianna gave a weak salute as Kara climbed into her car, and

then she walked several more spaces before getting into her SUV and dropping her head on the steering wheel. Even though Kara's heart was in the right place, Dianna wished she would stop trying so hard to make her life better. How could things possibly get better when her entire life was slipping through her fingers?

CHAPTER FOUR

*D*ianna didn't need another hassle. She didn't need *another* stressful moment in her life, but that was exactly what she was getting. Jason had come home for the holiday, and she and her sons had immediately sat around the kitchen table, where they debated how to handle their first holiday as a broken family. The discussion had gone downhill quickly, and both her kids were pissed off.

"I'm not going," Sam said for what Dianna was certain was the tenth time since they started discussing their plans. "No way in hell I'm acting all *Brady Bunch* with that cunt."

Dianna closed her eyes. "Do *not* use that word in my house."

Jason threw his hands in the air. "Well, we can't just not see Dad."

Sam lifted his brows sarcastically. "Yes, we can."

"*Mom*, tell him."

Dianna shrugged her shoulders. "He's seventeen, Jas. He can do what he wants."

Sam pushed himself up. "Except say cunt."

"Except *that*. Where are you going?"

"Megan's parents invited me to go out to dinner with them tonight. They feel bad that I've been abandoned by my father."

"All right, listen," she said. "I'll have dinner ready whenever you plan to be here. All you have to do is tell me when you are going to your dad's dinner. That is all I need to know."

"I'm not," Sam said. "Don't wait up. I plan on staying as late as I can to avoid the empty shell that was once my home."

Dianna chuckled as he left, but her grin faded when she noticed Jason glaring at her. "What?"

"You let him get away with everything."

She didn't say what she was thinking, but she silently considered how much her eldest son sounded just like his father in that moment. Mitch always seemed to have a disapproving tone when speaking of Sam, who preferred his guitar and friends to books and studying. "What exactly is he getting away with?"

"What are you going to tell Dad if Sam doesn't show up for Thanksgiving?"

"*I'm* not going to tell your dad anything, Jason. That's not my job anymore. All I need to know is when you guys plan to eat *here* so I can have dinner ready."

"So, you're just going to let Sam skip out on spending any part of Thanksgiving with Dad?"

"What do you want me to do? Drag him over there and

supervise his every move, just so that he spends quality time with your dad and his new girlfriend?"

Jason lowered his gaze. "Fiancée."

Dianna's stomach dropped like a rock, and a sour taste filled her mouth. *Fiancée?* They weren't even divorced, and Mitch was engaged? She swayed in her chair as her heart slammed against her ribcage.

"He called this morning to let me know." Jason's voice was quiet, as if saying the words softly wouldn't inflict as much pain on his mother. "He said he was going to wait until after the divorce was final, but she found the ring, so... I'm sorry, Mom."

She gave him a pathetic attempt at a reassuring smile, even though her eyes had filled with tears. "It's okay."

"It's not. It's not okay. What the hell is wrong with him?"

Dianna hushed him as she reached out and stroked his hair, but as he always did when she tried to comfort him, he shook his head and snuffled back his tears.

"Sam's right. We shouldn't go. Grandma will understand. I don't want to meet her. I don't want to pretend like I'm okay with this. It sucks. *Dad* sucks."

"But he's still your dad. No matter what happens, what he does, or...who he marries, he's still your dad."

Jason stood and pushed his chair in. "Let's do our usual Thanksgiving thing. Parade in the morning, eat around lunchtime, and then we'll help you get the tree set up. Okay?"

"Okay."

"I told the guys I'd be over to hang out. I'll see you later."

"Bye. Jason?"

He stopped walking away and faced her.

"I love you."

"Love you, too, Mom."

Then he was gone, leaving her sitting alone at the table. She was tempted to call Sam. His anger over the engagement must have been the reason he refused to spend the holiday with his dad. She hated, absolutely loathed, that Mitch was so thoughtless toward their children.

How did he think Jason and Sam would react to their dad walking out on their mom and getting engaged to someone else so quickly? How could he think this would be okay with his sons?

Almost as much as she hated what he was doing to the boys, she hated that he could still hurt her. But her lip began trembling as she ran the news of his engagement through her mind again.

sh

Paul smiled when he saw Dianna sitting at the same table where they'd last shared coffee and conversation. He'd considered calling her several times, but every time he'd hesitated, not sure what he would say. When she'd called him, he'd smiled as soon as he saw her number on the caller ID. She'd sounded a lot less excited when he answered, but he didn't let that bother him. However, when she looked up at him, her skin was pale and she had bags under her bloodshot eyes. She looked worse now than she had sitting on the witness stand talking about her husband's affair.

"Hey," he said tentatively.

"Hi." Her voice was hoarse, and she cleared her throat before speaking again. "I was waiting for you before I ordered."

He waved a waitress over. "Do you know what you want?"

"Just coffee. Thanks."

He placed their order as Dianna stared blankly out the window. Whatever was going on, she definitely wasn't okay. Several minutes later, the waitress filled their coffee mugs and set a brownie and a slice of cheesecake on their table.

She looked at the plates and then creased her brow at him.

"You looked like you could use something sweet."

Her lip twitched, but she didn't fully smile.

"What's wrong?"

Tears welled in her eyes and rolled down her cheeks, and Paul let out a slow breath. Nabbing a napkin from the stack on the table, he handed the far-from-soft paper to her as she took a few slow breaths.

"What happened?"

She lifted her gaze to him, and even more tears fell down her cheeks. "They're getting married."

The words stole his breath. For a moment he had a flash of standing on a beach, Michelle smiling up at him as she vowed to be his wife for the rest of their lives. But the memory faded quickly, and he was back in a café staring at Dianna. He pushed his plate away. "That was fast, huh? I mean, we're not even legally divorced yet."

"Neither are we." She looked down at her wedding bands.

He looked at his as well, and he had to wonder why he was still wearing the gold band. It wasn't like either of their spouses deserved the show of loyalty a wedding ring represented. But he hadn't been able to remove his yet, and apparently neither had Dianna. At least not until this moment, when she tugged the bands off and tossed them aside.

"I thought you should know," she said quietly.

"I guess we really didn't mean that much to them after all, huh?"

He glanced up and immediately felt like a jackass for his comment. Her face scrunched and her lashes grew wet with tears as her lip quivered.

"Oh, God, I'm sorry, Dianna. I shouldn't have said that."

"No, it's true." She snatched up a napkin, dabbed at her eyes, and took a breath.

"But I shouldn't have said it."

"How could he just walk out of our marriage and into another one without a second thought? He couldn't. Not if he cared. Not if he..." She gasped in a failed attempt to calm herself, and more tears fell down her face. "Not if he loved me. Even just a little bit."

Grabbing her hand, now devoid of her wedding rings, Paul squeezed it tightly in his. She used the other hand to cover her face. Sliding from his booth and into hers, he ran his hand over her back and did his best to soothe her. After a minute, she sniffed and reached for another napkin.

"I'm sorry." Her voice was hoarse. "I thought I was done crying over this."

"When did you find out?"

"This afternoon. He told the boys. Jason told me."

"How are they handling it?"

"Better than me. I just don't understand." She lowered her head, and her long dark hair fell like a curtain, hiding her face from Paul.

He tucked the strands behind her ear. A tear had fallen down her nose and was on the verge of dripping from the tip. He used the knuckle of his pointer finger to wipe it away. "I don't either. I don't know what they wanted from us."

She put her hand to her face to hide her emotions, but she didn't seem to be able to control the ragged breaths she was taking. Paul didn't know her, didn't know a thing about her, but seeing her heart breaking in front of him was tearing him apart. He slid his arm around her and handed her more napkins.

"I'm sorry," she said after several minutes.

"It's okay."

"No, I didn't ask you here to dump on you like this."

He squeezed her shoulder. "I don't mind." Oddly, he didn't. Soothing her somehow kept him from thinking too much about how much this was hurting him. He'd loved Michelle—maybe too much, like she'd said, but he tended to be an all-in kind of guy, and just because she'd left didn't mean he'd pulled his heart out of their marriage yet. Part of him, for reasons he couldn't quite understand, kept expecting her to change her mind. Though, he was certain—or so he hoped—that he'd be too smart to take her back if she did. Michelle being engaged, however, seemed to be the slap in the face Paul had needed to accept that his marriage was indeed over.

Dianna finally glanced over at him. "I swear I don't normally get hysterical in public. This is so embarrassing."

"No, it's not. You were just dealt a pretty hefty blow."

"I don't know if I'm going to survive this. It's killing me."

"You will survive. I'll make sure of it."

She flicked her gaze to him. "That's very noble, Paul, but you have your own problems."

He stared at her for a long time before he clutched her hand. "This is a tough time we're going through, and we need all the help we can get. We'll take turns being miserable, huh?"

She offered him a slight smile. "Well, I certainly took advantage of my turn today."

"And I'm sure I'll take advantage at some point, too."

She took a deep breath and seemed to relax a bit. "I spent so much time falling apart, I didn't even ask. How are you? I kind of dropped a bombshell on you."

He lowered his face and exhaled slowly. "I'm not surprised, I guess. She's not the type to take care of herself."

"It still hurts."

He nodded as he processed the knowledge that his wife was getting married. They were silent for some time before he pulled his hand from hers and lifted his cup to his lips. His arm was still around her as he sat silently, drinking his coffee.

She picked up her fork and took a bite of the brownie. "Maybe this will fill the black hole of agony I have inside, hmm?"

"If that doesn't work, try brandy. It has amazing healing powers."

"I'll try that tonight when I should be baking pies and wrapping presents, but I can't even..."

"What?"

Dianna sighed and put her fork down again. "Nothing."

"Come on. Don't shut down on me now. What were you going to say?"

"Our Thanksgiving tradition is to watch the parade, eat, and then we put up the tree and stuff it full of presents. By the time we go to bed Thanksgiving night, Christmas has taken over the entire house."

"He may not be there, but your kids are. You can still do all that."

She gnawed at her bottom lip as she nodded.

"That's not it, is it?" he pressed. "There's something else?"

Her cheeks flushed. "I, uh, I got a job after Mitch left, but...I can't afford to stuff a tree full of presents this year. I can barely afford *any* presents this year." An embarrassed-sounding laugh left her, and she shrugged. "They understand. They're old enough to know about finances and all that, but it doesn't make it any easier for me. I've always been able to provide for them.

Well, Mitch has always been able to provide. I guess *I* never was."

"You provided them with plenty."

She nodded. "I got them a few movies and CDs, things like that, but it's a far cry from the laptop and gaming systems they've been asking for. They're going to be so disappointed in me."

Paul was quiet as she lowered her face. As she reached for another napkin, he reached for her discarded wedding bands. There were three rings: a plain gold band, one with a large marquee cut diamond, and a band—likely to celebrate an anniversary—that was filled with diamonds. Sliding the rings onto the tip of his finger, he examined them for a few moments. "You could sell these."

"Not good for anything else, are they?" she asked after a moment.

He stood, dropped the rings into his pants pocket, and then reached for his coat. "Come on."

"What are you doing?"

He helped her to her feet and held her coat open until she put her arms in the sleeves.

"Where are we going?"

Instead of answering, he took her hand and tugged her out of the café and down several doors. A bell jingled to announce their arrival as he pulled her into a small pawn shop. The man behind the counter, an elderly gentleman who reminded Paul of his father, welcomed them.

"How much for these?" Paul deposited Dianna's rings on the

glass display case. "And this." It was a struggle to get his wedding band over his knuckle, but once he did, he set it down next to hers.

After fifteen minutes of bartering, Paul guided Dianna out of the store and toward his car. "I know this guy who runs an electronics store. He'll have what you want for your boys."

"Paul, we didn't get enough to get what they want. I mean, you did a great job haggling with that guy, but do you have any idea what a new laptop costs?"

He opened the passenger door for her. "Trust me. We have enough."

She stopped in front of him and tilted her head in that sympathetic way she had the day of his trial. "I hate to take the wind out of your superhero cape, but we don't."

"This guy we're going to see—I worked a deal that kept him from serving a very long jail sentence. He said he owes me. We're going to take him up on it. Trust me." He winked at her. "We have enough."

"You're going to pull in a favor from a criminal to get my boys Christmas presents at an extremely discounted rate?"

"He was never convicted."

Her lip trembled again, but this time she smiled as tears filled her eyes. She hesitated, as if unsure of herself, before throwing her arms around his neck and hugging him tightly.

Paul had suggested that Dianna fill her emotional void with brandy, but the best she could do was a cheap bottle of wine. The boys were in the den cussing at each other over a game while she kept herself busy pretending that it wasn't one of her favorite nights of the year. They had decided not to go to Mitch's, which had caused him to call her nonstop. She'd finally unplugged the landline and turned off her cell phone. She half expected him to show up at the house, but he hadn't. Other than that, Thanksgiving had been peaceful, and knowing she had presents to put under the tree, as she had every year since her sons were born, had made her first holiday as an almost-divorcee much easier to get through.

Turning her cell phone back on, she ignored all the pings of new messages and missed calls. She snapped a photo of the tree and sent it to Paul with a message.

It's beginning to feel a lot like Christmas, thanks to you and your criminal clientele.

She'd barely put her phone down when it rang. She was expecting it to be Mitch again, but her phone identified the caller as Paul.

"Hey, you."

Instead of responding to her greeting, he said, "The tree looks nice."

"Thanks. Did you have a good day?"

He let out a loud sigh. "Not in the least."

Dianna took a moment to analyze his voice. "You sound a little drunk."

"Nah, not too much."

"Paul?"

"I tried calling earlier. I wanted to tell you Happy Thanksgiving." He was speaking more slowly, as if trying to sound sober but doing a terrible job.

She creased her brow. "I turned my phone off earlier."

"Oh."

"What did you do today?"

"I just…you know…stayed home."

"Alone?"

"Yeah. Yeah, it was fine. The kids had stuff going on with their mother, and I didn't…" He exhaled again. "I wasn't up for company."

"Are you up for company now?"

"You don't have to—"

"We're in this together, remember?"

Paul was quiet for so long, she began to wonder if he had hung up on her. Finally, he rambled off his address and gave her confusing directions.

She walked to the den and waited to be noticed, but Sam and Jason were too entrenched in a video game. "Hey, guys, I'm going to take some leftovers to a friend. I'll be back in a while, okay?"

They mumbled responses, confirming what she already knew—they wouldn't even miss her.

CHAPTER FIVE

*P*aul opened his door before Dianna climbed out of her car. He'd been standing in the window, brandy in hand, waiting for her. Actually, he'd been standing there most of the day, trying to ignore the fact that his day wasn't filled with the sounds and scents of the holiday.

"I hope you're hungry." She held up two covered dishes. "I brought plenty to eat."

"I'm starving."

He gestured for her to enter, taking the dishes from her as she passed. She toed off her shoes and looked around his contemporary living room, with its orange-red accent wall and abstract sculptures stuck in white box shelves. He followed her gaze around the room and realized he probably should have cleaned up a bit before she arrived.

She slowly turned her eyes back to him.

He laughed quietly. "Not what you expected?"

"Not exactly."

"The mess or the colors?"

She lifted her brows. "Both."

"I haven't been much in the mood for cleaning. As far as the ugly-ass walls, I told you she's everywhere here. *'Contemporary is where it's at.' Pfft*! I don't think she knew what the hell she was talking about. If I hadn't owned this place when we got married, we'd have been living in some horrible warehouse loft downtown. She did the best she could to make this place into what she wanted, but she hated the house as much as I hated her fucking decorating."

Dianna creased her brow, and he ran his hand through his hair and then gestured to the right toward the kitchen. He sat at the island while she started unloading his dinner. She didn't ask. She simply started opening cabinets and looking for what she needed, and he let her.

"Remember when you said you were good at decorating?" he asked.

She found the plates and set one on the counter. "Yeah."

"Can you help me?"

She stared at him for a long time, probably gauging just how much he'd had to drink. Rather than confess the excessive amount of alcohol in his system, he took another gulp and set his near-empty glass aside.

"I can hire someone, I guess."

"No. I can help. I *will* help. But ask me when you've had a little time to sober up. Is it okay if I make coffee? I'd really like some."

He nodded and sat back as she figured out the coffee pot. He could have helped, but he didn't seem to have the energy. He'd tossed and turned the night before, rolling his life over and over in his mind. Thinking about every moment he could recall with Michelle, from the day they met right up to the moment she informed him she was leaving.

"Paul?"

He lifted his face and blinked several times, reconnecting with the present.

"Are you okay?" Dianna asked softly.

"Sorry. My mind wandered."

"Do you need to lie down?"

He shook his head slightly. "I'm okay."

She set a mug in front of him. "Drink this."

"Actually—"

She grabbed the glass of alcohol he'd been consuming before he could. "Drink the coffee."

He looked into the mug. "Maybe this wasn't such a good idea. I'm not going to be very good company."

"Well, your not-so-good company is still better than what I had at home. The boys have been hiding out in the den playing video games since the tree went up. Let me reheat you some dinner, and we'll talk, okay?"

"I don't really want to talk."

She started scooping food onto his plate. When the plate was in the microwave, she set silverware and a cloth napkin in front of him. By the time she pulled out a second mug and filled it for herself, the microwave dinged. She slid the plate of warmed food onto the counter and then took the seat next to him at the island. "You look like hell."

He responded by stuffing his mouth full of mashed potatoes. "Are these homemade?"

"Yes."

"They're delicious."

"Thanks. Have you been drinking all day?"

"Yes. But I'm not drunk."

He took an oversize bite of stuffing and chewed it slowly while she took a drink from her mug.

He swallowed as he pushed his turkey around on his plate. "How are you sleeping, Di?"

"Not so great."

"Me either."

"Have you tried sleeping pills?"

"They don't work."

She ran her hand up and down his back. "Today is hard."

"Every day is hard. Today is just worse." He took a drink of his coffee.

"I wish I had some way to make it better."

"You're hurting, too."

"I'm having an okay day today."

He took several more bites before pushing the plate away. "That was great. Thanks."

"Do you want pie?"

"Pumpkin?"

"Of course." As she served him dessert, she poured him a second cup of coffee.

"You don't have to stay," he said as she put the drink in front of him. "I'll be okay."

Dianna set a slice of pie next to his mug. "I'd like to stay. If you don't mind."

He stuffed his mouth rather than answer. She sat next to him, curled her hands around her mug, and looked around the lime-green kitchen as she'd done the orange-red living room.

"I hate all the bright colors," he said. "She loved them, said they made her feel alive. They just give me a headache."

"We can tone it down."

"And the furniture. I feel like I'm living in a goddamned magazine."

"We'll fix it, Paul."

He slid his mug away and put his elbows on the counter. Digging his hands into his hair, he held his head and took a few breaths. "I'm sorry. I know you don't need to hear this."

"Hey," she whispered. She cupped his cheek with her palm as she turned his face so she could look into his eyes. "We agreed we were going to help each other through this, didn't we?"

"Yeah."

"You helped me when I was a complete mess. You held me while I broke down, and then you helped me figure out what I needed to do to provide Christmas for my kids. You helped me. Now, let me help you."

She took his hand and pulled him from the stool. He wrapped his arms around her, and her arms went around his waist as he hugged her tightly. He didn't know how long he held her, his face buried in her long, dark hair, but it wasn't nearly long enough. He only eased his hold when she pulled away.

"Where's your room?"

"That way." He nodded to the hallway.

She guided him through the dimly lit house and into his bedroom. "Lie down."

He stretched out, resting his head on a pillow and sighing with a mixture of exhaustion and defeat. Dianna sat on the edge of the bed and ran her fingers over his hair. The move surprised him, not because she touched him but because it was so nurturing—maternal. It was soothing in a way he hadn't been soothed in longer than he could remember.

"Close your eyes," she whispered.

He reached for her other hand and held it tightly as he let his eyelids drift shut. "Talk to me," he whispered.

"About what?"

"Anything. Anything that isn't about her."

She hesitated, as if she couldn't think of a topic that wasn't about their cheating spouses, but then her soft voice surrounded him. He smiled slightly when she started going on about the weather. That was a safe topic. Michelle couldn't weave her way into a discussion of the forecast. He listened to Dianna's soothing tone as he drifted off to sleep, and when he dreamed, rather than seeing his wife leaving him, he dreamed of leaves changing colors and walks under big, brightly colored umbrellas.

sh

Normally Dianna would spend Black Friday hounding sales at the mall. This year she sat at the kitchen table with bills sprawled in front her while her calculator proved what she already knew. She didn't have enough money to cover what she owed.

She'd been so excited when Paul had pawned their wedding rings for cash and helped her buy Sam and Jason presents. What she should have done was taken the money straight to the bank. Her sons didn't *need* the gaming system and laptop. They *needed* electricity.

Stupid. Just one more stupid thing she'd done.

She picked up her bank statement and looked at the balance in her savings account.

What savings account?

She'd all but emptied it over the last six months: skimming it to get by, paying for an attorney, and helping Jason with living expenses at school.

Maybe it was time to take Kara's husband up on his offer for a job answering phones at his marketing firm. She hadn't yet because of her damned pride. But her determination was losing out to the desperation of watching the gap between what she'd earned and what she owed grow on a weekly basis.

The doorbell rang, surrounding her in that sad sound that was so fitting to her life lately. Gathering the sheets of paper in front of her, she tucked them in a folder, slammed it shut, and pushed herself up.

All Dianna could see of the man standing on her porch was that he was holding a gigantic bouquet of white lilies. She checked the driveway and smiled when she saw Paul's car. Her spirits instantly lifted, debts forgotten, as she looked at the flowers again. She couldn't remember the last time she had received fresh-cut flowers, Mother's Day most likely, and she doubted they had been as beautiful as the bouquet he was holding.

She opened the door. "Well, hello to you, too."

He lowered the flowers and grinned as if he were as unsure as a teen on his first date. "Hi. I hope it's okay that I just dropped by."

"It's fine. What is all this?"

"I'm sorry about last night."

She stepped back to let him in the house. "These are beautiful," she said when he handed her the bouquet, "but there's nothing to apologize for."

"I was an ass."

"I thought you were quite charming, actually."

"How so?"

"The slurred grumbles, the shoveling of food, slurping of coffee." In an attempt to hide her grin, she dipped her head and sniffed a flower.

His lip curved. "Sarcasm in the face of my apology. Cute."

Dianna chuckled softly. "I'm teasing. You had a bad day. There's nothing wrong with that."

"I shouldn't have dragged you into it."

She gestured for him to follow her. "I'm glad you did."

"Because you're an emotional masochist?"

"Because it got my mind off my day. Did you sleep?"

"I did. It was early this morning when I woke. I had coffee and watched the sun come up. And then I noticed that my house was significantly cleaner."

"Less cluttered, maybe. I didn't actually clean anything. I just picked up a bit before I left."

"Well, thanks."

"Only two more holidays to get through, and then we can breathe easy until Valentine's Day. Won't that be fun?" She opened a cabinet above the sink and stretched, trying to reach the top shelf where she had several vases, but it was no use. Before she even asked, Paul stepped beside her and grabbed the largest one. She filled the vase with water, removed the paper from around the flower stems, and dropped them into the intricately etched glass. As she was arranging the lilies, he held a small envelope out to her.

Dianna brushed her hand on her jeans and then opened the envelope. Inside, she found a gift card to a salon.

Paul was smiling excitedly, more so than she'd ever seen from him. "You said you wanted a makeover. At the café the day of my hearing. I owe you more than flowers for yesterday."

She turned her attention back to the card. "Paul, this is too much."

"No, it's not. You helped me. Probably more than you realize."

It was too much. She hadn't done anything that he hadn't done for her, but neither of them needed the stress of bickering over a gift card. "Thank you."

"You can use that to do whatever it is that women do when they say they need a makeover."

"Usually we shave our heads and get piercings in strange places."

"Oh. Well, then never mind. " He snatched the card from her hand.

"No take-backs." She grasped the card just as quickly as he had and laughed. "I was just about to make myself a turkey sandwich. Care to join me?"

"That sounds good."

"Grab us some plates and glasses." She pointed to a cabinet as she walked to the fridge.

"So Thanksgiving was a total bust. I can't wait for Christmas to roll around."

"Shall we make plans now? You can get up and start drinking by nine, and I'll be over by one to sober you up? It can be our new tradition."

"God, I hope not." He scoffed. "One holiday like that was pathetic enough, don't you think?"

She set some leftovers on the counter as she looked at him. "It wasn't pathetic."

"It was. I hate this so much."

"Which part?"

"All of it. I can't stand to be around anybody because I know they feel sorry for me. 'Poor Paul. If he had only listened when we told him what a slut he'd married.'"

Dianna stopped moving and looked at him. "Did they say that?"

"Not in so many words, but I got the gist."

She started pulling slices of turkey from a container. "Well, everyone was shocked by Mitch's betrayal. No one saw it coming." She put the meat in the microwave and pushed start. "As for my friends, Kara is really the only one I see anymore. I guess that's for the best anyway. At least with everyone avoiding me, I don't have to see the pity on their faces."

"Oh, yes. The pity is the worst."

"Wait until word spreads that they're getting married. It's going to get so much worse. I haven't told anyone but you. Not even Kara. I don't know why. I just can't bring myself to say it."

"You will when you're ready."

She shook her head. "It's so humiliating. Mitch is getting married. My *husband* is getting married. To someone else." No matter how many times she said it, it just didn't seem real.

"You okay?"

"No." She frowned. "But I will be. I just need to get through the next few weeks."

Paul wrapped his arm around her shoulder. She hesitated only for a moment before she leaned closer until she could drop her head onto his shoulder. His hold tightened, and she put her arm around his waist, soaking up the brief reprieve from her misery.

"I'm so tired of feeling like this," she said quietly.

Paul ran his hand over her hair and turned his face, as if he were going to kiss the top of her head, but hesitated when sneakers squeaked to a stop on the linoleum. Dianna pulled from Paul's embrace just as Sam threw his hands up.

"It isn't bad enough my married father is engaged to a ho. Now my married mother is hanging all over some strange man in the kitchen? So much for the innocence of my childhood."

"Sam," she called when he turned on his heels to leave the room.

"Can't talk now, Ma. I gotta call my therapist."

She looked at Paul after Sam disappeared. "He's kidding. It's his way."

"Cute."

"It can be. Sometimes." She walked to the microwave, which had beeped sometime before. They constructed their sandwiches as she filled him in on some of her son's references to his tarnished youth.

Paul laughed as they carried their plates and drinks to the living room. "Where does he get that sense of humor?"

She sat on one end of the sofa while he situated himself on the other.

"Believe it or not, I can be quite funny when I'm not having my heart and soul obliterated by my husband. I've been lucky so far, but he still has a few more months to get himself suspended from high school and blow all his scholarships."

"Naw, I bet he's a good kid."

"He is. Both my kids are very good."

"Mine, too. They have their mother to thank for that."

She glanced at him and saw raw guilt on his face. He was certainly very good at beating himself up. She wondered if he'd always been that way or if this was a by-product of his divorces.

"I like the tree," he said, changing the subject.

The artificial spruce stood over seven feet tall and sparkled with white lights buried beneath years' worth of memories in the shape of handmade ornaments.

Dianna followed his gaze. "I love all the decorations from when they were kids. Unfortunately, it reminds me how old I am. Oh, speaking of decorating..." She grabbed a stack of magazines off the coffee table. "I got these the last time I was going to redecorate. It's been a couple years, but it should give you some ideas."

His laugh sounded awkward. "Oh, right."

"Do you still want help?"

"I don't know. I think I might just sell. Get something that doesn't have all those ghosts shuffling around."

"Well, you still should paint over all those gaudy colors, so you might as well pick something that you like. Most real estate agents say to go with something neutral and light."

The misery that played across his face as he dropped his sandwich onto his plate tugged at her heart. She picked at the crust on her bread as she thought about how her bedroom seemed to taunt her at night and her living room ridiculed her as she sat alone watching television. As much as she wanted to stay in her house, she wanted to leave. With Mitch moving on and getting remarried, it seemed pathetic that she was so stagnant. The time had come to let go. So why the hell was she still holding on to everything he'd left behind?

"You okay?" Paul asked, pulling her from her thoughts.

She gnawed at her lip for a moment. "Do you remember when you offered to call your brother and ask him to help me get a car?"

"Yeah."

"Well, I know nothing about cars. I don't even know what I should ask when looking at one. That was Mitch's job. It sounds stupid now, but that's just how it was. He handled things like buying cars and fixing the house, and I"—she shrugged—"I made things pretty. So if you'll go with me to see your brother, I'll make your house marketable."

"I go with you to test-drive a few cars, and in exchange you are going to paint my house?"

"No. *We* are going to paint your house. I'll just take care of the colors and decorating."

He considered her suggestion for a moment. "How about you pick out the colors, and I pay someone to paint?"

"Even better. Deal?"

He nodded his head. "Deal. Finish up so we can go."

"Go where?"

"Car shopping."

Her eyes widened. "Now?"

"Well," he said picking his sandwich up, "after lunch."

Paul's little brother was nothing if not a know-it-all, and Matt certainly seemed to think he knew everything at the moment. From the time Paul and Dianna had walked into the dealership, Matt kept glancing at Paul, smirking as if he'd discovered some great truth.

Dianna had been firm on the highest monthly payment she could afford, and while she was gathering up her paperwork to trade in her SUV, Paul had called his brother and struck a deal. Matt agreed to have several nicer sedans ready for her to test-drive, and when she chose one, he'd offer her the same discount he'd offered members of the O'Connell clan in the past.

Matt immediately surmised that Dianna was Paul's girlfriend, and even though Paul insisted she wasn't, his little brother winked and gave him the thumbs-up the very first time Dianna turned her attention to the cars he'd lined up.

Dianna sighed, pulling Paul's attention back to her. He stopped glaring at his brother and watched her lift her pen from the signature line.

She looked at Matt and gnawed her lip for a moment. "Are you sure about this price?"

She wasn't stupid. She had to have known she was getting a discount, but Paul hadn't discussed it with her, and he wasn't going to give her the chance to bow out because he was calling in a favor for her.

"Year-end clearance," Paul offered.

Dianna glanced between the brothers before scrawling her signature on the last required spot, and Matt slid the keys to a much more sensible sedan toward her. She hesitated but then grinned widely as she curled her fingers around the key ring.

"Thanks, Matt." Paul stood and held his hand out.

Matt took his brother's hand but was smiling at Dianna. "I hope you enjoy the new car."

"Oh, I'm sure I will."

Paul started to leave, hoping to make his exit before Matt did or said something stupid. He should have known he never stood a chance.

Matt slid around his desk as they walked out. "Are we going to see you next Sunday?"

Dianna glanced at Paul, clearly confused, and Paul moaned.

"I told you I'm not going," he said.

"You can't miss the family Christmas. Annie will freak."

"Christmas already?" Di asked.

"Family tradition decrees that the second Sunday after Thanksgiving is the O'Connell family Christmas," Paul said. "Annie is our older sister. She thinks since Mom is no longer with us, it's her job to see me through my divorce. The only thing is, she doesn't have a nurturing bone in her body and her so-called support comes off rather condescending."

Matt laughed but stifled it when Paul frowned at him. He cleared his throat and focused on Dianna again. "He's not completely off the mark."

"The family Thanksgiving was bad enough," Paul said.

"He barely stayed long enough to eat," Matt told Dianna. "And then he refused to join any of us on Thanksgiving Day."

Paul tensed his jaw muscles. *Not now, Matthew.*

"That's my fault, I'm afraid," Dianna said. "He spent Thanksgiving with me."

Matt's eyes lit as if he'd just gotten the confirmation that he had been seeking ever since Paul first introduced Dianna, and Paul had to wonder which was worse: his family thinking he was sulking, or his family thinking he'd spent the day with a woman.

"Oh." Matt gave Paul that know-it-all smirk again. "Why didn't you tell us you were spending the day with a *friend?*"

"Because it's none of your damned business." Paul put his hand to Dianna's elbow and steered her toward the door. "Thanks for your help. Sorry we can't make it—"

Matt dismissed his brother's refusal and followed them outside. "It's next Sunday at noon, Dianna. Lunch and then our traditional white elephant gift exchange—ten-dollar limit. We are a funny bunch, so the more outrageous the gift, the better. Last year I walked away with a pair of British flag underwear."

Dianna laughed. "Very nice. But," she said looking up at Paul, "I don't think I'll be there."

"Of course you will. As soon as I tell Annie I met Paul's new girlfriend, she won't let up until he agrees to bring you."

Dianna put her hand to her chest, clearly surprised by Matt's assessment. "Oh, we're not dating."

Matt shrugged. "That doesn't matter. See you next weekend. Paul knows where. Oh, and if you try to duck out, I have your phone number in that nice big stack of paperwork."

"Enough," Paul warned. "I'll be there, but don't drag Dianna into it."

Matt laughed. "Seriously, though, you should come. It'll be fun."

Paul snorted as he gently pushed her toward her new car.

Dianna giggled as they climbed in. "Stop scowling. You don't have to go."

"Oh, yes, I do. He wasn't kidding about Annie."

"I'm sorry. I thought telling him you were with me would help. I didn't think he'd jump to the conclusion that we were dating."

"He came to that conclusion the minute we walked in the door. My family isn't happy unless they are nosing around my personal life."

She bit her lip but couldn't stop her grin from spreading. "Would you like me to go with you?"

He watched her adjust the rearview mirror. "If you come with me, Annie is going to make a big deal about it. No matter how much I insist we aren't a couple, she will give you the third degree."

Dianna focused on him. "That's a small price to pay to make it so you can tolerate being around your family again."

His frustration faded a bit. "Really?"

"Really."

"Thank you."

"You're welcome." She started the car. "Now that we have my new car taken care of, we need to go pick out paint colors."

"Wait. You said *you* were going to pick out paint colors."

"I am." She winked at him. "I'm just taking you with me."

CHAPTER SIX

*P*aul frowned at his brother. Matt held up a to-go bag from one of their favorite local hamburger places, but Paul wasn't impressed.

"What are you doing here, Matty?"

"Just thought I'd swing by. Catch the game."

"There is no game."

"Oh. Well, maybe a movie, then." He pushed his way into Paul's house and kicked off his shoes. "Grab us a few beers, will ya?"

Paul exhaled as he closed his front door and headed for the kitchen. There was absolutely no point in trying to fight what was about to happen. Grabbing two bottles from the fridge, he took them to the living room and dropped onto the sofa next to Matt. "Get it over with."

"What?"

"The game of twenty questions you plan on playing."

Matt at least had the decency to try to look offended. "I just wanted to hang out."

Paul grabbed a burger and an order of onion rings. "She's just a friend going through the same shit I am, and we're trying to help each other through it. No sex or heartstrings attached."

Matt nodded. "That's a pretty big favor you called in for her. Asking me to give her a car at cost."

"And I appreciate it. If you need me to cover some of the loss, I will."

"We'll make it back selling her Suburban."

"Good."

Matt shoved a few fries into his mouth. "She's pretty."

Paul sighed at the abundance of lettuce and tomatoes on his sandwich. "You know I hate this shit on my burger."

"So take it off, big boy. You didn't answer me."

"You didn't ask a question."

Matt scoffed. "Sorry. Dianna's pretty, *isn't she?*"

"Actually, I think she's beautiful. She's reminds me of Mom in a way."

Matt snickered, and Paul glared at him.

"Mom was gracious and kind. She always put us first. Dianna is like that. Mom didn't deserve all the crap Dad pulled, and Dianna doesn't deserve what her husband is putting her through. She's strong, but she needs someone to help her, even if she doesn't want to admit it."

"And you've decided to be that someone."

Matt's tone told him all he needed to know. It wasn't an observation. It was a warning.

"She isn't like Michelle, if that's what you're getting at."

"How do you know?"

Paul shook his head. "I'm not doing this, Matt."

"Doing what?"

He took a big bite of his sandwich. "I'm not discussing my fuck-ups with you," he said around the mouthful.

"I wasn't talking about your fuck-ups."

"You were getting there."

"I just want you to be careful. Is that so wrong?"

Paul frowned at him. "For the last few years, you've been subtly telling me how wrong I was to marry Michelle. You never once took into consideration that I actually loved her."

"That's not true."

"The hell it isn't." He squirted a packet of ketchup on his onion rings.

"I know you loved her. But she was using you from the get-go."

"And I was just too stupid to notice?"

Matt dropped what was left of his burger and wiped his hands. "You were blinded by her. The rest of us were on the outside looking in. We had a better vantage point. We hated watching her hurt you for so long, but you wouldn't listen. In case you didn't know this about yourself, you can be pretty damned stubborn."

Paul smirked. "That's an O'Connell family trait apparently."

"I don't want you to get back into a situation like that."

"I'm not."

"You can see why I might think that, right? I've never even heard you mention this woman, and then all of a sudden you're asking me to do her a favor. That's not like you."

Paul swigged his beer as he considered how much to tell his brother. "Look, I'm not giving you details, because...I don't want to, basically. You're being too damned nosy for my liking."

Matt chuckled. "Okay."

"She was married for over twenty years. She stayed home raising kids and taking care of her family while her husband worked to support them. Then one day, he left. Just like that. Now she's got two kids to support and all the bills that she had before but no husband to help her out. She's doing the best she can, but she had this huge car payment dragging her down. I knew I could help her."

"But why is it your job to help her?"

Paul shrugged. "I was a mess Thanksgiving. Okay? There, I admit it. I was drinking myself into a stupor, and she came over and did her best to talk me through it. We're both going through hell, but we're trying to make things a little easier for each other. And nowhere is sex, love, or money involved in that. Okay?"

Matt nodded. "Okay. I just don't want to see you get hurt again. Not every woman is after your classic good looks, you know?"

Paul rolled his head back and groaned. "Jesus, you sound like Annie."

sh

Paul let out a catcall whistle when Dianna opened her front door. "Hubba hubba."

Heat started at her neck and quickly rose to her newly dyed hairline and flushed her face. "*Stop.*"

"I like it. Very nice."

She ran her fingers through her freshly cut strands. She'd used the gift certificate he'd given her to have long layers put back into her hair and have the color dyed a shade lighter than her natural chestnut with a hint of auburn. She had walked out of the salon feeling years younger. When she got home, she'd even put on makeup. She hadn't done that in months. She'd added just enough mascara and eyeliner to bring out the brightness of her blue eyes, used a bit of concealer to hide the seemingly permanent dark circles under her eyes, and dabbed on a little lipstick.

She hadn't paid close attention to her appearance since Mitch left. Realizing the creases in her forehead had somehow grown deeper and the lines around her eyes and mouth more obvious dampened her spirits, but she pushed the criticism aside and relished having an updated look.

"I can't thank you enough, Paul. Seriously, I so needed this."

"You look beautiful. Even more beautiful," he quickly amended. "Thanks for inviting me to dinner. It smells great."

She grinned. "Well, I owed you. I hope you like eggplant parmesan."

"Sounds perfect."

She took a bottle of wine from him as he hung his coat, and then they walked to the kitchen. While he lifted the lid off the sauce and tasted it, she dug out a corkscrew and glasses.

"Is this homemade?" he asked, going in for another spoonful.

"Yes."

"Amazing. Do you make everything yourself?"

"Not everything." She grunted as she pulled the cork out. "Mitch preferred homemade, and I had the time, so I did whenever possible. It's a habit now, I guess."

Paul lifted his glass after she filled it. "Well, here's to hanging on to the good habits."

She clinked her glass to his and took a drink. Paul got plates down while Dianna returned her attention to the stove.

Leaning against the counter, he took a drink of his wine while she strained the pasta. "I have a confession to make."

"Uh-oh."

"I didn't bring the wine just for dinner. I was hoping to get you drunk so I could take advantage of you."

Dianna turned and lifted her brows at him.

"I need to go Christmas shopping, and I really suck at that. I thought if I got enough wine in you, you'd agree to help me."

"Oh, yes, I can see how you'd need alcohol on your side. Women *hate* shopping." She smiled when he laughed. "I was planning on going to the mall tomorrow after we left Annie's if I had time. I need to get a few more small things. Want to tag along?"

"Perfect. And it will give us an excuse to bail."

"You're worrying me a bit." She topped off his food with some sauce. "Are they going to sit me at a table with spotlights and grill me?"

"That's not completely out of the realm of possibility." He accepted the plate. "Michelle left a bad taste in their mouths. I wouldn't be surprised if any woman I ever introduced to them in the future had to go through a lie detector test."

Dianna sat across from him with her own plate and watched him cut into his dinner. He had taken three big bites, moaning his appreciation each time, before he stopped chewing.

He eyed her. "What?"

She chuckled when she realized she'd been staring. "It's nice to cook something I like and have someone enjoy it rather than complain and then go make a sandwich."

"Anybody who doesn't appreciate your cooking is an idiot." He started to fill his mouth again and then stopped. "Wait, we're talking about *him* right? I don't want to call your kids idiots."

"Well, them, too, but they're kids. They aren't supposed to like good food. I meant him."

"Well, he's an idiot."

"Indeed." Dianna cut into her dinner. "Tell me more about your family."

He told her about his siblings as they ate. Matt had opened the car dealership right out of college, and Annie went to work for a real estate agency after high school. Five years after that, she branched out on her own. The other realty office closed, but

Annie's was still going strong. She'd never married but had a daughter. The father had never been in the picture. Matt, on the other hand, was happily married and spoiled his two girls rotten.

Paul's sons, Sean and Toby, sounded eerily similar to Dianna's boys. Toby was quite serious, while Sean had always been the class clown. Paul had never been close to his boys, but now that Michelle was out of the picture, he wanted to try to fix that.

In turn, Dianna told him of her love of music. Once upon a time, she'd hoped to give lessons, but she'd never found the time. Jason had never cared to learn, but she'd taught Sam to play the guitar, though the piano was her favorite.

Once dinner was done, Dianna filled a container with leftovers and put it on the counter for Paul to take home. The dishwasher door squeaked as Paul opened it, and Dianna stopped gathering their plates from the table as she turned to him.

She watched him rinse a pan before setting it inside the machine. "What are you doing?"

He glanced back over his shoulder. "Helping you clean up. Is that wrong?"

"No. No. That's right. That's very right. Thank you."

"He didn't do that either, huh?"

"And get his hands dirty? God, no."

They worked together to clean up dinner, and then Dianna led him to the living room. They sat on the sofa, and Paul listed off who he intended to buy presents for when they went shopping the next day while Dianna wrote their names on her shopping list.

"Any idea what you want to get them?" she asked.

Paul sank back into the sofa and rolled his head back. "Not a clue. I can't even begin to tell you how much I hate Christmas."

Dianna gasped dramatically. "What?"

"The stress, the panic, the pressure. It's horrible."

Her smile faded as he ran his hand through his thick silver strands. "I know it's been a tough year, but—"

"It's not that."

"What is it?"

He looked at her, and the depth of sadness in his gray eyes made her heart hurt. "The only good thing about Christmas is the food."

She held his gaze for a moment before letting her questions go and smiling. "The food is amazing."

"Will you be spending Christmas with family?"

"No. My family is in Oregon. I met Mitch in college. We moved here after he graduated. He grew up here."

"Did you graduate?"

"Nope. I did get pregnant, though. I planned to finish after we got settled, but it just never happened. Mitch had a good job, and I wanted to be home with Jason, and then Sam came along. I always thought I'd go back once they were both in school, but then there was PTA and classroom volunteering and sports. I never found the time to finish my degree. I'm certainly kicking myself for that now."

"Don't. You were with your kids when they were growing up. That's important. You have a bond with them that I'll never have with my kids." His lack of relationship with his sons was clearly weighing on his mind.

"It's not too late. If you want a relationship with your boys, you can make it happen."

He stared at the tree, but she didn't think he was actually seeing it. "They're in college. They don't need me now."

"Yes, they do." Her voice was soft but firm. "Trust me, they do. It's never too late to be a father. Will they be there tomorrow?"

"No. They're both back at school until Christmas break."

"Well, when they get home, do something fun, something different than you normally would do. It'll give you something to talk about."

"Maybe." He shook his head after a moment, as if to rid it from his thoughts. "So what did you study in college? Music?"

"Music and English."

"English?"

She scrunched up her nose. "I'm kind of a nerd."

He laughed. "Well, working in a bookstore must be heaven for you."

"It's more stocking shelves than analyzing poetry, but I like it." She finished her wine. "I'm going to get more. Would you like some?"

"Sure."

She nodded toward the remote and took his empty glass from the coffee table. "Why don't you find us a movie to watch? I'm over talking about depressing shit."

CHAPTER SEVEN

*K*ara gasped loudly. "What are you doing on that site?"

Dianna turned from the sink where she was washing the last of the dinner dishes. Kara was staring at her laptop screen. She'd forgotten to close the window she'd been browsing earlier. "I have to start selling stuff if I'm going to pay the bills."

Kara's eyes went wide. "Did you put your address online?"

"No. But I'll have to give it to whoever wants to come look at what I posted."

"Don't. You. *Dare*. Are you insane?"

"It's not like I put out a sex ad, Kare. I'm selling some furniture."

"Do you know how many crazy people are just waiting for some beautiful single woman to sell some furniture? You'll be raped and murdered within a week."

"Oh, my God." Di laughed. "You watch too much *Nightline*."

She sat in her chair and pulled her laptop to her. "Besides, you're one to talk. Didn't Harry just lecture you about personal safety after you hired a drug addict to do some work at your house?"

"He wasn't a drug addict. He just...had a problem. And I'm not talking about me. There are perverts out there who answer these ads just to case out a house and see if they have a potential victim. Stonehill isn't a bubble. There are lunatics here, just like everywhere else. I cannot believe you put an ad on Craigslist."

Dianna's frown deepened when Paul stepped into the kitchen, his eyes just as wide as Kara's.

"You did *what?*" he demanded.

"She put her address on Craigslist."

Dianna rolled her eyes. "No, I didn't. I set up an account so I could sell some things. She's acting like I asked someone to come kill me."

"You might as well have," Kara said.

"Just...stop," Dianna said. "Paul, this is Kara, my overlord."

Paul took Kara's hand when she extended it. "I've heard a lot about you."

Kara rolled her eyes to Dianna. "None of it good, I'm sure."

Paul grinned as he sat at the table. "Not *all* of it was bad."

Kara snorted. "I bet."

"If you'd quit hovering like I'm a child, I'd have nicer things to say about you."

"And if you didn't do things that endanger your life, I wouldn't hover."

"She's right," Paul said. "If you're going to sell something online, do it through your social media. At least you know the people."

"And have everyone know just how bad things are? No, thanks."

"Hey," Kara said firmly, "there's no point in trying to save face if some weirdo cuts your head off."

"*Jesus*," Dianna said. "You really do watch too much TV. Is he going to decapitate me or rape me?"

"He'll probably decapitate you and *then* rape you, smart-ass."

"Not all murderers are men, you know," Paul offered. "That's a pretty broad stereotype, and as the only male in the room, I'm slightly offended."

Dianna chuckled and looked at Paul. "When did you get here?"

"Just now. Sam let me in on his way out. Listen, if you don't want to list your stuff on your profile, I'll put it on mine, but don't use some online sales site. It isn't safe."

Dianna frowned. "Fine. I'll take my ad down."

"Thank you," Kara said with a nod. "Do it now, please."

She grumbled under her breath but went in and took down what she'd posted earlier in the evening.

"What are you selling?" Paul asked. "I'll see if anyone I know is interested."

"A leather sectional sofa, a piano, and a full-size bedroom set."

"You're selling your piano?" Kara asked softly.

"Yes." Though she didn't elaborate, she was sure the

expression on her face spoke for her. She didn't want to sell it—she didn't want to sell any of it. But she was out of options. Silence hung in the air, heavy and thick, while Dianna messaged Paul and Kara the photos and information on the items she was selling. "Do me a favor and tell anyone who asks that I'm remodeling instead of destitute, okay?"

She pushed herself up and walked to the sink to fill a glass of water but didn't miss the glance that Kara and Paul shared. She'd have asked them both to leave if it weren't so rude to do so. She'd spent the day determining what big items to sell and then researching what other people were selling similar furniture for so she wasn't asking too much or too little. She'd been depressed and gloomy, and as she always did, Kara acted like it was her responsibility to cheer her up with food and drink.

Overeating had worked briefly. For a while Dianna actually forgot that her life was in shambles. But it came back around the moment Kara had realized Dianna's secret plan for getting by. Her guests were quiet, which seemed to make it all that much worse.

"Di," Kara started in her let-me-solve-everything voice.

She slammed the glass down and turned to face them. "Were you just dropping by, Paul, or did you need something?"

"Hmm? Oh. I, uh, I hit up Goodwill today and got a few things for the party."

Kara's eyes lit. "What party?"

"Oh, Dianna agreed to suffer through my family Christmas

gathering. We do a white elephant exchange. It's pretty lame, but I can't get out of it and didn't want to go alone."

"It's not like that," Dianna said as soon as Kara's eyebrows lifted.

"I didn't say anything." Kara put up her hands to show her innocence. "Did you hear me say anything?"

"I didn't hear a peep," Paul said.

"You were thinking it. I know how your mind works. Paul helped me out. I'm helping him out. End of story."

"Okay." Kara pushed herself up. "End of story. Well, I have to go. I don't want to interrupt you *helping* each other out."

Dianna's mouth opened, but then she closed it. Anything she said would only encourage Kara, and Paul's quiet chuckling certainly didn't help matters.

"Don't egg her on," Dianna chastised.

"I didn't do anything," he said.

She made a face at him, but then Kara was standing between them.

"Listen," she said quietly, "don't sell your piano. You'll regret it so much."

"I need the money."

"I will help you if you need it," she whispered, "but *don't* sell the piano. Don't let him take anything else away from you."

Dianna knew Kara and her husband would help, but she just couldn't accept charity from friends when she had other choices. So far, she'd been making it with those other choices.

Kara turned to Paul. "It was nice meeting you."

"You, too." He pushed himself up from the table and watched her leave. He looked at Dianna, and she was certain he, too, was going to offer to swoop in and save her. He just had that air about him. He had probably been a knight in shining armor in a previous life.

"I'm sorry about her," Dianna said before he could delve into her troubles. "She's become a bit overbearing since Mitch left."

"She's still not as bad as Annie."

Dianna laughed, but it was uneasy.

"I know it's not my place, but—"

She closed her eyes. "If you're about to offer me money, please don't." Looking at him again, she could see the concern on his face. "Everybody keeps offering me money like I'm a charity. I don't want people tossing cash at me to appease their guilt. Mitch hasn't been gone that long. I'm still trying to figure this out, but I will, okay? It's hard—it's really hard—but I can't be dependent on handouts to get by."

"Okay," he said quietly. "But I want you to know—"

"*Paul.*"

He crossed the room and lowered his face so she had nowhere to look but his eyes. "I know how devastating it has been to lose your husband's income and to try to maintain your home and your lifestyle for your kids. You're doing your best, I know that. But sometimes a little help doesn't hurt. I'm not going to hand you money, but if you need it, I can give you a loan or we can work something else out."

Her heart simultaneously lifted and sank a little more with

every word he'd said. He didn't even know her, and he had more concern for her and her kids than Mitch had shown since leaving. It was as heartwarming as it was mortifying. It was a crazy mix of both, and she didn't know if she should hug him or cry.

Finally, she managed to grin. "Well, I haven't reached the point of prostitution just yet, if that's what you mean by *working something out*, but I'll keep your offer in mind."

He held her gaze, but after a moment, he chuckled. "Let's hope neither of us get so bad off that prostitution is our only option."

"Let's hope."

His smile was still soft as he held her gaze. "Piano, huh? You play?"

"Not for a while. The piano was a gift from my parents a long time ago, but it just sits there taking up space now." She exhaled and looked down at herself before he pushed and she had to tell him playing music just depressed her now. She drew a breath. "So, where are these gag gifts you bought for the party?"

"Before I forget," Paul said the following Sunday. He dug into his pocket and pulled out several folded bills. "For the piano."

Her heart sank as she looked at the wad of cash. "You sold it already?"

"My friend's daughter just started lessons."

She bit her lip as she took the money from him. "Thanks."

"He's hoping to surprise her for her birthday. Would you mind if it stays here for a while?"

She shrugged. "No, that's fine."

"Good." He smiled. "Are you ready?"

"Um. Yeah." She tucked the cash into her purse, and then he helped her into her coat and followed her out to his car.

"Don't be nervous," Paul said. "Annie can come off as pushy, but underneath it she's very sweet."

Dianna glanced at him from where she sat in the passenger seat of his car. "I wasn't nervous...until you started constantly telling me not to be nervous."

He smiled. "Sorry. You look very nice, by the way."

She looked down at her beige slacks and then at his jeans. Underneath their winter coats, she wore a coral-colored blouse and several long gold necklaces to dress her outfit up while he wore a T-shirt under a sweater jacket. "Am I overdressed?"

"No. You're perfect."

"I feel overdressed."

"You look beautiful."

"They're not going to be mean, are they? They'll be nice even if they don't like me, right?"

He reached across the car and squeezed her hand. "They're going to love you, sweetheart. Trust me."

Dianna's teeth stopped working over her lip at the term of endearment and intimate touch. "Sweetheart" had rolled off his tongue like he hadn't even considered his words, and though he pulled his hand back quickly, she could still feel the heat of his touch. His smile was wide across his lips, and she had to wonder if he even realized what he'd said. He'd called her "sweetheart." And even if he hadn't meant it intimately, it had made Dianna's heart skip a beat and a feeling wash over her that was something like...*belonging*. Like she belonged here. With Paul. Going to meet his family.

Belonging somewhere was something she hadn't even realized she'd been missing.

She exhaled when he pulled into a driveway several minutes later. Stonehill wasn't exactly the slums. The mid- to upper-class Des Moines suburb was still one of the fastest growing areas, yet it somehow managed to keep its small-town feel. Most of the houses, while large, were modest, but the house she found herself looking up at was one of the nicer ones she'd seen. She had felt nervous before, but now she felt completely out of her element. Paul was a lawyer. Matt and Annie both owned businesses. They were all clearly successful in life. All Dianna had done was raise kids and fail at her marriage. What was she even going to talk about with these people?

She swallowed hard. "I feel like they're all going to be judging me."

Paul parked behind several other cars. "Oh, they will be, but only because I screwed up so badly when I married Michelle."

"Okay. That did *not* help ease my nerves."

He reached over and squeezed her hand again. "Just be

yourself, Di. Even if they don't like you, which they *will*, it doesn't matter. We're not dating."

"Right."

Paul climbed out of the car. He opened the back door and grabbed their gifts while she got out, her mind racing with anxiety.

"Do they know how we met?"

He closed the car door. "Not yet, but I'm sure they will before the day is over."

"Oh, God."

He laughed and took her elbow to guide her to the front door. He pushed it open without knocking. "Hello?"

Dianna took a deep breath when several people said his name from the other room. A woman several years older than Paul rushed into the foyer as he was helping Dianna out of her coat. She stood only to Dianna's nose, making her at least six inches shorter than Paul. She was blond and had a soft curve to her face, but she looked as intimidating as he had warned. Dianna knew this was Annie.

She looked at Dianna as if her brother weren't even there. Her gaze, the same steel gray as Paul's, was piercing and suspicious. Dianna smiled and extended her hand. This wasn't a date. She and Paul were barely even friends. Like Paul had just said, it didn't matter what his family thought of her.

So why did she so desperately feel the need to gain Annie's approval?

"It's nice to meet you, Annie. Paul has told me so much about you."

Annie finally acknowledged her brother with a frown. "I'll just bet he has. The pleasure is all mine. Trust me. Come on. Donna and I are hiding in the kitchen with the food and wine while the men discuss football and other testosterone-infused subjects."

Dianna looked back at Paul when Annie started pulling her away. He shrugged, as if he were innocent, but Dianna suspected he'd known exactly what was going to happen before they'd even arrived.

Annie led her into the kitchen, where she was instantly met with the scents of Christmas dinner. Ham and rolls and spices from the pies assaulted her, making her feel at home. She was almost able to relax until the woman standing at the stove turned. Her stare was almost as distrusting as Annie's had been.

"This Paul's girl?"

"Dianna, this is Matt's wife, Donna." Annie filled a third wineglass and looked at Donna. "Looks like a deer in the headlights, doesn't she?"

Donna chuckled. "Better than looking like a tramp heading out for a night on the town. That wife of his," she said to Dianna, "showed up for her first family dinner in a minidress and stilettos."

"I considered wearing a minidress," Dianna deadpanned, "but I haven't shaved since September, and I didn't feel like breaking out the weed whacker."

Annie laughed as she handed Dianna a glass of wine. "You're already better than the last one. Now sit down and let us grill you."

Dianna grinned. Mostly because she was realizing that Paul hadn't over-exaggerated Annie's behavior at all. But unlike Paul, Dianna could appreciate where Annie was coming from. Paul had been through hell, and here he was bringing a new woman to Christmas.

"How'd you meet?"

"I'm going to let Paul tell you that one."

Donna turned and cocked a brow. "Shit. You're not one of his clients, are you?"

Dianna chuckled as she recalled the small, timid man who had sold her electronics at a much-discounted price. He was as far from the stereotypical criminal type as Dianna could have imagined, so she could guess the horror that Donna and Annie might have at the thought of her needing Paul's defense.

"No. I'm going through a divorce as well, so…" She lifted her glass as if to make a toast. "Divorcees unite." She gulped the white wine as Donna and Annie exchanged glances.

Donna sat next to Annie. "How long were you married?"

Dianna guessed that was a question she was going to get asked a lot now. People rarely wanted to know how long she'd been married when she *was* married. Now that it was over, the length of her marriage seemed to define her. "Twenty-two years."

Donna's eyes widened. "Wow."

"And now you're dating someone who is also going through a divorce?" Annie asked. "That seems like a disaster waiting to happen."

"Oh, no. Paul and I aren't dating."

Annie narrowed her eyes. "If you aren't dating, why did Paul bring you today? Family dinner generally means family or those who could become family."

"Actually, Matt invited me. Paul was helping me trade in my SUV because I didn't have a clue what I was doing. Matt asked if I was going to be here. I think Paul didn't want to be rude so he extended the invitation."

And he didn't want to face you all alone. She swallowed more wine instead of adding that last thought.

Donna slammed her hand down. "I asked Matt if that's what happened, and he said it wasn't. What a dolt."

"So you aren't interested in Paul?" Annie asked.

"He's very nice and he's been very kind to me, but no. My divorce isn't even final. I'm not ready for all that."

Annie sat back. "I apologize if it seems like we're two mother hens, but we've had no choice but to sit back and watch Paul get walked all over for the last three years. He can spot a lie before it's spoken where his clients are concerned, but when it came to his wife, he put on blinders and then shoved his head in the sand for good measure."

Donna sighed loudly. "He was in complete denial about how horrible she was to him. She used him so badly, and when she was done, she just tossed him aside. At least now she has a new sucker to leech off and Paul can finally be rid of her."

Dianna lifted her brow and downed what was left in her wineglass.

"It's put Paul through the wringer, though." Annie finished her glass as well and refilled hers and Dianna's.

"So how long have you and Paul known each other?" Donna asked as she pushed herself up when a timer dinged.

"Uh, just since October. Do you need help?"

"Nope, you sit right there and endure our questions until we're satisfied that you aren't some backstabbing, greedy bitch we're going to have to scare off like we should have done to Michelle."

Dianna chuckled. "I get the feeling you didn't care for her much."

Annie moaned. "The only thing I liked about her was... Never mind. I can't think of anything."

"She had pretty hair," Donna offered.

Annie made a face. "There was that."

Dianna drew a breath. She was tempted to ask more about Michelle, just because her own morbid curiosity was dying to know everything about her, but she pushed the urge down. "Well, no one has ever accused me of backstabbing or being greedy. At least not to my face."

Annie laughed. "That's something. So tell me more about yourself. What do you do? Who do you know?"

"I work at that little bookstore on the town square. And

unless you've got kids in high school sports, chorus, or band, we don't run with the same crowd. My life revolves around my kids and their activities...or it did, I guess."

"Soccer mom," Donna said.

"Until recently," Dianna confessed. "I had the perfect life, perfect marriage, perfect everything, right up until I didn't."

Annie stared at her for a moment. "Who left?"

Back to her divorce. "He did."

"Did you see it coming?"

"Nope. It was a complete shock."

"It was for Paul, too. The fool."

Dianna finished her second glass of wine. "So, you know all about me now." She lifted a brow at Annie. "Your turn. Why didn't you ever get married?"

Annie held her gaze, as if warning her to back down, but Dianna didn't, and Annie conceded. "Men irritate me."

Donna snorted. "Everyone irritates her."

"Everyone irritates me," Annie reiterated with a shrug. "I just never found someone who made me want to make the sacrifices necessary to be married. I love my work, my daughter, my life. I can take care of myself. So, until I meet someone who adds to that instead of takes away from that, I have no interest in men."

Dianna looked at Donna. "How long have you and Matt been married?"

"Ten glorious years."

"They're enough to make you sick, too." Annie topped off

her wine. "They're one of those couples who actually like each other."

Dianna laughed. "Well, congratulations. Apparently that's very rare."

"You mentioned kids," Annie said, turning the focus back to Dianna.

"Two boys. Jason is at the University of Iowa. Sam will be headed there next fall."

"And they play sports?"

"Every single sport they can get into. I'm actually thankful they'll both be in college soon. I can take a break from sitting on cold bleachers."

"Baseball?"

"Oh, yes. They've both played since Little League."

Annie grinned, and Donna chuckled.

Dianna looked between the two. "Why is that funny?"

"Paul was quite traumatized by a baseball game in his youth," Annie said. "You should be fully aware of it so you can tease him if you're ever around when he's watching a game."

"Tormenting him over this is a long-standing family tradition," Donna added.

Dianna couldn't help smiling. She'd been accepted. If she hadn't, they wouldn't be sharing secret family traditions. She felt a little guilty, like she was betraying Paul's trust, but she wouldn't have to if he were sitting here with her instead of making her fend for herself. "How does one go about getting traumatized by baseball?"

8h

By the time Paul walked into the kitchen, looking hesitantly at the women, Dianna, Annie, and Donna were laughing so hard Dianna could hardly breathe.

"Look who's here. His ears must have been burning," Donna said before returning to the stove.

Paul cringed. "Why do I sense trouble?"

Dianna tilted her head innocently. "Annie was just telling me a little bit about you. That's all."

Paul's eyes widened as he looked at his sister. "You didn't."

Annie put a hand to her chest, barely hiding her mischievous grin. "What?"

"You told her about the baseball tournament." He groaned when all three women started laughing again.

"Don't be embarrassed." Dianna lifted her glass as if to hide her smile. "It was a long time ago."

"And yet my sister still tells the tale."

"If you'd listened to me when I said you couldn't borrow pants from someone two sizes larger than you—"

"Mine were dirty."

"—they wouldn't have fallen down and you wouldn't have cost the team two runs and ultimately the game."

"Thanks." He walked to the table and snatched a cookie off a platter. "I can't believe you're telling her this."

Dianna playfully glared at him. "That's what you get for trying to throw me to the wolves."

He stuffed a Christmas-tree-shaped cookie into his mouth. "I did no such thing."

Paul glanced at his sister. The way she was smiling—with amusement and approval rather than the plastered-on, forced smile she'd always given him when Michelle was around—warmed his heart. He was far too old to be seeking the approval of his sister, but it felt good to see her genuinely smiling at him.

"Took you long enough to come check on her," Annie said. "I could have chewed up your girl and spit her out ten times over."

"I wasn't worried. I knew you'd like her," he said, as if Dianna wasn't sitting right there.

"I'm sure." Annie's voice had softened from teasing to gentle. "Go tell everyone to wash up. Lunch is ready."

"Yes, ma'am."

Paul called the family to the table, and when Dianna emerged from the kitchen carrying a dish, he took it. "So it went well?"

She put her hand on her hip and tried to look angry, but he could see she wasn't. "You abandoned me."

"You were laughing at me."

She nodded. "Yes, we were." Reaching out, she pulled a blond hair that matched that of his two young nieces from his sweater. "And what were you doing while I was winning over your protectors?"

"Having a tea party with the girls. I bet Donna and Annie were easier on you than those kids were on me. I didn't lift my pinky. I was nearly banished."

Di giggled. "You should have better table etiquette."

"Obviously."

He pulled out a chair for her as his family started piling into the room and the table filled with food. He sat next to her as conversations overlapped and people settled in for their annual dinner. It was the first holiday meal in years where he felt relaxed and welcomed instead of defensive. He didn't feel the need to justify having this woman by his side.

"So, Paul." Annie handed him a dish of green beans. "When I asked Dianna how you two met, she said I had to ask you."

The other conversations stopped as everyone focused on Paul. He dropped a spoonful of beans onto his plate and looked at Dianna. "She tells you my most embarrassing moment ever, and you can't even tell her how we met?"

"Oh, man," Matt said, "Annie told you about the baseball game?"

"She did." Dianna smiled brightly. "I'm really bummed there aren't any photos, though."

"Thanks." Paul passed her the dish. "I appreciate the support."

Dianna took the beans from him. "I do what I can. Anyway, I thought the tale of our paths crossing was better told by you. You were the one who sought me out."

"Did you meet online or something?" Donna asked.

"It was much less orthodox than that," Dianna said.

"Wait a second," Matt said from across the table. "I didn't make the connection before. Friedman? Dianna *Friedman*. The ex-wife."

"There's no ex about it," Dianna said. "Not yet anyway."

"What ex-wife?" Annie passed the dish of potatoes to Paul.

"The one who testified. At his hearing," Matt clarified.

The weight of everyone's stares pressed down on Paul, as well as a resurgence of the guilt he still felt over having asked Dianna to share with the court how she'd caught her husband having sex with Michelle.

Annie looked from Dianna to Paul and back again. "So you guys met when Paul asked you to testify?"

"After the hearing, we had coffee and spent a long time talking about our marriages and divorces and...bonded over our misery," Paul offered.

"Now we all get to stare at you and make you really uncomfortable." Matt clearly was trying to lighten the tension at the table.

Dianna laughed.

Paul tried, but he found it difficult. "Neither one of us was expecting our sudden changes in marital status. We both have some things that we weren't prepared to handle, but we realized we can help each other with those. I helped her buy a car. She's going to help me redecorate."

"Thank God," Annie muttered.

"I'd been a housewife for over twenty years. I never had to do things like negotiate a car sale. Paul has been so gracious in helping me take on all these new responsibilities. I owed him Thanksgiving dinner."

"Well, you've paid your debt after today," Annie said. "It's a damned shame what they did to you two, but I'm glad you have

each other to get through it. Now that we have that settled"—
Annie nudged Paul—"we can get back to telling stories about
you."

sh

Paul considered not answering the phone. If he didn't, though,
he would have to have this conversation face-to-face. He was
actually surprised it took his sister this long to call him. He'd
dropped Dianna off several hours ago. He had expected the
inquisition to start much sooner.

"Hey, Annie," he said, settling on the couch so he'd be
comfortable as his sister analyzed his life.

"She's nice."

Paul chuckled. Not even a greeting, just right to the heart of
the matter—Dianna. "Yes, she is."

"Seems sincere."

"I think so."

"She's funny."

Paul rolled his head back, wishing Annie would just get to
the point. "Yes."

"It was considerate of her to help clean up."

Ah, a jab at Michelle. "Dianna is very considerate."

"I remember when you told me about the hearing. How bad
you felt for her. I can see why. She doesn't deserve what her
husband did."

"No, she doesn't."

"You should bring her around more often."

Paul lifted his head. Annie had never said that before, not about a single woman Paul had ever dated—and he wasn't even dating Dianna. "We're not in a relationship, Annie."

"Yet."

He sighed and ran his hand over his face. "*Really?*"

"What?"

"No woman you've ever met was good enough for me. Even Laurel—who, by the way, definitely got the short end of the stick on our marriage—was faulted beyond repair in your eyes. But this woman, whom I'm not even dating, is the one you want me to start bringing around more often?"

"Every other woman, Laurel included, looked at you with dollar signs in their eyes."

"Come on, Annie. I'm not a millionaire."

"No. But you do well for yourself, and it shows. I don't want my little brother with a woman who is more attracted to his wallet than his heart."

"How do you know Dianna isn't? Hmm? You spent a few hours with her."

"And in that short amount of time, I saw more genuine concern for you than I ever saw from either of your ex-wives."

Paul considered her words, recalled the way Dianna constantly—albeit gently—steered the conversation in a new direction anytime Matt, Donna, or Annie tried to put Paul under their scrutiny. She'd been so clever at it, he'd hardly noticed.

"Well, I may have told her that I'm tired of you guys nitpicking my mistakes."

"Nobody—" She cut herself off. It was an argument he suspected she didn't want to have any more than he did. "We love you, Paul. We don't like seeing you hurting. Today was the first time you looked happy in a very long time. You even laughed a few times. You may not have noticed, but we did. We all did. And it was obvious she did that for you. So. You should bring her around more often. Even if you aren't dating. *Yet*."

Paul opened his mouth, but Annie ended the call before he could respond. Dropping his cell phone onto the sofa, he picked up the remote and turned the television volume up. He didn't hear Bruce Willis delivering sarcastic lines, however. His mind was wandering back over the afternoon spent with his family. Annie had said it was the first time he looked happy in a very long time, and he had to admit, after the initial uneasiness wore off, it probably was the first time he'd *been* happy in a long time. He'd been surrounded by his family, and they'd all been able to relax and enjoy each other. That hadn't happened for years, it seemed.

Now that Michelle was out of the picture, things were returning to normal. He was happy to be around his family without them scrutinizing him. That's all it was. His happiness had nothing to do with Dianna. He *refused* to let his happiness be about Dianna.

CHAPTER EIGHT

*D*ianna was unloading a bag of groceries when her cell phone rang. She set a bag of apples aside as she pulled the phone from her pocket. She read her attorney's name on the screen, and her heart plummeted to her stomach.

She held her breath as she connected the call. "Hello?"

"Dianna, it's Derek Jenson. I hope this isn't a bad time."

She looked around the empty kitchen. "No, it's fine."

"I just wanted to call you and let you know the paperwork just hit my desk. I'll send you a copy today, but it's done. Your divorce is final."

The wind left her, and she couldn't seem to refill her lungs. "Thank you," she whispered.

"If you need anything else—"

She hung up before he could finish. Finally, her body resumed function, and she inhaled sharply. Her mouth started to water as her stomach turned. The breakfast she'd eaten just an hour or so before, a bagel and two cups of coffee, surged violently, and the bitterness of bile burned its way up her throat. She darted into the bathroom, salivating as the need to throw up overcame her.

She slammed the door behind her and dropped to her knees in front of the toilet. Luckily her hair was pulled back in a bun so she didn't dip it into the water or coat it with vomit as she lost control and retched violently. She vomited again, and then a third time, continuing until there was nothing left in her stomach and she was simply heaving.

Curling up, she hugged her legs and dropped her forehead to her knees as she took slow deep breaths, letting her mind wrap itself around the finality of her marriage. After a long time, she managed to pull herself from the floor to the sink, where she rinsed her mouth and splashed cool water on her face.

At some point, she collapsed on the sofa, where she alternated between feeling numb and wishing the world would stop spinning and her suffering could end.

"Mom?" Sam's tone sounded concerned, as if he'd called out several times.

Dianna blinked and looked up at him.

"What's wrong?"

She tried to smile, but tears fell from her eyes. Of all the horrible things she'd had to tell him the last six months—Dad left, Dad's seeing someone else, Dad filed for divorce—this was probably the worst.

"It's final," she whispered. "We're divorced."

His face sank more and more with every word she said. When she finished, his mouth was hanging open, like she'd dealt him some reality he hadn't been prepared to handle.

Dianna stifled down the emotions that were trying to erupt from her. She didn't think she had any more in her. Her chest ached, her throat burned, and her head throbbed from the sobbing that had racked her body throughout the day. But here it was again, threatening to overwhelm her. She swallowed again, one more attempt to steady her voice before speaking. "I'm sorry, babe."

"Don't be. Dad's a dick." His voice was hard. "He always has been."

"Sam."

"No, Mom. Screw him. And his cunt fiancée." He walked around the sofa and plopped down next to her. "You didn't tell me not to say the C-word."

She sighed. "No. I'll let you call her that today. It's fitting today."

Sam stared at the pile of tissues on the coffee table. "When did you find out?"

"This morning."

He was quiet. He always grew quiet when he was processing information. "Have you been sitting here like this all day?"

"I'm okay."

"No, you're not."

She bit her lip when she saw tears sitting on his lower eyelids, threatening to run down his cheeks.

"Don't lie to me, Mom. I can handle it."

She ran her hand over the back of his head. "I know you can. But you shouldn't have to."

He looked down and wiped at his face, and Dianna's heart broke all over again. A sob escaped her, which triggered one from Sam. Nothing was worse than seeing her boys cry, and as much as Sam tried to laugh life off, he was sensitive. This was hurting him, which made it even worse for her.

He took a breath. "Do you need something? Coffee? Something to eat?"

Fresh tears fell from her eyes as she considered how proud she was of him. He'd picked up more hours at work so he didn't have to ask her for money, he'd started taking out the trash, and over summer, he'd mown the lawn without her pestering him about it. He'd stepped up and helped her in more ways than she could have ever foreseen.

And now, as his world was coming apart, he was asking if she needed something. It broke her heart and filled her with pride at the same time. He looked away when she sobbed again.

"I'm sorry, Sammy. I thought I would be stronger than this."

"You are strong, Mom." His deep voice cracked. "You always have been." He wiped his eyes on his sleeve and looked away from her. "I suck at this stuff. I'm gonna call Kara."

"No. Honey, I love Kara, but I don't need her hovering right now. I just don't." She ruffled his hair and took a breath. "I'm all right. I'm having a bad day, but I'm okay. We're going to be okay. You and me and Jason. We're okay."

"Have you told Jas yet?"

She shook her head. "No. I wanted him to get through all his classes first."

"It's almost five. He's been done with classes for a while. I'm going to call him."

Dianna tried not to let her surprise show. Almost five? She really had been sitting there all day. A sense of defeat started edging in on her depression. "Are you sure? I don't know how he'll take it."

"He'll be okay. Dad probably already called him anyway. He always tells Jason everything. Can I use your phone? My battery died."

She handed him her phone and watched him leave. Leaning back on the couch, she exhaled slowly. She had told herself that she wasn't going to cry, she wasn't going to fall apart, and more than anything, she wasn't going to admit how broken she was. She'd done all of the above.

"Damn it," she breathed as another round of tears found her. She curled up on her side as exhaustion surrounded her. She'd gotten through the worst of it now that she'd told Sam, and if she were honest, she was glad he was telling Jason. She felt guilty letting him do it, but she was relieved, too. It was one less time she'd have to say the words.

Paul brushed Dianna's hair back from her face. "Di," he said softly when she barely stirred.

She drew a deep breath before her eyes fluttered open. Her face was pale except for the dark circles under her red and swollen eyes. His heart broke for her. He'd give anything to take the pain from her eyes and see her smiling like she had the day before at Annie's house.

He pushed more of her hair back and forced a supportive smile to his face. "Hey, sweetie."

"Paul?" Her voice was slurred and cracked.

"Hi."

Her lip trembled, and she took a gasping breath. "I'm divorced," she whispered, and tears instantly filled and then fell from her eyes.

"I know. Sam called me."

She closed her eyes. "I told him I'm fine."

"Well, I can see why he disagrees with you. You most definitely are not fine."

Her shoulders shuddered, and a muted sob rolled from her. "He took it so hard."

Paul frowned as he wiped a tear from her eye, just so another could fall. In that moment, he wanted to hunt Mitch Friedman down and beat the crap out of him.

Stretching onto the couch with Dianna, Paul tucked her body against his. Once he was situated—one arm curled under his head because there wasn't any other place to put it and the other around her back—he kissed her head. "Sam is going to be okay."

She buried her face in his chest. "I couldn't even comfort him."

"He didn't want you to comfort him. He wanted to take care of you. He just didn't know how."

"Where is he?"

"I sent him out for some dinner."

"Oh, God." Her body rocked with another cry. "I didn't even feed my son."

Paul tightened his hold on her. "Stop. He's fine. He's doing okay. I may be in trouble, though," he said, trying to lighten her mood. "I gave him cash and told him to get whatever he wanted and to bring something back for us."

"He'll probably come back with nothing but junk food."

"That'd be okay, huh? At least for tonight."

Dianna exhaled loudly before pushing her face deeper into Paul's chest. "I fell apart. I completely fell apart."

"It was a rough day."

"It's not like I didn't know this was coming."

"It's still hard."

"How can I not be married anymore? How can it all just be over?"

He hugged her closer. "Because he's a goddamned fool."

He held her close, brushing his hand over her hair until she finally stopped crying. When she was quiet for a few minutes, he whispered, "Sam should be back soon. Why don't you clean up before he gets home? Show him you're going to be okay."

She nodded and then tightened her hold on him before he could get up from the sofa. "Thank you. For everything."

"You're welcome." He rolled to his feet and then reached for her. When she was in front of him, looking up at him with raw desperation, he cupped her face in his hands. "You're going to get through today, and then you'll get through tomorrow and the next day. You're going to be okay." He hugged her one more time.

She held him as well and took a few deep breaths before easing away from him. He walked with her, his arm over her shoulder, until she went upstairs, and then he walked toward the back of the house. In the kitchen, he pulled out three plates and utensils. He'd just finished setting the table when Sam walked in with a bucket of chicken and a bag of sides.

"Mom's favorite comfort food," he announced, setting their dinner on the table. "How is she?"

"She's all right. She'll be down in a minute."

Sam shoved his hand into his pocket and pulled out a handful of bills. "Here's your change."

Paul lifted his hand in dismissal. "Consider it a delivery fee."

Sam hesitated, but only for a moment, before shoving the cash back into his pocket. "Thanks. And thanks for coming over. I didn't know what to do, and she didn't want to see Kara."

"I'm glad you called. Really." Paul pulled glasses out of the cabinet and filled them with water.

"It's been forever since we've had fried chicken. Mom better hurry before I eat it all."

Paul put the glasses on the table. "I'll see what's keeping her." He left the kitchen and trotted up the stairs. He knocked on the only closed door and slowly pushed it open when he didn't get a response. He stuck his head into her bedroom. "Di?"

She stepped out of the master bathroom wearing a tattered robe over a T-shirt and a pair of yoga pants. Her hair was pulled back and her face was clean, but her eyes were still red.

"Sam brought chicken."

"I don't know if I can eat."

"You can." He took her hand. "You have to. Deep breath."

She did and then let it out slowly. As she did, her tears returned. "Thank you for being here."

"You're welcome." He pulled her gently, but she didn't budge.

"How can I face him?" She shook her head. "I'm such a failure."

"Hey," he said sternly. Putting his hand to her chin, he forced her to look at him. "I know you feel like the world is crashing down on you right now, but you are stronger than you realize. And you are showing Sam what it means to be strong."

"By falling apart?"

"By not giving up. You're overcoming a gigantic obstacle right now. And he sees that. You didn't fail him. You didn't let him down. You're proving to him that his mother can get through anything, even if she has a bad day now and then."

Her lip trembled as he slid his hands down her arms and clutched her hands.

"Come downstairs," he whispered. "Show him you're going

to be okay. Then we'll get you tucked into bed, and when you wake tomorrow, you'll get up and you'll do it again, knowing that eventually, it's not going to hurt this much."

She nodded, and he led her down to the kitchen.

She hugged Sam as he stuffed a chicken breast into his mouth. "Thanks for dinner."

"It was Paul's idea," he said around his mouthful.

She sat in the chair between them as Paul served her. "Did you talk to Jason?"

"He's okay," Sam said. "Dad had left him a message."

"A *message*? Like a voice mail?"

"Yeah. Jason was pissed about it, but he was okay."

"God." She planted her elbows on the table so she could rub her temples. "Who leaves a message like that for his kid?"

Sam tossed his chicken down as he frowned.

Paul set a plate in front of her. "You can't control what he does," he said softly.

She nodded and smiled weakly at Sam. "I'll call Jas later. Thanks for checking on him. I really appreciate it. And thanks for the chicken." She pulled her plate closer and poked aimlessly at her potatoes.

Paul filled his own plate as he asked Sam about school and college, trying to steer the conversation as far away from Mitch and divorce as he could.

sh

"I guess he asked to use my phone so he could call you," Dianna said after Sam went upstairs to finish his homework. She sat at the table while Paul put their plates in the dishwasher. He had refused her help so she could call Jason, who insisted he was fine and he'd have to talk to her another time since he was on his way out. Dianna wished she could believe him. She knew better, though. He just didn't want her to know he was upset.

"I think so." Paul put the last of the dirty utensils in the rack. He closed the dishwasher and ran his hands under the faucet to wash them. As he leaned against the counter, he dried his hands on a dishtowel.

She laughed softly at the image of him dressed impeccably in slacks, a dress shirt, and tie while he did her dishes. It was so out of place it was amusing.

"Be careful, Di," he said, tossing the towel down. "You're smiling."

"You must be tired," she said. "You've had a long day."

"Not as long as yours." He crossed the room and held his hand out. "Come on."

He bypassed the living room where she expected him to take her and guided her upstairs. "Get ready for bed," he said as they entered her bedroom.

She considered arguing but didn't. She brushed her teeth and returned to her room. He'd tugged the blankets back and stretched out on her bed, leaning against the headboard as he looked at his phone.

"That's my side," she said, her tone teasing.

He grinned before sliding to the left side of the bed. "My apologies."

She crawled into the bed beside him, and he moved down to lie behind her. He curled around her, his body pressed against hers. They stayed like that, him spooning her, holding her close without saying a word, for a long time.

"Thank you," she finally whispered.

"You're welcome," he said just as quietly.

She closed her eyes when he kissed the back of her head and entwined her fingers with his. "I don't think I could get through this without you."

"Yes, you could," he said softly. "You're stronger than you think."

She laughed flatly. "You keep saying that."

"Because it's true."

She rolled over so she could face him. The light coming in from the streetlamp was dim, but she could see his face. "I don't know what to do, Paul. I just don't know what to do."

He hushed her as he pulled her to him, hugging her against his chest. "You don't have to know what to do right now, Dianna. All you have to do is keep moving forward. The rest will come."

She exhaled slowly and wrapped her arms around him. "Will you stay until I fall asleep?"

"Of course."

Closing her eyes, she listened to his heartbeat as she drifted off.

he Monday Dianna had painters scheduled, Paul had handed over a prepaid credit card and made her promise not to do anything contemporary to his home while he stayed with Matt for the week.

By Thursday, the entire interior of his home had new, lower-key colors. The living and dining rooms were now a soothing blue shade, which contrasted against the new bright white wainscoting and trim. The kitchen and bathrooms were almond with the same bright white on the cabinets. The almond color carried into the guest room as well. His room, however, was a deep saffron yellow that he'd picked out.

By Friday, Dianna was putting the finishing touches on his home. The only photo he'd had out was of him with his sons, but it was several years old. She'd asked Annie to e-mail a few newer pictures. Those were now printed and framed and hanging on the living room wall where Michelle had previously hung box shelves filled with statuettes.

The room looked completely different. It looked homey and comfortable. It looked like a room where Paul belonged.

One final walk around the house, and she was confident in the work she'd done. The last touch was the Christmas tree she'd set up in the corner of the living room. He hadn't had a single sign of the holiday in his house, and she was determined that he not let the season pass by ignored as he'd tried to do with Thanksgiving.

The doorbell rang, and she checked her watch. She wasn't expecting Paul until after five, and it was just after three. She smiled when she spotted Annie standing on the porch. Dianna pulled open the door. "Hey."

"I'm being nosy." She stepped in and looked around the living room. "Holy shit, Di. This is amazing."

"Do you think Paul will like it?"

"He's going to love it. This color is fantastic." Annie wandered through the house, commenting on various touches Dianna had added. In Paul's bedroom, she stood at the foot of the bed and nodded. "So. When can you start?"

Dianna creased her brow in confusion. "Start what?"

"My freelance decorator keeps screwing me over. Once you start, I won't need her anymore. Of course, you realize you won't be staging houses full-time. I need you to help in the office mainly. Answering the phone and scheduling appointments.

Nothing you can't handle. You'll basically be an assistant to the agents."

"Oh, Annie, it's very sweet of you—"

"I don't do sweet. I do practical. You need a job that pays better. I need an office administrator who can decorate. I can't be everywhere at once. You're one of the few people I'm not related to that I actually like. I have a low tolerance for bullshit. I trust that you're not going to give me any bullshit."

"Look, for whatever reason, Paul has taken me under his wing, which, believe me, has saved me more than once in the last few months, but this isn't a familial obligation. He has some kind of unfounded guilt over Mitch leaving me high and dry, but my post-divorce hardships are not his problem. And they certainly aren't yours."

Annie looked at Dianna for a few moments before starting out of the bedroom. "Has Paul ever talked about our parents?"

"Just that your mother passed away when you were all fairly young."

"Did he tell you that I turned into a mother hen and just about drove them crazy?"

"Yes. But he said it with love."

Annie snorted. "I bet." She stopped in front of the bare Christmas tree and looked at the boxes of ornaments and ribbons. "Dad was a drunk. Not a mean drunk, just a drunk. He couldn't hold down a job to save his life. Or to feed his family. Paul was just twelve at the time. He took on two paper routes to try to make enough to feed Matty and me. I took over cooking, cleaning, and worrying, and Matty did whatever he could. We had this kind of silent pact to take care of each other because, even if we never said it, we all knew Dad couldn't raise us. Paul grew up working and negotiating to keep a roof over our heads and the utilities on. He was always taking care of us. He put himself through law school because he didn't want any of us to have to go without again."

"That must have been hard on all of you."

"It was. But we survived. And we all learned how important it is to take care of each other. You're taking care of my brother, so I'm going to take care of you. Paul says you have been looking for a full-time job. I'm looking for a full-time office admin. If you don't like the job, quit. But I promise you, you will be able to make ends meet for you and your boys."

Dianna nodded slightly. "Okay. Thank you."

"So, when can you start?"

"Um. Next Monday?"

"Next Monday it is."

"Annie?" she called when the woman started to leave.

Annie turned and lifted her brows curiously.

"Is the thing with your father the reason Paul doesn't like Christmas?"

"Dad never celebrated after Mom died. We tried to keep traditions alive, me more than Paul and Matt, I guess. But it was never the same. I think it just reminds him of that."

"Maybe I shouldn't..." She gestured toward the tree.

"Leave it. Give him something good to think about this holiday. I'll be in touch about the job."

"Yes, ma'am."

Annie closed the door behind her, and Dianna exhaled heavily and looked at the tree again. She debated only for another moment before pushing the doubts from her mind and focusing on the good that had come from Annie's visit. She had a full-time job. Starting next Monday, she would once again have the means to take care of her kids.

sh

Paul couldn't help but smile as Dianna stepped out to greet him when he started up the stairs to his house. "That's some grin," he said, meeting her at his front door.

She chuckled. "I have news."

He lifted his brows, but she shook her head.

"Let's have a look around first," she said. "I hope you like it."

He looked past her at the now blue and white walls of his entryway. The vibe was immensely better already. "Wow. This is amazing." He stepped inside, set his briefcase down, and wriggled out of his coat, which Dianna hung on a hook by the door while he kicked off his shoes and unbuttoned his suit coat.

They walked into the living room, and he stopped when he noticed the tree. He hadn't planned on decorating for the holiday, but somehow it seemed right. She seemed nervous, so he gave her a smile and a reassuring nod.

She led him through the house, showing him the bathroom and his new bedroom. The colors were much more soothing, much more *him*. She'd made his house feel like a home again. "You did a great job, Di," he said, looking at his new bedroom furniture. "I love it."

"Well, come on. We still have to see the kitchen."

"The kitchen." He grinned. "You mean the source of that amazing smell?"

"Lasagna."

"Oh, man. If you tell me that's homemade, I'm going to have to declare this the best day of my life." They walked into the kitchen, and he gasped dramatically. "No more lime-green walls."

She grabbed a pot holder and opened the oven. "New dishes, too."

"Nice. This is just amazing. Thank you." He filled two wineglasses while she went to work on serving dinner. "Tell me your big news."

She glanced back and bit her lip. "Annie stopped by—"

He stopped pouring and looked at her. "Oh, no."

"No, it's good. She liked what I did to the house and offered me a position."

"Di—"

"It's good, Paul."

He sighed and bit back his warning. He didn't want to rain on her parade, but Annie was far from easy to work for. Instead he nodded. "Congratulations."

Her smile returned. "Thank you. Matt didn't drive you crazy this week, did he?"

Paul had artfully sidestepped any conversation Matt had attempted to have about Dianna over the last week. He'd called and heard her voice and managed to keep it limited to "checking in" on how the redecorating was going. He hadn't wanted Matt to know how much time he and Dianna were spending together. Actually, Paul hadn't even realized it himself until he forcibly stayed away from her. He'd missed her over the last week—missed her laugh and her cooking and just being around her—and that was something he hadn't wanted to admit to himself or his nosy brother.

He shrugged and shook his head as he dug into his lasagna. "No, he didn't drive me too crazy."

CHAPTER TEN

"You didn't have to do this," Dianna said as she and Paul were led to a table at her favorite Italian restaurant.

Paul held out a chair for her. "I wanted to do this."

She eased down. "Well, thank you. I appreciate it."

He sat across from her. "So tell me more about your first day working with Annie."

She shrugged. "There really isn't more to tell. It was confusing at first, but I think by the end of the day I started to get the swing of things. I only dropped two calls, which Annie forgave me for, and I even got the appointment reminders out. I think I'm going to like it."

When a waiter approached, Paul ordered an entire bottle of wine. Dianna almost protested, but something about his demeanor made her stop.

"I've been rambling on about my day. I haven't even asked

about yours yet."

He shrugged and diverted his gaze. "I have a court date coming up, so I've been doing a lot of research and note-taking. Trust me, your day was much more interesting."

She wanted to press but changed the subject instead. "So, Christmas is just around the corner. I thought maybe you'd like to come over for dinner. Unless you're doing something with Toby and Sean."

"No, I'll see them Christmas Eve. Would, uh, would your boys mind?"

"I don't think so. They have to go to Mitch's after dinner, so it's not like you'd be interfering with some great family tradition. Ham and all the fixings. Sound good?"

He nodded as he shifted his silverware on the table. "Sounds great. What time?"

"We usually eat about one."

When their waiter returned, he filled their glasses with wine, set the bottle down, and asked for their order. Dianna chuckled as she realized they hadn't even looked at their menus. She ordered eggplant parmesan, and Paul ordered lasagna.

His amusement faded quickly, though, and he swirled the liquid in his glass.

She reached out and took his hand. "Are you okay?"

"Yeah, fine."

She started to press, but he shook his head.

"I'm fine."

Obviously he wasn't but didn't want to talk about it. "So, this friend of yours who bought my piano. Any idea when he wants it?"

"No. Is it in the way?"

"No, I just kind of feel guilty hanging on to it since he paid for it."

"Have you been playing it?"

She hadn't touched the instrument. Knowing it was going to be leaving her broke her heart, but for some reason it seemed important to Paul that she had, so she let a little white lie slip through. "Some."

"Good."

Dianna watched as he refilled his glass. He was being polite, but his heart wasn't in their conversation. He may have been sitting across from her, but his mind was elsewhere.

"Paul, what happened?"

He looked away and shook his head.

She reached across the table and covered his hand. "Honey, what is it?"

"I don't want to ruin your day, Di."

"Talk to me."

He focused on his glass, taking a moment to swirl the deep-red liquid. "It's final. I got the decree today at the office."

"Jesus, Paul." She squeezed his hand. "Why didn't you tell me?"

He gave her a slight smile. "This is your big day. I didn't want to ruin it."

"You couldn't possibly ruin it. Let's get our dinner to go. We'll take it home and—"

"No. Can we just... Can we enjoy dinner? Please? I'd really like to have a nice dinner with you."

She hesitated, wanting to push him harder, but nodded and delved back into her day, rambling about things that weren't all that interesting. She leaned back as their dinner was served. They cut into their food, and Paul immediately informed her that her lasagna was much better than what the chef had prepared. Then he finished off his third glass of wine. Dianna watched but didn't stop him as he filled his glass for the fourth time, and soon after he commented that he needed to flag the waiter down for another bottle.

Paul polished off his dinner and a second bottle of wine and then ordered dessert and a coffee. They talked about everything and anything, except his divorce. He held his liquor well until she urged him to leave the restaurant. Though it had been half an hour since his last drink, he was still wobbly on his feet. She apologized to the people next to them when he bumped into their table. Then she slid under his arm to keep him steady on the way out. She guided him to his car and took his keys without any resistance from him.

Paul stared out the passenger window as she drove toward his house. "I don't know why I'm letting this get to me. It's not like I thought she'd change her mind. They're getting married, remember?"

"Yes. I remember."

"Who the hell needs her anyway?"

They drove the rest of the way in silence. After parking in his driveway, she waited for him at the front of the car and then guided him up the steps and through the front door. He stumbled in, and as she hung their coats, he headed for the living room.

She pulled off her boots and walked farther into the house to find him sitting on the new sofa, his face buried in his palms as he took deep, loud breaths. She stood, not sure what to do, but finally sat on the coffee table and gently pushed him back. He fell, slouching on the sofa, as she reached down and slipped off his dress shoes.

"How long before they get married?" he asked as she set them aside. "A week? A month? Or do you think they went to the courthouse today?"

Dianna swallowed as she looked at where her wedding ring used to sit. She'd done a good job of not dwelling on Mitch's impending nuptials. She hadn't allowed herself to think of how quickly he'd gone from leaving her to being engaged to Michelle, let alone how quickly they'd get married once they both were free. But now, it was an obvious question. How soon before she was officially and legally replaced? "I don't know."

"I couldn't have tried harder. I couldn't have. I don't know what else I could have done."

His words broke her heart.

She'd felt the exact same pain not so long ago. Putting her hands on his knees, she did her best to comfort him as he'd done for her. "Nothing, Paul. You couldn't have done anything. She did this. It wasn't you. You are wonderful."

He laughed, but it was a bitter, disbelieving sound. He stumbled to his feet, and Dianna held out her hand, as if she could catch him should he fall.

"I'm a disaster," he said. "Everything I touch turns to shit."

"That's not—"

He turned and pointed at her. "*Don't!* You don't know. You don't know anything. Your life is just as screwed up as mine."

His words cut at her and made her wince. Sure, her life was a mess, but Paul was the one person who made her feel okay with that. It hurt to hear him point out her flaws.

He sighed and lowered his hand. He turned away from her and ran his hand through his hair. "I'm sorry, Dianna. I didn't..." He faced her, and the look in his eyes tore at her heart. He was so broken inside.

She wanted to wrap him in her arms and hold him until he stopped hurting. She opened her mouth, prepared to ask him to come back to the sofa so she could sit with him. But then he spoke again.

"Who are we kidding?" he whispered.

She waited, but he didn't expand on his question.

"Who are we kidding about what?" she asked.

"We act like we're moving on, like we're letting go, but we aren't. We aren't letting go. We're hanging on to the only part of them we have left—each other. We're clinging to the parts they threw away because it's all we have left. It's pathetic. *We're* pathetic."

Where his previous declaration had cut at her, this time she felt like his words would emotionally bring her to her knees. She pulled her lips into her mouth and pressed her teeth into them as tears sprang to her eyes. Was that what he thought? What he really thought? That she was pathetic? That she wasn't moving on? That she was just something that had been tossed away?

She blinked, and a tear fell down her cheek. "I'm sorry you feel that way," she whispered. "I thought we'd become friends, Paul. I thought we *were* moving on and letting go. Together. Like we said we would."

"Di—"

She pushed herself up. "Look, um, I don't think you should be alone, but maybe I'm not the one you need right now. Why don't you get ready for bed, and I'll call Matt?"

"No, please."

She stepped around him before he finished, going to get her phone from her purse by the door. Paul clumsily rushed after her, but she didn't stop until his fingers gripped her upper arms. His breath, thick with alcohol, rushed over her shoulder as he wrapped his arms around her and pulled her to him, pressing his chest against her back.

"I'm sorry," he said quietly and then buried his face in her hair. "I'm so sorry. Don't go. Please."

Dianna closed her eyes. "I just want to help you."

"I know." He loosened his hold on her, just enough that he

could turn her and pull her back to him. He cupped the back of her head as he slid his other arm around her shoulders, pulling her tightly against him. "I'm sorry. Please don't leave me."

"Okay," she soothed. She hugged him, and he squeezed her even more tightly.

After a moment, he leaned back and put his hands on her face. "I'm sorry. I'm so sorry."

"I know. It's okay."

He searched her eyes, and her heart did a strange little flip in her chest as his thumbs brushed over her cheeks.

He took a few deep breaths, exhaling them slowly. "Di?"

"Yeah?" she breathed.

"I think I'm gonna be sick."

She creased her brow, but then he swallowed hard and she pulled from him and reached for the front door. She got him to the porch and turned away, grimacing as he leaned over the banister and vomited into the snow. She laughed, more at herself than at him. For a moment, for just a few seconds, she'd thought he was going to kiss her. Closing her eyes, she shook the thought from her mind and ran her hand over his back. He retched several times before he stood upright.

"Better?" she asked.

He nodded and spit before sucking in the cold air. "I think so."

"Can you make it inside?"

"Yeah."

He put his arm over her shoulder and leaned on her as she

led him in. They went down the hall and through his bedroom. Dianna propped him against the bathroom sink and reached for his toothbrush.

While he clumsily brushed the regurgitated wine and lasagna from his teeth, she pulled the blankets back on his bed. She busied herself closing the blinds and curtains as she listened to the toilet flush and water run. When the bathroom door opened, she spun toward him and then sighed and looked away.

Paul, clad only in a pair of tight, pale blue boxer briefs, made his way to the bed and crawled in. Dianna closed her eyes and tried not to think of how damned good he looked. "I'm going to get you some water."

"No." He reached out to her.

"You need to get some water in you. Otherwise you're going to have a horrible hangover."

"Please. Stay."

She stared at him for a few heartbeats before caving and returning to the bed. She sat on the edge, but he pulled her down and tugged at her until she stretched out on her back beside him. Her heart skipped when he rolled nearly on top of her.

He put his hand on her cheek and stared into her eyes for a minute. "I didn't mean to be a jerk."

"I know."

"Don't leave me, okay?"

"Okay," she said breathlessly.

He slid down in the bed, resting his head on her shoulder and draping his arm over her stomach while his leg wrapped around hers.

Dianna stared at the ceiling for a long time. She should not be lying in his bed with him nearly naked. Even so, she ran her palm down his back. She almost felt guilty as she touched him. He was passed out drunk in his underwear, and she was gratuitously running her hand over his hot skin. However, the feeling of his arms around her and his heat sinking into her banished her guilt, and she ran her hand over him again. He snorted and she laughed slightly, but her lips fell when he hugged her even closer.

As much as she enjoyed having him so close, this was surely the pathetic part he'd mentioned earlier. Falling into this...*friendship*, if they could even call it that, had been so easy for them. It was so easy to have someone there showing affection and appreciation, but the affection wasn't real. They'd created a safety net, and she had consciously chosen to ignore that it was frayed. At some point, it was going to give and they were going to go tumbling down.

Paul jolted when his alarm clock started beeping. Holy. Shit. The sound echoed through his head like a gong. Rolling over, he stopped when he bumped into a body. Holy. Shit. Again. Just how much had he drunk? Oh, yeah, at least a bottle. Maybe two.

A quiet moan from the woman next to him was enough for

Paul to identify her. Stretching over Dianna, he slammed the snooze button on the alarm clock and dropped his arm around her as he collapsed onto the pillows. He smiled slightly, as much as he could manage with his massive hangover, when she snorted in her sleep and shifted closer to him. Burying his nose in her hair, he breathed in her scent as he tried to piece together the night before.

Screaming. Vomiting. Asking Dianna to stay with him.

Oh, shit.

He ran his hand over her stomach, relieved when he felt the material of her shirt. Okay. So they hadn't slept together. That's good. That's very good. Paul suspected she'd be offended if he couldn't remember their first time together.

First time? Where had that thought come from?

His alarm blared again. This time, Dianna jolted. Paul stretched over her again, silencing the obnoxious sound.

"Good morning," he muttered.

"Mmm," she moaned. But a second later, she gasped and sat up. "Shit! I didn't go home last night. Sam is never going to let me live this down."

"Hey," he called, but she darted from the bedroom and was down the hall, flipping on lights as she went, before he could even think of what he should say. She was holding her phone when she reappeared.

"Get dressed," she said. "I have to be to work in an hour or Annie will kill me." A moment later, she put the phone to her ear. "Hey, Sammy. I am *so* sorry. I'm at Paul's. We fell asleep."

Paul glanced at her, and she rolled her eyes.

"Not like *that*," she told her son.

Paul grinned as he imagined the sarcasm Sam was giving her. He stood up, and Dianna turned her back to him. He glanced down and, without an ounce of shame, realized he'd slept in nothing but his underwear. Even so, he opened a drawer and found a pair of house pants.

"Were you okay last night?" A moment later, she sighed heavily. "*Sam,* it wasn't like *that*. I'll see you tonight."

She ended the call and shoved her phone into her pocket as she glanced back at Paul. "How are you doing?"

He pulled a T-shirt on, and she seemed satisfied that she could face him again.

"I need you to take me home. Like, now."

"Why don't you just take my car?"

"How will you get to work?"

He raked his hand over his hair. Even that inflicted pain on him. "I'm pretty sure I'm taking the morning off. Can you pick me up on your lunch break and we'll get your car?"

"Are you going to be okay by noon?"

"Yeah. Um, I don't remember much about last night, but I seem to recall making you cry."

Dianna exhaled slowly. "You were drunk."

Damn it. "That's no excuse. What did I do?"

"You said our friendship is a façade."

"Shit, Di, I didn't mean that."

She worked her lip between her teeth for a moment. "If you do—"

"I don't."

"But *if* you do," she said firmly, "you need to tell me. I deserve to know where I stand with you, Paul. I deserve the truth from you."

He nodded his agreement, even though it hurt like hell to do so. If anyone deserved his honesty, it was Dianna. Crossing the room, he stopped in front of her. "I'm telling you the truth. I don't think this is a façade. I don't remember what I said last night, but it was the alcohol and the emotion talking. It wasn't me. I'm so sorry."

She looked down. "It's just... I don't know up from down anymore. Just when it seems like things are getting better, they fall apart again, and things *have been* getting better. I keep waiting for the other shoe to drop."

"I know that feeling." He put his finger under her chin and lifted her face so he could look into her eyes. "I'm—"

"Don't apologize. It's done. I just... I don't want to count on you if you're going to disappear once you can stand on your own."

Paul smiled as he brushed her hair from her face. He didn't think he could walk away from her if he wanted to. "That's not going to happen. We haven't known each other for long, but I care about you, Dianna."

She gave him a slight smile. "I care about you, too."

"Whatever I said, please believe it was my reaction to the divorce. Not to you."

She nodded. "I have to go. I can't be late."

"Go. But, Di?"

"Yeah?"

"Don't dwell on this all day. Don't let my stupidity ruin your day."

"I won't."

"Okay." He leaned forward and kissed her forehead. "I'll see you for lunch."

"Go back to bed. You look like hell."

"Thanks."

She laughed quietly and then turned to leave.

Paul stood, not moving, until the front door closed. Dropping his head, he exhaled heavily. The fog of sleep and alcohol was still clouding his mind, but it wasn't lost on him that he'd awakened far more concerned about upsetting Dianna than about his divorce. Running his hand over his hair, he pictured her bright blue eyes looking up at him, her body beneath his, and wished more than anything else that their evening hadn't been ruined by his drunken stupidity.

CHAPTER ELEVEN

*D*ianna smiled brightly as she stepped aside and let Paul in. "Merry Christmas."

"Merry Christmas. Wow, it smells good in here."

"I'm glad you agreed to come for dinner." She took his coat and hung it up while he set a present on the table next to the door. "I made way too much food, as I tend to do."

"Are you sure it's okay with the boys that I'm here?"

"Yeah. It's fine."

That may have been an exaggeration. Sam refused to believe that Dianna and Paul weren't dating. Jason, on the other hand, scoffed and rolled his eyes whenever Paul was brought up. Apparently Dianna wasn't supposed to even date—not that she and Paul *were* dating—despite the fact that Mitch was now engaged.

She had threatened Jason's life if he was rude to Paul and Sam's life if he even hinted at his suspicions of their relationship status—which he shared relentlessly after Dianna accidentally fell asleep at Paul's house. A night she tried not to think about too much, and not just because her son liked to embarrass her. Whenever she thought too much about how Paul had wrapped himself around her, she tended to blush and her heart would start racing.

Paul followed her into the kitchen, where she was finishing up dinner.

"Do you need help with anything?" he asked.

"You can take those dishes to the table."

As he carried a casserole dish out of the room, she pulled her phone from her pocket and sent a text to Jason, who was on the other side of the house.

Come eat. And be nice!

As Paul returned to carry another dish out, she whipped the boiled potatoes with milk and butter. She pulled the rolls from the oven, put them into a basket, and carried the dishes to the table. She smiled when she saw the three men in her life chatting. Jason even looked moderately tolerant of Paul. She sat at the table as they started passing food, and peace washed over her for the first time in months. Not just a *sense* of peace, but *real* peace, *real* contentment. It had been a wonderful day. The boys had been thrilled with the presents Paul had helped her get and had even gotten her presents in return, which had never happened before.

They felt like a family despite Mitch's glaring absence. They'd laughed and torn into presents and had a huge breakfast, just like they had done every year since they were old enough. She'd thought of Mitch but was able to push him from her mind and focus on happier things. Now, as she watched the boys fill their plates and Paul once again complimented her on how good dinner smelled, she realized she was happy. The emotion took her completely by surprise and brought a surge of tears to her eyes. She tried to blink them away, but Sam hesitated in handing her the potatoes.

She put a spoonful on her plate and passed the dish to Paul.

"I'm okay," she whispered when he, too, looked at her with concern.

She watched as they dug in and must've gotten lost in the moment, because Paul reached under the table and put a hand on her knee, squeezing it gently. She looked at him and smiled before picking up her fork and stabbing at her ham. They all laughed at the story Sam was telling, and by the time dinner ended, even Jason seemed relaxed. It was more than Dianna could have asked for, more than she had expected from her first Christmas as a divorcee and single mother.

She wanted to reach out and take Paul's hand in hers, she just had the urge, but as she did, she recalled her insistence that there was nothing going on between them. Instead, she gathered her dishes and stood. "Anybody ready for dessert?"

"We have to head out if we're going to get to Grandma's on time," Jason said bitterly, causing Dianna to pause and look at him. "I guess we can't put off meeting that woman forever."

Sam turned his attention across the table to Paul. "Any tips on how to survive your ex-wife?"

"Toss her something sparkly to distract her."

Dianna raised a brow at Paul. "Don't encourage this."

Paul put his hand to his chest as if offended. "What did I do?"

"Look," she said to her kids, "you may not be happy about this situation, but you can't change it. Don't make it worse than it is. This"—she waved her hand—"*woman* is going to be your stepmother eventually. You may as well get used to that."

"Fat chance." Jason pushed himself up.

She didn't argue. She had done all the defending of Mitch that she felt obligated to do. She watched them leave and then carried a stack of dishes to the kitchen.

"Well, today wasn't as bad as it could have been," she said when he followed her, carrying two dishes. "I was afraid Jason was going to glare at you the entire time."

He grinned. "I bought him off."

She creased her brow as she snapped tops onto the containers for storage. "How so?"

"While you were finishing dinner, I gave them both gift certificates to the game store at the mall."

"Paul!"

He laughed. "Hey, it worked. Are you okay? You kept fading during dinner."

She put the food in the fridge and faced him. "I was just thinking that I'm okay. I'm actually, really, honestly okay. And I'm glad you were here."

"Me, too."

They finished cleaning up from dinner and then headed to the living room. Dianna pointed at the last wrapped present under the tree. "You want to open that?"

He followed her gaze. "For me?"

"Mmm-hmm."

He hurried to where he'd left her present and carried it to the tree. "Come on."

Dianna walked across the room to sit with him in front of the tree. She grabbed the box she had wrapped for him. "You first."

He opened the box and pulled out a CD of mixed jazz music and a small handmade booklet. He opened the booklet and chuckled. "Coupons."

"*Magic* coupons."

He flipped through the computer-printed slivers of paper. "*Good for one eggplant parmesan.* I like that. What else did I get with these? Lasagna. Laundry. Awesome. You know I hate doing laundry."

She chuckled. "You've told me. I'm sorry. I just couldn't afford to get you something better."

"No." He smiled sincerely. "This is great. This is perfect. This is better than anything you could have bought. And this CD..." He looked over the back. "Some of my favorites are on here. I love it."

"I hope so."

"I do. Open yours."

She pulled the big box onto her lap and couldn't stop her smile from spreading as she tore it open. She lifted the top off a box, pushed the tissue paper aside, and pulled out a plush, teal-colored robe.

"Your other robe looked like it deserved to spend the rest of its life in retirement."

She giggled as she thought of the old tattered garment that had been given to her on Mother's Day when the boys were still in elementary school. "It's seen better days."

He pulled her to her feet and held the robe open while she slipped her arms into the wide sleeves. She turned and folded the front closed and then tied it with the sash.

"Lovely," he said.

"I like it. It's very..." She stopped speaking when she shoved her hands into the pockets and felt an envelope in one. Pulling it out, she looked at him with confusion.

"Oh, that? That's actually for both of us."

She tore the envelope open and found two season passes to the community theater. "Paul," she breathed.

"You said you wanted to spend more time at the theater. I enjoy shows as well, so..."

"This is amazing. Thank you."

He shrugged. "That means, of course, that you have to take me."

"Oh," she teased, "I'll try to work you into my rotation." She untied the sash around her waist and laid the robe over a chair. "I made pie."

"Not yet. I'm stuffed."

They plopped onto the sofa, and Paul kicked off his shoes while she grabbed the remote control. She turned on the series they'd started binge-watching on Netflix, and they sat quietly through the episode.

"Hey, Di," he said quietly before she could start another.

"Hmm?"

"There's something I've been meaning to tell you."

His tone seemed to indicate that he wasn't looking forward to whatever it was he planned to say. She sighed.

"What?"

Suddenly the front door opened and then slammed shut. She and Paul jolted and turned toward the entryway.

Sam stormed up the stairs without a word to them. Jason came in behind him, opening and closing the front door much more easily than Sam had. Dianna stood with Paul beside her, looking curiously at her son.

"They're getting married," Jason said, sounding like he could barely speak.

Dianna creased her brow. "We knew that."

"On New Year's Eve. At the stroke of midnight."

Dianna's breath left her in a rush, like she'd been punched in the gut. Paul put his arm around her shoulder, and she leaned against him for support.

"They want us there," Jason said. "Sam made it pretty clear we had better things to do."

Dianna opened her mouth, but she couldn't speak. No words

came out. Her mouth just gaped and stayed that way.

Jason looked away. "I'm going to check on Sam."

He left the room before Dianna turned to Paul. He looked as shocked as she felt. Just when she was doing better. Just when she was content.

A tear fell from her eye, and he wiped it away. When his own tear ran down his cheek, she reached up as he had done and dried it. Using his hold on her head, Paul pulled Dianna to his chest and wrapped her in his arms as they dealt with another blow from their exes.

sh

"So," Matt said, handing Paul a beer. "How's it going?"

Paul took a long drink as he looked at the television. Matt had shown up at his door under the pretense of wanting to watch the football game, but Paul didn't need Matt to tell him the real reason he was there. He'd stopped responding to Annie's phone calls. He was tired of reassuring her that he was fine. She didn't believe him, but surprisingly, he actually was doing okay.

It was Dianna he was worried about. She'd finally seemed to be doing well. She'd said she was okay on Christmas, and he thought she really was. Then Jason dropped the bombshell, and it was like her feet had been kicked out from under her again.

Swallowing a mouthful of cold brew, he nodded. "It's fine, Matt. Just like I told your sister."

"*Our* sister. And Annie isn't the only one worried. Donna thinks you're in denial about how upset you are."

"Because I'm not wallowing in self-pity?"

Matt smirked. "You have a way of doing that."

"Screw you." Paul lifted his hand in frustration as his team lost the ball. "Idiots."

"You seem to be handling things well."

"Because I am. You know, I have friends for these kinds of chats."

"You also have family," Matt reminded him. "And we were finally starting to see you on a semi-regular basis, but the last few days, you've gone back into hiding."

"I'm not in hiding."

"She's getting married, Paul. In a few days. That's gotta sting."

Paul took another drink. "You know what, Matty? It does. But I finally figured out that Michelle's behavior has nothing to do with me. She's shallow. She's narcissistic. The sting I feel is more at my own stupidity than the lack of affection she felt for me. She's going to do to this guy the same thing she did to me. Wrap him up, turn him around, and then leave him for the next thing that comes along. It's what she does."

Matt nodded. "I'm glad you see that. How's Dianna handling it?"

Paul sighed. "Not well. She's trying to be strong for her kids, but she's pretty torn up."

"And, uh, how do you feel about that?"

"What do you mean, how do I feel about it? I don't want to see her hurting, if that's what you're getting at."

"How do you feel about her being torn up that her ex is getting remarried?"

Paul set his beer down. "I hate that he can still break her heart like that."

Matt was quiet for a minute. "Is she heartbroken?"

Paul nodded as a gloom he couldn't quite explain settled over him. "Yeah. She seems to be pretty devastated."

"That sucks, huh?"

"Yeah, it sucks. She doesn't deserve what he's put her through."

"No, I mean... If she's devastated, that means she still cares about him. If she still cares about him, she's not ready to move on, and if she's not ready to move on..."

Paul eyed his brother. "What?"

Matt took a long swig from his bottle. "Just...don't get invested in a woman who isn't ready to invest in you. That's all."

Paul sighed and returned his attention to the television. "I wish you and Annie would stop trying to put Dianna and me in a relationship. We know we aren't ready. Neither one of us has even tried to go there, and we aren't going to. So just...drop it."

He glanced at Matt, who was giving him a look like he didn't believe a word he was saying.

"Drop it," Paul said again.

CHAPTER TWELVE

The week after Christmas had been an emotional blur. Dianna had gone from angry to depressed to perfectly fine and then went through it all again, over and over. Somehow, though she wasn't quite certain how, she had ended up in a crowded ballroom at the local casino on New Year's Eve with a pilot named Mike giving her googly eyes while she scanned the faces for Paul.

Mike put his hand on her shoulder. "Did you hear me, Diane? I said we should go someplace quieter so we can talk."

She'd already corrected him on her name three times. She wasn't doing it again. "I don't think my date would appreciate that."

"C'mon. What kind of guy leaves a beautiful woman standing alone on New Year's Eve?"

"He just went to get more drinks."

Mike leaned close. "I've been watching you. And I keep thinking one thing."

"I bet you do," she said through her frozen smile just as she spotted Paul pushing his way through a group of people. "There's my date. Gotta go."

Paul's gaze followed Mike as he moved on to another woman standing alone. "Who was that?"

"Um, that was Mike, and he's been watching me all night and thinking *one* thing." She glanced back and shuddered. "Do not leave me alone again."

Paul grinned and ran his fingers over a curl dangling along the side of her face. He'd been doing that all night. He seemed to be mesmerized by that particular strand of hair. She didn't mind. The first time it had been gentle and sweet. As the night grew older and they drank more, his hand became heavy and lazy. This time, he practically petted her face, and she chuckled.

"You look beautiful. Did I tell you that?"

His voice was a bit thick but not slurred like Mike's had been. And when Paul complimented her, it pleased her instead of making her feel icky. Rather than feeling like meat on a platter for Mike to pick over, Paul's words warmed her inside.

"Yes, you did. But you can keep saying it." She took another drink from the glass in her hand. The bartender was either making the drinks taste too good or she was officially too drunk to taste the alcohol. She could have finished off the drink in the time it took her to walk to the bar and order another.

Paul had made several trips to get alcohol beyond their

initial stop upon arriving at the party. He'd had just as much scotch as she'd had vermouth and gin, only she was clearly feeling hers more. The martinis were starting to systematically dismantle her common sense. She was probably eyeing Paul the same way Mike had eyed her, but she didn't care. He was handsome as hell in his gray dress shirt with the top two buttons open, exposing his neck and tempting her to kiss his smooth skin.

She sighed, begrudgingly dragged her gaze upward, and grinned when he smirked at her. Yeah. She was *definitely* looking at him like Mike had been looking at her. She giggled and leaned into him. She was going to have a hell of a hangover with a strong dose of embarrassment in the morning if she didn't slow down. Part of her said it was time to switch to water, but the other part of her reminded her it was New Year's Eve and her husband was getting married.

The band started playing an old Eric Clapton song, and she pushed all logic and ideas of remorse from her mind. She pressed her chest to Paul's and put her lips to his ear under the guise of making sure he could hear her over the chattering of the crowd, but the truth was she just wanted to feel his body against hers. "Dance with me."

He slid his hand to the small of her back, and they both drank what was left in their glasses and then set them aside. He guided her through the crowd until they found space on the dance floor. Paul wrapped his arm around Dianna's waist and pulled her close. Her head was already spinning from the alcohol, but she thought she could pass out when she inhaled his scent and the heat of his body started to seep into her.

She had a fleeting thought that they weren't ready for any kind of relationship, but she discarded it just as quickly as it sneaked up on her. She wasn't going to listen to reason tonight. Not tonight. They moved as one to the song, and when it ended, Dianna silently prayed they would play another ballad so he wouldn't have to let her go. Instead, the lead singer announced it was one minute to midnight. The crowd cheered, but Dianna felt like she'd been kicked in the gut.

No. It wasn't midnight. It couldn't be midnight. Not already. Burning-hot tears sprang to her eyes, and she tried to stop the tidal wave of pain that was rushing over her, but she was instantly consumed and pulled into an ocean of misery. She gasped as the mask of happiness she'd been wearing all evening shattered and exposed the truth. She was heartbroken. She sagged against Paul, she dropped her head to his shoulder, and she shuddered in his arms as a sob erupted from deep within her.

He leaned back and put his hands to her cheeks. His face sank when he looked at her.

"They're getting married. Right now."

He used his thumbs to wipe her tears away, but more fell. He wrapped her tightly against him, and she clung to him. The crowd around them started counting down from ten, and her shoulders began to shake as every number felt like a dagger cutting at her soul. People cheered as a new year began, but Dianna cursed the moment. A moment she would never forget.

The moment she stood devastated, surrounded by horns and kissing couples, while the man she had loved for so long married someone else.

"Let's go," Paul said in her ear.

"I'm sorry. I didn't mean to ruin our night."

"You didn't."

She scoffed and scanned the happy crowd. "I wanted tonight to be ours, to be our good memory. I didn't want it to be about them."

The band started playing "Auld Lang Syne," and Paul looked down at her. He cupped her face and put his forehead to hers. She covered his hands with hers for a moment and then stroked her fingers over his hair and cradled the back of his neck. As the song ended and people cheered, Paul dipped his face down and captured Dianna's mouth with his. The kiss may have started out as a friendly welcoming of a new beginning, but their lips lingered and then moved in unison as Paul and Dianna simultaneously deepened the connection.

She wrapped her arms around his neck as he slipped his arms behind her back. He pulled her to him, held her tightly, and brushed his tongue over her mouth. She parted her lips in response and danced her tongue drunkenly along his. It was a desperate, hungry kiss that she felt all the way down to her groin. When she was breathless, she leaned back and met his gaze. His eyes mirrored what she was feeling—confusion, desperation, and sadness mixed with a heavy dose of lust and the recklessness that too much alcohol tended to bring.

She thought she should apologize for kissing him like that, but then he leaned down and drew her into another tongue-tangling kiss. In that moment, nothing else in the world mattered.

A body bumped into them, knocking them apart and back to the reality of standing in the middle of a crowded dance floor.

Paul looked down at Dianna and slowly grinned. "How's that for creating our own memory?"

She traced her fingertips along his jawline. Her heart pounded in her chest. Not just from the kisses they'd just shared but from what she was about to say. "It's a start."

She stared into his eyes, and an entire conversation passed between them without either saying a word. Sleeping together was a terrible idea. One they shouldn't even be considering. But they were hurting, they were lonely, and they were both tired of feeling that way. They reached an unspoken agreement. She wrapped her arm around his waist, and he draped his over her shoulder as they left the party and walked through the casino toward the attached hotel.

With a hotel room keycard in one hand and the other pressed low on Dianna's back, Paul guided her to the elevator. He pressed the button to summon a car and slid his arm farther around her waist. She smiled up at him, and his insides twisted with desire. Moving in front of her, he cupped her face and ran his thumbs lightly over her cheeks. She gripped his hips and pulled him closer.

Pressing his mouth to hers, he kissed her gently instead of delving into the passion they'd shared before. He lightly traced her lips with his tongue until she parted them. Holding her close, he tasted her, inhaled her scent, and absorbed her warmth. After the elevator door opened, he stepped back and guided her inside. He pushed the button for the fourth floor and leaned back against the railing, pulling her with him. Searching her eyes, he sought out any doubt she might be hiding, but she closed the gap between them and pressed her mouth into his before he could get a read on what she was feeling. Like the kiss at the party, this one was on the verge of exploding. Moving his hands lower, he cupped her bottom and pulled her closer.

She gasped against his mouth. There was no hiding his reaction to her. The car jerked to a stop, and Paul threw his arm out to stop the doors from closing before they could step out. He looked at the sign showing which rooms were in which direction and pointed her to the left. They walked past several doors until he stopped and unlocked one. He pushed the door open and gestured for her to enter first. She found a light switch and flipped it as she stepped by him.

He took his time closing and locking the door, watching as she walked farther into the room. He had to wonder if she had any idea how amazing she looked in her knee-length black dress and high heels. He'd guess that she didn't, which only added to her appeal. She wasn't trying to seduce him, yet he wanted her more than he could remember wanting anyone. His body was aching with need for her. Not just physical contact, but Dianna. His body was aching for *Dianna*.

She looked around the room, pausing when her attention landed on the bed. Paul tossed the keycard on the desk, followed by his wallet and keys. He held her gaze for a moment before closing the distance, standing just inches from her.

He searched her eyes. "Are you sure?"

"Are you?"

He answered by digging a hand into her long hair and pulling her to him. He crashed his mouth against hers and thrust his tongue between her lips, desperate to quench his thirst for her. She clung to him, meeting his passion. She fisted his shirt in her hands as Paul tore his lips from hers. He moved his hand down her hip and over her thigh as he used the hand in her hair to gently but firmly tug her head back and expose her neck.

She panted out his name as he licked at her flesh and lightly sank his teeth into it. He tugged her skirt until his hand was under the fabric, and then he lifted her thigh. Dianna ground her groin against his.

His body was twisting inside, tightening with need. His erection pressed against her as she tightened her leg around him. Having her like this was better than he'd imagined, more than he'd fantasized. He released his hold on her hair and, gripping her other thigh, lifted her. Her legs wrapped around him as he took several steps and gently deposited her onto the bed.

Sliding his hand up her body, he cupped her breast, eliciting a moan from her. She clung to him as he kissed the cleavage along her neckline, gently nipping and licking the top of her breasts. She pressed her heel into his behind, encouraging him to press against her, and he did so willingly.

He leaned back, hovering over her as he'd done once before. He'd had too much to drink that night, too. He'd said things that had hurt her. Trying to push the memory from his mind, he stroked her hair from her face. Her cheeks were flush, her lips puffy from their kisses, and when she lifted her eyelids and looked at him, she did so through what appeared to be a dreamy haze. He ran his hand over her hair again, and she smiled.

"You're so beautiful," he whispered. "I wish you knew how beautiful you are."

She laughed softly, but her smile faded and her brow creased when he sighed.

Damn it. He couldn't do this. Not like this. Not when they were shit-faced and hurting. Not when, less than half an hour before, she'd been crying over her ex-husband. He wanted her. His body was damn near begging for her, but he couldn't—wouldn't—make love to her under these circumstances.

She seemed to sense his change of heart because her face sagged and she looked away.

"We can't do this," he whispered. "I'm so sorry. I want you. I do. So much. But, Dianna…"

"Don't. Please." She closed her eyes and turned her face away as she released her hold on his body.

He put his hand to her face and waited for her to open her

eyes. When she did, a tear fell, and he brushed it away. "You are much too important to me to do something you are going to regret later."

"I won't—"

"You will. You're hurting, and you're thinking this will help. And it probably would. At least for tonight, but tomorrow you'd regret it, and then you'd resent me. We've had too much to drink. Too much hurt. Too much everything to be thinking clearly. We're *not* thinking clearly. We can't do this."

She shifted beneath him, and he rolled away from her. Sitting on the edge of the bed, he took a deep breath in a futile attempt to regain control of his body. "I'm not going to lose you because we did something rash. I care about you too much."

"I'm sorry," she breathed.

"Don't be." He looked over as she sat beside him and adjusted her dress. "I wanted this, too, but it's not a good idea."

Her face was even more red now, and a tear had trailed down her nose, threatening to drip off the tip, but she swiped it away and sniffed.

Damn it, he felt like an ass.

"I want to make love to you," he said, his voice softly pleading. "I do, but I want it to be for the right reasons, and that can't possibly be the case tonight."

"No, you're right. You're completely right. If we…" She stopped and cleared her throat. "It's just so unfair."

"What?"

She lifted her face, finally meeting his gaze. "He's happily remarried, and I'm...getting rejected...again."

"I'm not rejecting you."

"Oh." She pushed herself up. "Excuse me for misunderstanding."

He frowned as she walked to the window and looked out. "You still love him."

"You still love her."

"So we have no business doing this. Because if we do, one of us, maybe both of us, will get hurt. I don't want to hurt anymore, Dianna."

"I know. I shouldn't have thrown myself at you like that."

He smiled softly. "I'm fairly certain you weren't alone in that. I meant what I said. You mean so much to me. I'm not going to lose you now."

"You mean a lot to me, too. And I don't want to lose our friendship over one night." She finally turned and looked at him. "Can we just chalk this up to drunken stupidity?"

"That's exactly what we're chalking it up to." He slowly stood, hesitating when he wobbled a bit on his feet. "I can't drive, but if you don't want to stay, we can call for a ride."

She nodded. "That would be best, I think."

He walked to the phone and called the front desk. He requested a car service pick them up, but when he was told how long the expected wait time was, he changed his mind. Turning as he replaced the phone in its cradle, he shrugged. "We can either stay here or wait about two hours for the next available car. Apparently we aren't the only ones ready to go home. I can call Annie. I'm sure she's sober."

She gnawed at her lip for a moment. "No. No, don't worry about it. We've shared a bed before. I think we can manage it again. Just..." She grinned sheepishly. "You know, stop begging me to have sex with you."

They laughed quietly, but it was an awkward, uncomfortable sound from both of them.

Paul released a few buttons before he tugged his dark gray dress shirt off and held it out. "Put this on. You can't sleep in that dress."

He left her to change and closed the bathroom door behind him. He looked at his reflection. His mouth was red from kissing her. He licked his lips. Part of him wanted to throw the door open and tell her he'd changed his mind. To hell with the consequences. He wanted to be buried deep between her legs as she clung to him. He wanted her holding him as he thrust inside her. He wanted her writhing beneath him as she called his name. He'd been so close to that—so close to living out something he hadn't even realized he'd been wanting so badly.

"You idiot," he whispered to his reflection.

He splashed cold water on his face, brushed his teeth with the hotel-provided toiletries, and used the bathroom before washing his hands and easing the door open a crack. "May I come out?"

"Yeah," she answered.

He left the bathroom, and regret hit him again. She was

putting her phone on the nightstand, wearing his dress shirt and looking like a goddamned goddess. Her pale legs were naked, reminding him of what he'd given up. He ran his hand over his hair, cursing himself for having a conscience.

"There are toothbrushes on the counter," he said when he finally managed to look into her eyes.

"Perfect." Dianna shuffled her way into the bathroom.

The alcohol in Paul's system was definitely starting to catch up to him. His head was heavy and his mouth dry. He cracked open a complimentary bottle of water and chugged half of it before setting it on the nightstand next to her phone. He glanced back, made sure the bathroom door was closed, and then slid out of his slacks. He draped them over a chair with Dianna's dress and climbed under the covers.

She came out of the bathroom, and he tried to ignore the tension radiating between them.

"How loud are you going to snore tonight?" she asked, sitting on the edge of the bed.

"I don't snore."

Dianna laughed with disbelief. "Sure." She turned off the light and tugged at the covers.

"Hey," he whispered as she settled into bed.

"Hmm."

"I need to tell you something. About your piano."

She turned her face over her shoulder, her eyes wide as she looked up at him. "Oh, God. Does your friend want his money back?"

Paul exhaled. "There was no friend."

"What?"

"I bought the piano."

Dianna turned all the way onto her back. In the dim light that was streaming in through the opening between the heavy curtains, he could see something that looked like guilt playing on her face. "You did what?"

"I didn't want you to sell it, so I bought it. I was going to tell you Christmas Day, but then Sam and Jason came in."

"Paul, that's too much."

"No, it's not."

"It is."

"It wasn't about the money. It was about you not having to lose anything else to that man. He has taken too much from you already."

"I'll pay you back."

"No. I did it because I wanted to."

Dianna rolled onto her side. "Why?"

He creased his brow. "Why what?"

"Why are you being so good to me? You don't owe me anything."

He hesitated but then ran his hand down her arm. "I owe you everything. I would be a mess without you. Happy New Year, Di."

She smiled. "Happy New Year, Paul."

sh

Dianna woke up to Paul pressed against her back. She cleared her throat and moaned miserably as she reached for the phone to check the time. Almost ten. Shit. She put the phone down, debating if she should get up or sleep for a few more minutes, when it rang.

"Hey, Sam," she answered quietly.

"Guessing you're with Paul?"

"Yeah."

"You sound like shit, Ma. Did you party or what?"

She looked over her shoulder. Paul was still asleep behind her. "We just stayed up too late."

"Spare me any details, okay?"

"Sam." She didn't have it in her to argue with him about how she and Paul were just friends. She cringed at the memory of the night before and the realization that she probably couldn't honestly make that assertion anymore. "How was your night?"

"Dad sent a text at about ten asking if we were showing up at the ceremony."

Dianna closed her eyes and exhaled slowly, bracing herself for tales of her husband's—*ex-husband's*—wedding.

"I told him no. I mean, I'd told him that when he made his big announcement. But anyway, guess what?"

"Hmm?"

"He backed out."

Her eyes shot open, and she winced at the ache it caused throughout her head. "What?"

"Nobody showed up, at least not on Dad's side."

Dianna shouldn't smile. She shouldn't laugh. But she couldn't help the giggle that sneaked out, and a smile spread across her parched lips. "Oh, no."

"Dad sent me a text saying he was disappointed in me. I replied that I was even more disappointed in him. He didn't respond."

"Oh, Sam, that wasn't nice."

"Screw him, Mom. He doesn't get to shit on our lives and expect me to support him."

"I know, honey. It's the way he is."

"Anyway. I was just checking in since *once again* you didn't come home or bother to call and let me know where you were. That gives me two freebies, you know…"

She closed her eyes and rubbed them. "And I'm sure you'll use them between now and the end of summer."

"Most likely. When are you going to be home?"

"I don't know. If you need me—"

"I can change my own diapers."

"Then I'll be home later this afternoon."

"Hey," he said before she could hang up. "I don't care if it's wrong. I'm glad he didn't marry her."

"Bye, Sam." She ended the call and looked behind her.

Paul was now on his back, but he was still asleep. They'd have to check out of the room soon. She needed to wake him, but she didn't. She rolled onto her back and lay there, replaying the night before through her mind. Midnight, in particular. She'd thrown herself at Paul. Wantonly. Without a care for what the morning would bring. Thank goodness he'd had enough sense about him to stop where they were headed. He'd been right. She would have regretted it.

"Was that Sam on the phone?" he asked sleepily, pulling her from her humiliating thoughts.

"Mm-hmm. You won't believe what happened at the wedding."

"The earth opened up and swallowed the happy couple?"

"Nobody showed up to see Mitch get married, so he called it off."

Paul laughed softly. "I bet she had a fit."

Dianna chuckled as well. "We shouldn't laugh. That's not right."

"It is right. It's well deserved."

"Maybe." They were quiet for a few moments before she rolled away.

"Where are you going?"

"The bathroom."

"Come right back."

Dianna closed the door and used the toilet. She sighed at herself in the mirror as she washed her hands. She splashed her eyes, rinsed away some of the residual makeup that she hadn't bothered to clean off the night before, and then brushed her teeth.

Feeling somewhat refreshed, she walked back into the bedroom and collapsed on the bed. "I feel horrible."

"Me, too. Are you hungry? We should have time for room service before we have to check out."

"Sure."

"Order pancakes and sausage," he said, getting up. "And gallons of coffee."

She called in their order and then curled under the covers.

Mitch hadn't gotten married. Why had that lifted her spirits so much? Vindictive pleasure in knowing he must be miserable? Or was it something else? She certainly wasn't expecting him to come back to her. And if he did, she'd tell him to get lost. Or at least she *hoped* she would. She deserved better than the way he'd treated her. She deserved to be treated with respect and consideration, the way Paul treated her.

When the bathroom door opened, she forced her focus onto her phone, scrolling through her social media feed as he pulled his slacks on. There were tons of pictures of people celebrating the New Year, but the one she stopped on was her own. Paul and her *before* the drinking began. She hadn't noticed, at least not too much, but they actually made a good couple.

"Did you order?"

She lifted her brows in question. "Hmm?"

"Breakfast." He fell onto the bed.

She looked at him and stuttered for a second. "It should be here in a few minutes."

He tucked a second pillow behind him. "How do you feel about them not getting married?"

"I don't know. I was just trying to sort that out. I'm glad they didn't, but I don't know why. I think it's a bit vindictive."

Paul exhaled loudly. "I can't help but smile a little as I picture her face when he told her he wasn't going to marry her. Of course, unless they split over this, it's just a postponement. They'll get married eventually."

"Yeah, but knowing they were just as miserable as we were last night makes me feel a little better."

Paul nodded in agreement and drew another deep breath. "So…about last night. Are we going to analyze what happened or just chalk it up to alcohol and let it go?"

"I don't know. What do you think?"

"We were hurting, and we crossed a line that we shouldn't have."

She worked her lip between her teeth for a moment. "I worry that it will change things between us. We've managed to become really good friends, but…"

"But if we kissed once—well, several times—it's bound to happen again?"

"It usually works that way." She drew a breath, trying to get a reading on how he felt about that.

He smirked. "And here we are having sleepovers in hotel rooms."

She laughed, but she didn't break away from the uncomfortable gaze between them. "If you hadn't stopped things last night…"

"Yeah." Paul was quiet for a few seconds. "I have this really bad habit of jumping in with both feet and worrying about the consequences later. I forge ahead and never realize what's going on around me. I did that with my first wife. I did it with Michelle. And, if we're honest, I'm doing it with you."

"Yeah, you are. I'm not complaining." She smiled. "But I think maybe we've probably traveled into relationship territory without realizing it."

He nodded. "And we have no business being there."

Dianna sighed, disappointed that he wasn't more open to exploring what they could be together, even though she agreed that it probably was a terrible idea.

"I have this mixed up kind of co-dependency. I need to take care of someone to feel complete. Not that I don't care about you or want to look out for you, but...it might be more selfish than I realized. You know?"

"Annie told me about how things were after your mother passed."

He lifted his brows, clearly surprised. "She did? Why?"

"I think she just wanted me to have a better understanding of who you are, probably to avoid this very situation that we are finding ourselves in."

He seemed to consider her words. "She thinks it's her fault that I'm like this."

"*Like this?* You say it like it's a bad thing, Paul. It's not. Looking out for other people isn't a shortcoming."

"It is when I take it too far. And I always take it too far. I pushed Michelle away—"

"Don't. Please don't. She's a selfish bitch, okay? If she weren't, she wouldn't have gone after a man who had a family. She wouldn't have hurt you and me and my kids. You're a wonderful man, Paul. You really are. It wasn't you."

He looked up at her. "Well, it sure as hell wasn't you either. When I'm with you, everything feels so easy, so right. I feel like we could be great together. But we're still tied to them, whether we want to be or not. We can't consider any kind of relationship right now. We'd just hurt each other."

"I know."

"I feel like a jerk for kissing you and then—"

"Hey, I kissed you, too." She sighed heavily. "So what should we do? Just forget last night? Pretend it didn't happen?"

"Can you do that?"

She forced a smile to her face. "You're a pretty good kisser, but yeah, I think I can get over it. But there is one small issue that we keep brushing aside."

"What?"

"There is an attraction here, and if we keep letting our guard down, something is going to happen. Is that because we're moving toward something or because we're convenient to each other right now?"

Paul ran his hand over his face and exhaled loudly. "Honestly?"

"Honesty would be great," she whispered, even though she was starting to dread his answer.

A sweet smile curved his lips. "I'm so attracted to you I'm

about to lose my mind. You're amazing. Inside and out. Pulling away from you last night was damn near torture, but I have to take time to figure myself out. So do you. We have to finish this process of grieving and moving on before we drag anyone else into our misery."

She nodded. "You're right. Despite how much I wanted to be with you last night, he was on my mind. You deserve better than that."

"We both do. I don't know when we'll be ready, but it isn't right now, and I don't want to lose you because of this."

She smiled and took his hand. "I'm not going anywhere."

Paul jumped up when room service knocked on the door, and Dianna exhaled slowly, forcing out the overwhelming sense of disappointment their conversation had stirred.

CHAPTER THIRTEEN

*D*ianna slammed the bill folder shut and rubbed her eyes. She had one more week until payday. She could make it. It would be tight, but she could make it. She was just so damned tired of trying *so* hard all the time. Everything felt like a struggle now. She had bills that were due by the end of the week. Bills she couldn't pay. Luckily she'd managed to get caught up with what Paul had paid her to redecorate and the money for the piano so nothing was going to get shut off. At least not this month.

She hated living like that, but she didn't seem to have much choice in the matter. Which brought her back around to the thing she avoided thinking about until the first of every month rolled around. Her mortgage payment.

Though her car payment had decreased significantly, she still was struggling when the house payment was due. Even though Annie was paying her significantly more, she didn't make enough to ever get ahead. She was living paycheck to paycheck, and the house took much more than its share. As much as she hated to admit it, it was time to let her home go.

She could still remember her and Mitch's excitement when they moved in. Stonehill was an up-and-coming suburb of Des Moines. It was quite the coup to say they lived there. The house had been perfect. As soon as they'd stepped inside, she'd looked at him and he'd smiled at her, and she knew he felt the same. It was the perfect place to spend the rest of their lives. Rubbing her eyes, she silently insisted she wasn't going to cry.

"Hey, Mom," Sam said when he walked into the kitchen.

"I didn't think you would be up yet."

"I have to work in a bit."

She searched her mind, trying to think of the best way to break the news to him as he fixed himself a bowl of cereal. "Hey, Sam?"

"Huh?"

She swallowed against the tightness in her throat. "Remember when I said eventually I was going to have to sell the house?"

Sam glanced at her as he yanked the refrigerator door open. "Well, I never really liked this house anyway. The neighborhood sucks. It's full of thugs."

Dianna laughed softly as he talked about the friends he'd grown up around, the ones he still hung out with. "I've heard that."

"Well, you work for a real estate agent now, so I bet they can get us a kick-ass deal on a new place."

"Yeah, I bet."

He put the cap back on the milk after topping off his cereal. "You know, I'm going to be gone to school soon. You don't need this big house anyway. You need something small that you can take care of. I bet you can sell this for enough to pretty much pay for a new house. You won't have to"—he shrugged—"you know, stretch things so far to get by."

She sank her teeth into her lip as he sat across from her. "I'm sorry."

"For what?"

"For not being better at this."

"Don't do that. Okay? You're doing fine."

She swallowed hard, pushing her emotion down. "Thank you. I need to hear that every now and then."

"I have a couple hundred in the bank—"

"No."

"Just to help out—"

"No. I appreciate the gesture, Sam, but I'll figure it out. You're going to need that money when you get to school."

"Okay. But, you know, I'm the man of the house now, so...let me be the man."

She chuckled as he puffed up his chest and returned to his usual goofy persona.

sh

Kara collapsed on the sofa next to Dianna. "Why didn't you come to yoga?"

"Did you just let yourself into my house?"

"Yes. Why didn't you come to yoga? You haven't come for weeks. The old biddies have been chomping at the bit to hear about your date with Paul."

"I got busy. I didn't think they'd mind."

"What's going on, Di?"

Dianna curled her hands farther around her coffee mug. "What isn't going on?"

"Is this about Mitch?"

"He didn't get married."

"*What?*"

Dianna shook her head. "Nobody showed up so he backed out."

Kara snickered. "Serves him right."

"I almost slept with Paul, though."

Her grin fell. "*Almost?*"

"We kissed. A lot. There was a little groping and grinding."

"Nice," Kara teased.

"Yeah. But then he pointed out we were drunk and would regret it later. So we just passed out in a hotel room, and when we woke up, extremely hung over, we agreed that maybe someday but not right now. And that friend of his who bought the piano?"

"Yeah?"

"There was no friend. Paul just didn't want me to sell it."

"Wow. So chivalry isn't dead, huh? Any other news from the last three days you'd like to share?"

Her lip quivered. "I've decided to sell the house."

"Oh, baby," Kara said softly. "I'm sorry."

"I can't keep putting it off. It's like a rock around my neck dragging me down."

"You'll find something great."

Dianna nodded. "Yeah, I'm sure. What about you? How was your New Year's?"

She smiled. "Oh, you know. Harry and I just stayed in. *Alone.*"

Dianna snorted. "You two are too much."

"You were missed at yoga, though. I think your love life has become the glue that keeps that group together."

"Oh, God. That's so sad."

"Iris, that's Greek lady number one, the one right next to me, says that if Paul doesn't see what's right in front of him, he's a *vlaka*. I had to look that up—it means idiot. But, Karme, Greek lady number two, says that if it is real love, it will bloom in its own time and neither you nor Paul can push it. She also says her son Theos is a great catch. He's a chef at their restaurant and would cook for you every meal. That would be a nice change of pace, huh?"

"They really talked about this?"

"Yes, for the last two Saturdays. Today, Elle, the woman beside you, said that you probably weren't at yoga because you and Paul had finally hooked up and you couldn't stand to be away from him. I told her I didn't think so, but then I come here and you tell me you almost slept with him. How did that happen?"

"Um, about five or six martinis and a shattered heart at the thought of my husband marrying someone else made me think throwing myself at Paul would be a good idea."

"But you said you guys kissed."

She nodded. "We did, and then he pointed out it was very, very bad of us to do that."

Kara frowned. "Well, that's rude."

"But he was right. Then he told me that he bought my piano and he wants me to keep it."

"Which is romantic as hell."

"But then he said we should just be friends, and I haven't talked to him since."

"I guess if all else fails, you can call Theos. His mother says he's also very good at massaging feet. She apparently gets painful corns."

"Ew." Dianna cringed and sank down into her sofa. "I did not need to know that."

CHAPTER FOURTEEN

*D*ianna and Paul hadn't vocalized their intent, but a week had passed before they saw each other again, and after a week apart, it had come down to this: board games and a platter of snacks rather than a movie and shared bowl of popcorn and sitting on opposite sides of the coffee table instead of close together on the sofa.

Dianna shook her head as Paul put letters on the Scrabble board. "That's not a word."

"Yes, it is. Just not in English."

"You can't do that."

He made a face at her and gathered up his mismatched letters. "I told you I'm not good at this game."

"You're a lawyer. How can you not be good at making words?"

"I've made plenty of words. You just don't like them."

"Because you can't use Latin. Do you want help?"

"No, thank you, Miss English Major. You just stay on your side over there with your seventy-point lead."

"Seventy-*six*-point lead."

"Whatever."

She laughed and then picked up her phone. "What's up, Sam?"

"First thing, I'm fine."

"*Okay.*"

"Second thing, don't freak out."

"Sammy?"

"I'm at the ER."

Dianna gasped. "What happened?"

"Some jackass ran a stop sign and T-boned me."

"Oh, my God."

Paul pushed himself up and rushed around the table to sit next to her. "What?"

"Sam was in an accident."

"Is he okay?"

"I'm fine," Sam said. "That was the first thing, remember?"

"He's at the ER."

Paul pulled her to her feet and took the phone from her. "Sam, are you at Stonehill Hospital?" He brushed his hand over Dianna's head as he listened. "Okay, we're on our way."

Paul helped Dianna get her coat, grabbed her purse, and shuffled her out to his car. He drove fast—but not dangerously so —and found a parking spot close to the emergency room doors.

He held her hand as they walked in. At the counter, he asked the receptionist about Sam.

"The doctor is with him now. I'll let them know you're here. Do you have a medical insurance card for him?"

Dianna shook her head. "He's on his father's insurance. He should have those cards on him."

"He didn't. We need that information as soon as possible." She slid a clipboard across the desk. "Fill this out and bring it back."

"When can I see him?"

"I'll find out."

Paul guided Dianna to a row of hard plastic chairs and sat next to her. "You need to call Mitch."

"Yeah, I know." She searched his eyes for a moment. "You can leave if you want. I'll call Kara. She can come sit with me."

"Do you want me to leave?"

Her heart sank. That was the last thing she wanted. "Do *you* want to? He'll probably bring Michelle."

He put his hand to her face. "Being here for you and Sam is more important."

She took a slow breath as she looked at the clipboard on her lap. "He's okay, right?"

"He said he was okay." He kissed her head for what she thought was probably the tenth time in the last twenty minutes. "Call Mitch, tell him to bring the insurance card. Then fill out the paperwork so the doctors know what they need to in order to help Sam."

Dianna swallowed and closed her eyes for a moment. She hadn't talked to Mitch in months. He'd called a dozen times on Thanksgiving when the boys didn't go to his family dinner, but she'd deleted his messages without listening to them. She hadn't heard his voice or seen his face since their divorce hearing. She needed a moment to center her strength. Once she did, she took out her phone and called his cell.

"Dianna?" he answered, his voice filled with confusion.

"I'm at Stonehill Hospital with Sam. He was in an accident."

"Shit, is he okay?"

"He said he was fine when he called, but I haven't heard from the doctor yet. They need his insurance cards, and Sam didn't have them on him. Can you bring yours?"

She closed her eyes when she heard Michelle's voice in the background asking what was wrong. Swallowing her anger at the woman, she listened to Mitch explain what was going on.

"I'm on my way," he said and then ended the call.

"He'll be here in a few minutes," she said to Paul.

He put his arm around her shoulder. "Get this filled out."

"I keep telling myself he's fine. I mean, he called and he sounded fine, but if anything ever happened to my kids..."

"I know. But he's okay, baby."

She took a breath and focused on the clipboard again. She filled out all of Sam's crucial information and medical history, and then Paul carried it to the receptionist's desk. Dianna was staring down the hall, so focused on silently beckoning for a doctor to emerge that she didn't realize Mitch was there until he stepped in front of her, blocking her view.

She looked up at him, and her stomach clenched. Funny how he looked the same. Like nothing had changed. Somehow she'd thought he'd look different.

"They need his insurance card." She nodded her head toward the receptionist. As she did, she locked gazes with Paul, who had hesitated on his way back to her side.

"How is he?" Mitch asked, pulling her attention back to him.

"I don't know. The doctor is with him now. He sounded okay when he called."

"Did he say what happened?"

"Somebody ran a stop sign and hit him. That's all I know."

He started to turn and then stopped and looked down at her. "How are you?"

"Fine. They need his insurance card."

Mitch turned and walked past Paul, but then, as he dug his wallet out of his pocket, he turned back and a look of confusion washed over his face.

"Last chance," she said when Paul approached her. "I promise not to be angry if you leave."

He sat next to her and wrapped his arm around her shoulders. "I'm not going anywhere. Besides..." He glanced around. "She's not here."

"She's probably around somewhere."

"I'll deal with it when she shows, *if* she shows. Hospitals aren't her thing, and she's probably not a real big fan of Sam's right now. He did contribute to the cancellation of her wedding, remember?"

She laughed softly. "Right."

"How are you doing?"

"I wish the doctor would come out. I just need to know he's okay."

"He's okay. He said he's okay."

She leaned toward him, and he kissed her head, as he'd done continually since she'd gotten Sam's call. She put her hand on his thigh and squeezed, absorbing his strength. She'd put Mitch so completely out of her mind she'd actually forgotten he was there until he cleared his throat.

He was staring at Paul. "I don't think we've met."

Paul stood, and Dianna's heart started racing again. She didn't think either of them would throw a punch, but she didn't expect them to laugh off the fact that Mitch had been the reason for Paul's very painful divorce. "Paul O'Connell."

Mitch looked surprised for a moment, but then his lips curved up slowly and he looked down at his ex-wife with a condescending smirk. "Right. I thought you looked familiar."

"She shared family photos?" Paul said. "That's sweet."

He returned his attention to Paul. "So, you two..."

His voice trailed off, but neither Paul nor Dianna elaborated. Not that she could if she'd wanted to. Her attention was bouncing slowly between the two men. Paul, though a few inches shorter, looked much more commanding than Mitch. She'd always thought Mitch was so confident and sophisticated, but standing next to Paul, he looked...normal. His hair, with its light color and receding line, made him look older than his forty-six years. The lines around his eyes aged him. In contrast, Paul's wrinkles made him look even more handsome.

She'd always put her husband up on a pedestal and held him in such high regard, but as her gaze moved back to Paul, she realized something she'd never seen in all these years. Mitch was, simply put, just an average man.

Movement drew Dianna's attention beyond the staring contest Mitch and Paul had gotten themselves into. "There's the doctor."

Paul helped her up as Mitch turned to face the physician. Paul's hands went to her shoulders.

"I'm Doctor Hillman. Sam is doing fine. He hit his head pretty hard, but nothing is broken."

Dianna exhaled and collapsed back into Paul. She reached up and covered his hands with hers. "Can he come home?"

"He sure can. He's getting dressed right now. He's got a few stitches, and he's going to have a pretty good headache. If you notice any confusion or anything like that, take him to see his regular physician. Otherwise, make an appointment with his doctor in a week to get the stitches taken out."

"That's it?" Dianna asked. "Just a few stitches?"

"He's going to be sore, but he's fine, Mom. You can breathe now."

She smiled. "May I see him?"

"Sure. Come with me. Uh, parents only in the trauma rooms,

please." He looked between the two men.

Dianna squeezed Paul's hands as she faced him. He nodded, as if to confirm what he'd been telling her. Sam was fine.

"I'll be back," she said.

"I'll be here."

She was perfectly content to walk to Sam's room in silence, but she should have known better.

"Is that the *boyfriend* Jason said you had over for Christmas?" Mitch asked once they were far enough from Paul to not be overheard.

"That's not your concern," she answered flatly.

"I guess that's why you were so vindictive in testifying against Michelle at her hearing."

She looked at him with an arched brow. "Vindictive? No, Mitch, I was being honest. I know it's a difficult concept for you to understand, but sometimes when people are asked questions, they tell the truth, and telling the truth is *not* being vindictive."

"You didn't have to testify."

"And she didn't have to sleep with my husband."

"So now you're sleeping with hers?"

Dianna shrugged nonchalantly. "Why not? At least I know he doesn't have a wife waiting for him at home, feeling terrible that her poor husband is '*working late*' yet again." She used air quotes around the words *working late*.

They walked the rest of the way in the quiet she had initially been hoping for.

"Well..." The doctor gestured toward a room.

He did a terrible job at hiding his grin, and Dianna felt her checks flush. She thought she should apologize to him for the little spat she'd just had with Mitch, but that was too much like apologizing to her ex-husband, and she wasn't about to do that.

"Sam's right in here," Dr. Hillman said. "His discharge papers will be at the front desk whenever he's ready to go."

"Thank you." She walked into the room and put a hand to her mouth as she looked at her son on the emergency room bed.

"Don't cry, Ma." Sam pulled his shoe on. "I'm fine."

"You scared me half to death."

"I told you first thing that I was fine."

"Like she was going to believe that," Mitch said. "You know how she is."

Sam ignored his father. "I got hit on the passenger side. It wasn't as bad as it could have been."

"Thank God."

He finished tying his shoe and then opened his arms. "Come on. Might as well get this over with."

Dianna wrapped him in her arms and hugged him tightly.

"Where's Paul?" he whispered.

"In the lobby."

"Bet that went over well."

She scoffed and then leaned back. She tipped Sam's head so she could look at the stitches along his left temple. Even though she knew he'd hate it, she planted a kiss on his cheek.

"*Mom.*"

"It's not as bad as I imagined," she said, running a thumb over his cheek to wipe her kiss away. "How are you feeling?"

"My head hurts, but I'm okay."

"How's the car?"

"Trashed. He hit my front fender. I'm pretty sure the axle got broken by the way the tire was sitting. I'm screwed. There's no way I can drive it, and it'd cost more to fix than it's worth."

"I'm sure you can drive Mom's Suburban while we get your car fixed," Mitch said. "She doesn't have any place to be."

Dianna turned around and glared at him. He was so out of touch with their lives he didn't even know he was making an ass out of himself. She shook her head and returned her attention to Sam. "The other person's insurance will pay something, but until then, maybe Matt will let you lease a car while we figure out what to do."

"Who's Matt?" Mitch asked.

He was once again ignored.

Sam's face lit. "You think he would?"

"I'm sure Paul would be happy to talk to him—"

"Wait," Mitch spat. "We don't need *Paul* to do *anything*, okay? I can take care of my son."

"Yeah, you've done a great job so far," Sam said. "The car I had, Dad, I could only afford because Mom matched me on what I had saved. Didn't know that, did you? You were always so concerned about me making my own way, you didn't have a clue that to get a job I needed a car to get me there. You always just expected Mom to drive me around, not caring that she had her own things to do. Or did you even know she had her own life?"

Mitch exhaled slowly.

"No, you didn't, because you don't know anything. You don't know how hard Mom's been working just to keep food on the table and the bills paid. You don't know how much she's been struggling to take care of me. You're so caught up in your own stupid life that you don't have a clue. You've *never* had a clue."

Mitch took a step to close the gap between him and Sam. "I'm still your father. I deserve some goddamned respect from you."

"Now is not the time," Dianna warned.

Mitch shook his head at her. "No, it is the time. It is the perfect time. I've tolerated him up until now."

"You've tolerated *me*?" Sam hopped off the table and stood tall, looking eye-to-eye with his father.

"You and Jason completely disrespected me by not coming to my wedding."

"You completely disrespected me, my brother, *and* my mother by walking out like we meant shit to you. Screw you. You wanted that life, well, you've got it. Take it, but don't act like we have to take it, too. And not that you care, but Mom is doing great without you. Anything she can't do for me, *Paul* can." He shook his head. "Go home to Michelle. We don't need you here." Sam stepped around Mitch and left the room.

Dianna followed him. "You okay?"

"Fuck him." Sam was angry, but he also sounded like he could cry.

Dianna wanted to push him to say more, but she didn't think

it'd be fair to bring him to tears when Mitch and Paul were around. She'd try to talk to him when he wasn't so upset.

"Go show Paul your war wound. I'll get your papers signed so we can go home." She watched Paul stand to greet Sam, and then she went to the front desk. "Discharge papers for Samuel Friedman?"

The woman slid papers across the desk and started explaining what Dianna needed to know if Sam showed signs of a concussion.

Dianna scrawled her name on the paper and tucked a copy into her purse. She walked back to where Sam was giving Paul all the gory details of his accident. "Ready?"

"Yup." Sam started for the door.

Paul looked at her. "Everything okay?"

"Let's just say he made it very clear that he doesn't want Mitch around right now."

"You can tell me about it later." He put his arm around her shoulders as they walked out.

Sam wasn't shy... They hadn't even made it to Paul's car before he was asking if Paul thought Matt could either lease or sell him a car for cheap. Dianna only half listened to their conversation as Paul backed out of the parking spot. Her heart skipped when she noticed Mitch standing at the doorway of the ER watching them leave, looking lost and confused. She shook her head slightly, forcing away any guilt she may have felt, and focused her attention on what mattered—Sam and Paul.

CHAPTER FIFTEEN

"Hell of a night, huh?" Paul hated seeing so much stress on Dianna's face. It seemed like she'd finally found solid ground to stand on, and now she was back to looking frustrated and confused. Not that he could blame her. Seeing her child in the ER, whether he was seven or seventeen, would be stressful, but he suspected her mood had more to do with Mitch than Sam. "Are you okay?"

"I think so." She sat heavily on the couch.

He sat next to her but kept a respectable distance. He'd been trying to be mindful of how much he touched her now that they'd determined they weren't ready for anything more. Of course, that had gone out the window when she'd gotten the call about Sam, but now that they knew he was okay, Paul was again trying to be aware of the space between them.

Dianna rubbed her brow. "Sam really laid into Mitch."

"Good. He deserves it."

"He's so clueless, Paul. I don't think he even knows what he did to us. He kept acting like everything was the way it was. He actually didn't even think that I'd be working. Apparently I should be able to survive on his incredibly gracious child support of a hundred and fifty dollars a month. He has no idea what our lives are like now."

"Did he ever?" Paul shrugged when she looked at him. "From what you've told me, it was almost like he was king of the castle and you guys were the commoners living in the kingdom. You took care of everything. He never had to think about anything."

"You sound like you're making excuses for him."

"I'm not. It's just...my first marriage. That's how we were. I worked and thought that's all I ever had to do. She ran the house, raised the kids, paid the bills. I didn't even know my kids. That's where Mitch is. Now that you aren't there, he's going to start realizing how out of touch he is with life but most especially with his own kids. Tonight was probably a big blow for him."

"He's such an idiot."

"That I can't explain."

She chuckled as she looked at him with that strong determination that she mustered up whenever things were going wrong, and his heart ached.

He stroked her hair. "What is it?"

"I just don't know how we're going to get him a new car right now."

"It would be great for Sam if Mitch stepped up, but if he doesn't, don't feel like you can't come to me."

"Thank you, but I'm not taking money from you."

"I just want to make this easier for you."

She slid her arm around him and snuggled close to him. He was helpless. He had no choice but to hold her back.

"This helps," she whispered.

"Yeah?"

"Yeah."

She rolled her head back to look at him. Her face was just inches from his, and a gust of warm breath hit him as she sighed. It smelled of the peppermints on the ER receptionist's desk, and Paul instantly thought about how her tongue would taste—cool and minty—against his. He dug his fingers into her side as they stared at each other, and finally he gave in and pulled her closer as he leaned down. Dianna dragged her hand up his chest and threaded her fingers into his hair as he pressed his mouth to hers.

Dear God, she tasted as good as he'd thought she would. Hot and cool at the same time, tingly from the peppermint, and as he slid his tongue over hers, she moaned in appreciation. He brushed his other hand, the one that hadn't been around her, up her side, and she arched into his touch. He broke free and licked away what was left of her kiss on his lips.

"How do you feel after seeing him?" The question had nagged at him, but he hadn't thought he'd voice it until it was out of his mouth.

"I don't know. I was too worried and angry to really process it. Has he always been that condescending?"

Paul smiled. "I wouldn't know."

"I think he has, and I just ignored it. Like I ignored everything else."

"Like he ignored you."

"I guess."

He brushed his thumb over her mouth. "I shouldn't have done that. I'm sorry."

"Are you going to apologize every time you kiss me?"

He smiled at her teasing, but his grin faded quickly and he traced her lips again. "I have a hell of a time controlling myself around you these days."

"That's such a terrible thing."

"It is when I'm determined to do things right from now on. I should go." He untangled himself from their embrace. "Call me and let me know how Sam is doing tomorrow. If he's up for it, we can go over to the dealership and figure out what kind of car he'd like. I don't know if Matt can do anything, but at least it's a place to start."

"Thank you, Paul. I would have been a mess if you hadn't been here tonight."

He wanted to kiss her again, but they'd probably sent enough mixed signals for one night. He took her hand and pulled her up from the sofa. They walked to the front door, where he slipped into his coat. When he was ready to leave, rather than a kiss like he wanted, he winked and reached for the door. "Get some rest, Di. You look exhausted."

She closed the door behind him. Huddled in his jacket, he

hurried to his car and slid in, cursing the cold January night. He started his car as the downstairs light went out. A minute later, the light in her bedroom filtered through the curtains.

He hated that he was going home alone. He wanted to slide into her bed and hold her all night. He didn't need more than that—he would be perfectly happy just having her body next to his. But then the nagging started in the back of his mind. They were getting in too deep, and someone's heart was going to get broken. He wasn't up for that, not so soon.

Pushing his loneliness and regret from his mind, he backed out of her driveway and headed home.

sh

Dianna wasn't surprised when she found Mitch standing at her door the next day.

"Morning," he said, giving her an uncertain smile as she opened the door. "The doorbell still sounds like a dying cow, huh?"

She stared at him, in absolutely no mood to make small talk.

"Uh, can I come in?"

Dianna hesitated before moving aside and gesturing for him to enter the house he hadn't stepped foot inside since the night he'd walked out, bags in tow, while she'd sobbed on the stairs. Despite catching him, despite knowing without a doubt that he'd had an affair, she'd begged him not to leave. What an idiot she'd been.

He gestured over his shoulder to the sign in the yard. "You're selling the house?"

"Yes."

He waited, likely expecting an explanation, but she didn't offer one.

"Is that your car out there?"

"Yes."

"You got rid of the Suburban?"

"Yes."

"Lots of changes in such a short time, don't you think?"

She cocked one brow at him. "Not as drastic as a new wife, but we all gotta start somewhere."

He sighed, that same disapproving sound he'd used for the last twenty-plus years. "Is Sam up yet? I thought we could go look at cars."

"I'll go get him."

"Wait, Di." He reached out but dropped his hand before touching her. "Look, I'm sorry about last night. I have no right commenting on your life."

"No, you don't."

He stuffed his hands into his pockets. "I know things are a mess right now, and that's my fault. I didn't sleep very well. I kept thinking about what Sam said. I didn't know things were so bad for you guys."

"Oh, come on. How could you not know, Mitch? You're a financial advisor, for God's sake. How did you think that we could afford to live on the hundred-fifty dollars a month child support you're paying? That doesn't even feed him. How was I going to make the house payment, and the truck payment, and the utilities, and the fees for his activities, and help Jason get by at school, and everything else? Don't tell me you didn't *know*. You didn't *care*."

"That's not true. I just... I never let myself think about it."

"Because it wasn't about you."

"Don't do that. I'm trying to apologize."

"Oh." She scoffed. "Well, excuse me. Let me just brush everything aside because you apologized. You want to know why he's so angry, Mitch? You want to know why your kids didn't show up for your wedding? Because you didn't just leave *me* for Michelle. You left them, too. You walked out of this house, and you never looked back. You left us completely in over our heads."

"They never asked me for money. If they weren't so damned proud—"

"It isn't pride, Mitch. For God's sake, are you so blind? Asking you for help is like telling you it's okay that you walked away as if we meant nothing to you."

"That's not how it was."

"Oh, spare me. I was standing right there." She pointed at the stairs. "I watched you leave. You haven't had a single concern for us since."

"Goddamn it, that is not true!"

"Then where have you been? Where the hell were you when I had to choose between paying the electric bill and feeding your son?"

"He was screwing his fiancée," Sam said casually. "Where else would he be?"

Dianna hadn't realized she'd been leaning toward Mitch and yelling in his face until she took a breath and stood upright. "Your father is here to see you."

"I heard."

Dianna went back to the kitchen where she'd been cleaning the stove when the doorbell rang. She scrubbed at a bit of burned-on food, taking her frustrations out on the glass top.

Bastard.

Sam walked in a few minutes later, and she shrugged. "Sorry. He made me mad."

"He deserves it. He wants to buy me a car. Like, not even demand that I pay half. He just wants to buy me a car."

She grabbed a towel and started drying her hands. "Well, you should let him do that."

"I'm going to. He, um, he wondered if you wanted go. He said we could stop at the grocery store on the way back. His treat."

She laughed bitterly. "No, thanks. You guys can go shopping. Get whatever you want."

Sam hovered at the door. "You okay?"

"I will be. Hey, Sam?" she called when he started to leave.

"Yeah?"

"Get lots of really expensive meat. We'll have pot roast and steaks this week. *His* treat."

He smiled. "Yes, ma'am."

He left, and she exhaled some of the anger brewing inside her. Maybe this was the eye-opener Mitch needed. Maybe he would start helping her take care of the kids now. Maybe things would be a little bit easier. She could only hope.

Her phone rang a few minutes later. "Morning," she said, trying to sound cheerful after seeing Annie's name on the caller ID.

"Hey, we've got a bite on the house. The other agent would like to show it in about an hour. Can you be gone?"

The reality of having strangers walk through her house hit Dianna like a sledgehammer to the heart. She suddenly couldn't breathe.

"Dianna?"

"Yeah. I can be gone in an hour. Could you maybe, uh… Could we look at some places? Do you have time?"

"Sure," she said enthusiastically. "Meet me at the office? I'll see what I can get lined up."

"Perfect. Thanks, Annie."

She ended the call and bit her lip. What if whoever looked at her house loved it? What if they made an offer? What if she actually had to sell her home?

She started to call Paul—she wanted to tell him about her confrontation with Mitch and ask him to go with her to look at houses—but she hesitated. They'd agreed to put some space between them, yet the first time they'd seen each other, they had ended up kissing. Even though he had asked her to call and check in with him, it probably wasn't a good idea to spend the day house hunting with him, especially when she was still so worked up over Mitch. Besides, she doubted he would appreciate Annie scrutinizing their every word.

She called Kara instead.

sh

After her long day, the last thing Dianna wanted was to deal with Mitch again, but when she pulled into the driveway, his truck was parked behind a sporty-looking red car. Sam must have worked Mitch's guilt to get that out of him. She was considering backing out, leaving them alone, when the front door opened and Mitch stepped out. That put an end to her debate. He was leaving, so she could go in and enjoy some peace. She took her time gathering her things, looking busy, hoping he'd climb into his truck and leave, but when she glanced up, he was walking toward her car. She sighed and silently prayed for strength not to kill him as he opened her car door.

"I like this," he said, nodding toward her car. "It suits you."

She stood in front of him and tilted her head. "Used and cheap suits me?"

He smiled, but his lips fell and he cleared this throat when he realized she wasn't joking. "Did you see that?" Mitch gestured toward Sam's new car. "He, uh, really knows how to twist a knife, doesn't he?"

She nodded slightly. "Mm-hmm."

"We went to the store and stocked you guys up on groceries," he said as she started to step around him. He laughed, but it was tense. "I had no idea you could spend so much on food."

She lifted her brows in response. "Well, how could you when you've never had to lift a finger to take care of yourself?"

His face sagged at her bitter comment. "Look, um, I am sorry, Di. That you've been struggling. I never wanted that. I'm going to call my attorney on Monday and make some changes to the child support. I'll get him to put in something for alimony, too."

She exhaled some of her frustration. "I don't want alimony, Mitch. If you can help take care of the boys, I can take care of myself."

He nodded. "I know you can. But you don't have to, not when I can help."

"Help the boys. You have no obligation to me, and I don't want to feel obligated to you. Okay?"

He held her gaze for a long moment before nodding. "Sam said you texted him that you were going to look at some houses today. Did you find anything?"

"I did."

He looked around the yard, at the tree where there used to be a tire swing for the boys, at the fire hydrant on the curb where they used to pretend they were firefighters, and then up at the house. "You really want to sell this place?"

"No, I don't, but my only other choice is foreclosure. I may not have your financial know-how, but that seems a bit foolish to me."

He frowned at her. "If you want to stay, you could refinance so the payments were less."

"That requires a down payment—"

"I'll help."

She rejected his offer with a shake of her head. "I don't want your help. Not for me, anyway. Besides, refinancing just means dragging out the payments. There's enough equity in the house that I can buy something smaller and actually afford the payments *and* groceries."

"But this is our house, Di. This is our home. This is where everything happened."

His words stung her, and her feelings of defensiveness and bitterness returned.

"*Our home? Our home*, Mitch? Yes, it *used* to be *our* home, but it isn't anymore. You got your fresh start. It's time I get mine, too, even if I have to make some hard choices to get it."

"I don't want you to have to sacrifice because of my choices."

"Really? Because I had to start making sacrifices the moment you left. This is my life now, Mitch, the life you handed to me. I am doing what I have to do to take care of my kids, and unfortunately, that means selling *my* house."

"Dianna, if you need money, I will give it you."

She smirked at him. "Oh, honey, that's so sweet of you. Really. But I doubt your new wife will want you keeping your old one tucked in your back pocket. Then again, she didn't mind sharing you before, did she?"

He flinched, like her words had cut him, and then he set his jaw.

She held her head high and stepped around him. As she walked toward her house, she realized what she'd told him was true. It was time for her fresh start. It was time to stop hanging on to the past so she could embrace the future. Whatever that may be.

She didn't look back as she walked away.

CHAPTER SIXTEEN

*P*aul smiled when Dianna looked up from the reception desk. She grinned in response, and a warmth spread through his chest.

"Hey," she said. "How are you?"

"Hungry. I was in the neighborhood for a meeting and thought I'd snag you for some Mexican food. You free?"

She glanced at the clock on the wall. "I will be in seven minutes."

"Perfect. Is my sister in?"

"Yes. Go on back. Would you like some coffee?"

"I know where it is." Serving clients may have been her job, but he wasn't going to have her waiting on him. He hung his coat on the rack and fought the urge to sneak over and kiss her cheek. Instead, he gave her a wink and walked back to Annie's office.

She glanced up when he walked in. "Fancy meeting you here."

"I came to steal Di for lunch."

Annie smirked but didn't say anything. "Tell her to come in here, will you?"

"Annie," he warned.

She dropped her reading glasses on the desk. "Oh, simmer down, Romeo. I just got an offer on her house. I want to discuss it with her."

"That was pretty fast."

"It's a great house in a great location."

"I wonder how she's going to take this."

"Only one way to find out."

Paul stuck his head out of Annie's office. "Hey, Di, come here."

She pushed herself up and walked to him. She was wearing black slacks and a navy blue fitted blouse, nothing spectacular, but damned if his body didn't think otherwise. He swallowed and forced his eyes to hers instead of taking in every curve of her body.

"We got an offer," Annie said as Dianna sat across from her. "They low-balled, so we should definitely counter."

Dianna's cheeks paled, and she stared at Annie for a few moments before nodding.

Annie continued. "Let's start with offering to drop the price two thousand and cover closing costs. Sound good?"

She sighed. "Sure."

"You okay?"

Dianna nodded again. "I thought it would take longer. That's all."

Paul put his hands on Dianna's shoulders, ignoring the way Annie watched him. "Remember how much easier things are going to be without that hefty payment."

She nodded. "The house with the loft that we looked at this weekend, can we look at it again?"

"I'll schedule something." Annie made some notes on the papers in front of her and slid them to Dianna. "Sign these, and we'll see what they say."

Dianna scrawled her name where Annie pointed and pushed the pages back. "Thanks."

"Let me check on when we can get into the loft house."

Paul took the seat next to Dianna and grabbed her hand. "How's Sam?" he asked softly while Annie made a phone call.

She sighed and flicked her gaze to him. "Sam's fine, but Mitch has been hanging around."

Paul's defenses went into overdrive. "Why?"

"Oh, you know, he's Dad of the Year and all that. He's so concerned about Sam and our finances and helping me make ends meet. He's just considerate like that." She scoffed and rolled her head back to look at the ceiling. "He's so very, very sorry for all he's put me through."

Paul squeezed her hand. She looked miserable.

"Sounds like you had a long weekend," he said.

"The house is available now if you want to have a look," Annie said, pulling them from their conversation.

Dianna looked at Paul. "Do you have time to look at my potential new residence?"

"Yeah. I'd love to."

They all shuffled out and climbed into Annie's car. Paul sat in the front and asked questions about any problems the property might have had. When Annie pulled into the driveway of the small house, Paul looked up at it. The red-stained siding, covered porch, and the tall maples in the front yard made it look like a cabin in the suburbs. The tiny home had been well cared for, and the upkeep showed in how it still appeared like a newer structure, despite its age.

"The roof looks nice. How old is it?"

"Less than five years," Annie said.

Dianna silently followed behind while Annie and Paul discussed plumbing and electrical while he looked at the hardwood floors that ran throughout and the newer appliances in the kitchen. The countertop had a few scratches but nothing terrible. The kitchen was clean and bright, and the window above the sink looked out over the long backyard that would be good for barbeques in the summer. The women stayed upstairs while he made a quick pass through the basement. The walls and floor were dry despite the melting snow outside. The space was open without any visible cracks in the structure.

Walking to the bathroom on the first floor, he looked at the old linoleum. The room wasn't in great condition, but maybe

Dianna could get someone to come in to lay tiles. The two downstairs bedrooms had newer carpet in muted tones that could match just about any color she put on the walls. In the master, a half bath guaranteed she wouldn't have to share a bathroom with her boys or guests.

"This is a good deal?" Paul asked his sister.

"I wouldn't show her one that wasn't."

He nodded. "Where'd she go?"

"Upstairs. Paul," she said quietly when he started past her. "What's going on with you two? You seem...more."

Paul frowned. "More what?"

She creased her brow. "You know what."

He ran his hand over his hair and looked toward the stairs. "Not now, Annie. In case you missed it, she's pretty damned upset right now."

"No, I haven't missed it. And I didn't miss how you were hovering, either."

"Hovering?"

"Hovering."

He shook his head and took the stairs two at a time. His heart saddened a bit when he found Dianna sitting on the window ledge, looking out over the yard.

"So?" she asked when he stood beside her. "What do you think?"

"It's great. It has a lot of updates that you won't have to take care of: roof, electrical, some plumbing work. The basement is in good condition. You could finish it eventually to get more space if you wanted. There's a lot of character, too. Little details that make it unique."

"I like the yard." She turned her attention to the window again. "I could do a lot of landscaping out there."

"It's close to where you are now. Not too far from work."

She drew a breath and looked at him. "Yeah. That's definitely a plus. I'm not crazy about the downstairs bath, though."

"It needs work, but that's just cosmetic. Everything is functional."

She gnawed at her lip. "That could be expensive."

He squatted in front of her. "Is that your only hesitation?"

She exhaled heavily and fisted her hands together. "As much as I can picture myself living here, I can't imagine living anywhere but home."

"It's hard. You've been there a long time. But you've said more than once it's become a burden. Your life will be so much easier when you don't have that mortgage payment weighing you down."

"I know."

"It's still tough," he whispered.

She sat up straighter, took a long, slow breath, and then exhaled. "I'm okay."

"I know you are. And you're going to keep being okay. This is just another thing you have to get through, but you will get through it."

She smiled faintly. "I'm glad you were able to see this place. I think… If the buyers accept my counter, I think I should make an offer on this one. I like it."

"Good. Should we get out of here? At least until we move you in?"

"Yeah. Let's go get something to eat."

He pushed himself up and pulled her to her feet, but instead of stepping away, he gripped her hands and held her gaze. "I know this is hard, but it's a great house. This place would be perfect for you. It really would."

"Yeah, I know." She inhaled deeply and nodded. "Come on. I'm starving."

"Think we should invite Annie?"

"I don't know. Did you see the way she was watching us in the office?"

He laughed. "She accused me of hovering."

Di giggled. "Well, you do. Just a little. But I don't mind."

"One more thing," he said before they started down the stairs. "What's going on with Mitch?"

She screwed up her face, as if she were disgusted. "He's feeling guilty and wants me to absolve him. Too bad for him that's not going to happen. Not anytime soon anyway. He'll stop coming around as soon as he gets bored. That's what he does."

"Are you okay with that?"

"He needs to fix things with Sam, Paul. I don't want my kids to go the rest of their lives angry with their father. I can tolerate him as long as he's there for Sam."

"Is he?"

She shrugged. "If he isn't, he's wasting his time. I'm not ready to forgive him yet."

Some weight lifted off his shoulders, but there was still a nagging deep in his gut. Paul didn't like Mitch sniffing around when Dianna was feeling so vulnerable. He didn't like it one bit.

sh

Dianna shook her head as she parked next to Mitch's truck. "What the hell?" As soon as she opened the front door, she was welcomed by the scent of steaks cooking. Angry as she'd been, the smell distracted her until she walked into the kitchen.

"What the hell?" This time, instead of feeling exasperated, she was furious. There wasn't an inch of counter space that wasn't covered in flour or sauce or some other spilled food product.

Mitch turned from the oven and smiled. "Hey. Have a seat and relax. I'm making dinner."

"Are you kidding me? Look at this mess."

He lifted his hands, which were covered in floral-print oven mitts. "I know. I don't have your finesse, but it's going to be delicious. Steaks, potatoes, and baked apples. All your favorites."

She wasn't impressed. "Don't you dare leave this for me to clean up."

She ignored his plea for her to wait and marched to the den, where she suspected she'd find Sam playing video games. There he was, without a care in the world.

"Your father is in there making a disaster out of my kitchen, and you're just letting him?"

"He wanted to make dinner. Who am I to argue with my parental unit?"

"Right. If your dad wants to cook you dinner, why the hell isn't he doing it at his house?"

Sam looked over at her and grinned. "I think he's planning to dump Michelle."

Dianna's heart flipped in a strange way she didn't quite grasp. "Then why isn't he making you dinner at Grandma's?"

Sam shrugged.

"We got an offer on the house today," she said more gently.

That got his attention. He sat up and actually looked at her. "Seriously?"

"I countered the offer. We haven't heard anything yet, but if they accept, we'll have to be gone in about a month."

"Great." He slouched down and un-paused his game.

"You remember the house I showed you online? I looked at it again today. I really like it. If you want to look—"

"It's not like I have to live there very long anyway."

She frowned at the angry tone in his voice. "Don't give me a hard time, Sam. I don't need it."

Dianna left him to his game when he didn't respond. She returned to the kitchen, where Mitch was pulling a casserole dish out of the oven. She was going to have to deal with his sudden appearance in her kitchen eventually. She might as well do so now. "What are you doing here?"

"I already told you. I'm making dinner. It's almost ready."

"What are you doing here?" She enunciated each word this time.

Mitch set aside the dish of apples he'd just pulled from the oven and took off Dianna's old oven mitts. "Can you stop looking so angry?" He set the mitts aside, not noticing that he knocked a dusting of flour to the floor. "I'll clean up the kitchen."

She tore her attention from the linoleum where the powder had landed and crossed her arms as she leaned against the doorframe. "Sam thinks you plan on leaving your fiancée."

He looked down for a few seconds and then lifted his gaze to hers again. The plea on his face was pathetic and made her cringe inside. He took several hesitant steps toward her. "Somewhere along the way, we got off track. We stopped appreciating each other. We stopped valuing each other and our family, but it's not too late. We can fix this."

Her stomach knotted around itself so tightly she couldn't breathe. *"What?"*

"I know it's going to take time. I don't expect you to just forgive me overnight, but"—he put his hands on her shoulders—"I miss you. I miss us. I want to come home."

She lifted her brows and smacked his hands off her. "You don't get to just *come home* whenever you feel like it."

"I know that—"

"I don't think you do. I don't care if you *want* to come home. This isn't your home anymore. I'm not your wife anymore. You divorced me, Mitch. You *divorced* me."

"I got caught up in something that wasn't real."

She laughed bitterly. "It looked pretty goddamned real to me when I caught you fucking her."

He at least had the sense to look ashamed of himself. "I'll never forgive myself for that. I saw how deeply I'd cut you, and I'll never forget it. But that's the thing that will keep me strong. That's the thing that will remind me how much I don't want to hurt you again."

"You know what? It's also the thing that keeps me strong, too. Because no matter what you say or do, *I* will never forget seeing you with her. *I* will never forget how you told me you were in love with her and that you were leaving me for her."

"I made a mistake, Dianna."

She shook her head. "You were all set to marry her three weeks ago."

"But I didn't."

"Because nobody showed up!"

"Because I realized it wasn't what I wanted. Come on, Di. After twenty-two years of marriage, I deserve a second chance."

"And I deserve to be with someone who wants to be with me."

"I *do* want to be with you."

"Because it didn't work out with her!"

"Because I love you. I love *you*. Don't you miss us? What we were together?"

"You destroyed what we were together."

"We can fix it." He smiled as he put his hands on her cheeks. "Honey, we can fix it."

She pulled his hands away from her. "There's nothing left to fix." She sighed when he ignored the sound of the timer beeping. Stepping around him, she grabbed a mitt and pulled a pan of rolls from the oven. She dropped the baking sheet on the stovetop and looked at the dinner he'd prepared.

Was she supposed to be so easily convinced? He cooked her dinner, and she should forget all the pain he'd caused her? She took a breath. "I'd like to you leave."

"Dianna."

"Leave. Please. Go."

"You wouldn't have to sell the house," he said quietly. "You wouldn't have to worry about money or how you're going to take care of the boys. You wouldn't have to work unless you wanted to. Things could go back to the way they were."

"They can't."

He put his hands on her shoulders and gently squeezed them. "They can."

Dianna shook his hands off her and faced him.

"Honey, they *can*. All those things we said we were going to do after the boys were gone, we can do them. We can add that sun-room you've wanted, like we've been talking about for so long. We can spend our mornings out there, drinking coffee and planning vacations. Just the two of us, like we said we would."

She ground her teeth together as he reminded her of the life she'd been looking forward to. The one she no longer had. "I got an offer on the house today." Her voice was tight with emotions she didn't want him to know she was feeling.

His face sagged for a moment, but then he forced his lips back up into a smile. "You don't have to accept it. You can turn it down."

"And do what? Continue juggling bills, hoping nothing gets shut off or repossessed? No, thanks. I've had enough of that to last the rest of my life. Look, I'm sorry things didn't work out with Michelle—"

"This isn't about Michelle."

"Isn't about Michelle?" She stepped around him, almost afraid that if she continued to stand so close to him she'd hit him. "You left me because of Michelle. You *divorced* me because of Michelle. I lost my husband, my security, my kids lost their lives as they knew them because of Michelle. I hate to break it to you, Mitch, but everything in my life right now is about Michelle."

"I made a mistake."

"No! You made a choice."

"You're still angry. I understand that. But you'll see. Once you calm down, you'll see that we belong together, and you'll know it's time for us to put this behind us."

"This? *This*? You say it so casually, like this is nothing. You didn't leave the toilet seat up, Mitch. You ended our marriage." She sighed and shook her head. "Just go. Go home to *her*."

"Let me clean up the kitchen."

"Leave it."

"It's my mess."

She glared at him. "I've gotten pretty damned good at cleaning up your messes."

He hesitated another moment and then walked out. She looked around at the counters and scoffed at the symbolism. The disaster was a very good representation of the emotions he'd just churned inside her. She wet a dishrag and went to work on cleaning the flour from the counters.

sh

Paul turned down his car radio as he pressed the speaker on his phone to answer Dianna's call. "Hey, I was just thinking about you," he said. "Did you hear back on your counteroffer?"

"Not yet. But that's not why I'm calling."

He didn't like the stress in her voice. "What's wrong?"

"Mitch was here when I got home."

Paul was quiet for several heartbeats. "What did he want?"

She was quiet. Too quiet. For too long. Finally, she said, "He's leaving Michelle. He wants to come home."

Paul's heart dropped. He wasn't exactly surprised by the man's change of heart, but he didn't think it would happen quite so fast. If Paul knew his ex-wife—and unfortunately he did—she'd been making Mitch's life hell for the last few weeks. He was likely fed up with her bitching and whining about the canceled wedding.

"Paul?"

He cleared his throat. "Are you okay?"

Again, she was silent for too long. "Angry. Frustrated."

Confused. She didn't say it, but her tone did.

His gut tightened. "Want me to come over?"

"Dinner will still be warm if you hurry."

"I'll be there in a few." He drove to her house, thinking of the last few weeks. How things had changed between them. They had crossed a line New Year's Eve. He'd thought he'd been doing the right thing by stopping them before they'd made love, but maybe he shouldn't have. Maybe he should have taken her, loved her, let her know how much she meant to him. Maybe he should have told her he cared about her more than he should. Maybe he should have put himself out there.

But he was so damned terrified of being hurt again.

Paul parked in her driveway and looked up at the house. It suddenly didn't seem so welcoming. Even so, he rushed through the snow up the sidewalk and pushed the door open. "Hello?"

"In the kitchen," Dianna answered.

He kicked off his shoes, hung his coat, and then headed for the kitchen. "Smells delicious."

"Thank my ex-husband. He was trying to butter me up."

"Doesn't sound like it worked."

She shook her head and filled a plate. "I'm furious. And I'm— Damn it," she seethed when she burned her hand on a casserole dish.

Paul pulled her to the sink and ran cold water over her fingers. Her lip trembled, and he exhaled slowly. He turned the water off then patted her fingers dry.

"He said he could come home and I could keep the house and I wouldn't have to work and life would just be fantastic, like his little indiscretion had never even happened. I pointed out that he was going to marry her, and he just shrugged it off like that was nothing. Like our divorce was nothing—just a little break he took from being my husband."

Paul set the towel on the counter and leaned back. He hadn't seen her this upset in some time. He wanted to hug her, but he didn't. He somehow didn't feel like he had the right.

Dianna closed her eyes. "He doesn't have a clue how much he hurt me, and no matter how I try to explain it, he'll never understand because all he thinks about is himself."

"Didn't he always?"

She nodded. "I suppose."

She lifted her gaze to his. He recognized the pain there as something that only Mitch could bring out in her. Her heart was breaking. Over *him*. Paul looked down and sighed.

"Sit down," he said. "I'll serve dinner."

She didn't sit. She reached for two glasses and started putting ice from the dispenser in them. "Sam already ate. He scarfed down his food and was gone before I even finished cleaning up the mess Mitch left."

Paul fixed their plates, and they sat to eat. Dianna stared at her food more than she ate as they sat in silence. He continually glanced at her, and when she'd catch him, she'd smile, but she was deep in thought.

"You're not hungry?" he finally asked.

"Not really."

He took her plate as he stood and cleared the table. She pushed herself up and went to the cabinet as he put her leftovers away. As she made coffee, he loaded the dirty dishes into the dishwasher. This was a routine they'd followed so many times it was habit now. However, he didn't think this night would end with them watching television, pretending they didn't want each other. There was something palpable in the air, and it wasn't their mutual attraction. She was upset. Frustrated. Hurt. Sad.

Paul washed his hands, used a towel to dry them, and then wiped the counter. Dianna smiled sadly when he hung the towel up and turned to face her.

"What?" he asked.

"Thank you."

He laughed softly. "I'm pretty great at loading a dishwasher, aren't I?"

"You are. You're pretty great all around, actually."

She stepped to him, put her head on his shoulder, and wrapped her arms around his waist. He slid his arms around her shoulders and stroked his hand over her hair.

"I'm sorry. I just need this right now. I can't believe I have to leave this place." Her voice was low, as if saying it quietly would make it less true. "I've had twenty years here, and now it's over."

He kissed her head. He loved kissing her head. Maybe the feeling was archaic, but when she was in his arms and he could put his lips to her hair, some part of his heart felt like she belonged to him. He liked that feeling—that she was his.

"I'm trying really hard to be optimistic. I just wish I had something to look forward to."

He squeezed her a bit closer to him. "You have things to look forward to. A lot of things."

"Like what?"

"If the offer pulls through on this one, in a month's time we're going to be moving you into a new house. You'll have a new place to decorate and make your home. I think we'll have to have some barbeques this summer. Doesn't that sound great? You, me, and our boys crammed around a picnic table full of food."

She leaned back and grinned up at him. "You're buying the food. I'd have to sell more than just my house to be able to feed all of you."

As they laughed, he brushed her hair from her face. He traced her ear with his fingertips as he touched her cheek with his thumb, and Dianna's smile fell as her lips parted. Her eyes darkened as he held her gaze. He wanted to lean in and kiss her, to feel her mouth on his. He wanted her to kiss him, hold him, and touch him like she'd done in that hotel room.

But that had been a bad idea a few weeks ago, and it was a worse idea now. He'd stopped them from making love because they both loved someone else. That hadn't changed. But now her someone else wanted her back.

He swallowed his churning emotions. "The coffee's done."

Her brow furrowed slightly, but then she stepped back and set about filling the mugs and stirring creamer into his. Paul accepted the drink she held out to him. They walked to the living room and sat on the couch, keeping the length of the sofa between them. She'd taken the Christmas tree down, but when he looked at the big bay window, he pictured them sitting there exchanging gifts. That memory, however, was quickly replaced by him holding her as she sobbed after finding out that Mitch and Michelle had set a wedding date.

Dianna's monotone voice pulled him from his thoughts.

"I hate how complicated my life has gotten. It used to be so simple. Even when I was being pulled in fifty different directions from all the activities the boys were involved in, I had some sense of balance. I'm so tired of feeling like everything is spiraling out of control." She snagged a tissue and dabbed at her eyes. "Just when I find my footing, something knocks me back down. I don't know how much longer I can keep going like this. I need things to stop being so hard."

Paul sat forward and put his coffee on the table. He stared at his mug for a long time as he weighed his response. He wanted to promise to take care of her. He wanted to take all her worries away, to tell her to lean on him—depend on him. He wouldn't let her down. He'd never betray her, or hurt her, or make her cry. He'd take her on vacations and buy her flowers. He'd make her feel wanted and appreciated.

Loved. He'd make her feel loved. Because he *did* love her.

Dianna sniffed, and when he looked at her, she was looking at the built-in bookshelf. "The day we moved in, I was unpacking a box of books. Jason was asleep upstairs. Mitch came in and gave me a dozen roses. He told me how happy he was, how he could never imagine us anywhere else. Now he's gone. And I'm leaving. It's like that moment never even happened."

And just like that, she reminded him she loved her ex-husband.

Paul swallowed his selfish desire to keep her and quietly said, "He's right, you know? Your life would be easier if he came home."

"What?" Her question came out in a whispered demand. She clearly hadn't expected him to say that.

He sat for a moment before turning his face to her. "You still love him, Dianna. And I don't blame you. You were with him for over twenty years. You had kids and a life. That doesn't just go away."

"Paul—"

"You can have your life back. You can stay in your house. You can stop worrying about how to take care of your kids and how to pay your bills. You can have the simplicity that you just told me you miss so much."

The muscles in her jaw clenched as she stared at him. "Yeah, I can have all that and a husband who doesn't think twice about cheating on me."

Paul lowered his face. "Maybe he learned his lesson."

"My God." She pushed herself up and moved around the coffee table. "You sound just like him. That's what he said. He's learned his lesson. He'll be better now." She stopped in front of the big window and faced him, her brow creased and her eyes hard. "He decides he's done living the life of a single man, and I'm supposed to...what? Be thankful? Stop caring that he tore me apart and just take him back? Goddamn it, Paul. I expected this from him, but you?" The anger in her eyes faded to sadness. "Don't you think I deserve better than that?"

"I do. I *know* you deserve better than that."

"Then tell me that. If you don't want me, that's fine, but don't just throw me back to a man whose betrayal nearly killed me."

He stood, crossed the room in a few strides, and put his hands to her face. He held her head as he stared into her eyes. "It isn't that I don't want you, Dianna. You're all I ever think of. Ever since we kissed, all I want to do is kiss you again. And more, so much more. I *do* want you. But I can't give you what you need."

She wrapped her hands around his wrists, clinging to him. "I don't want to leave this house, but that doesn't mean that I can't. I want to give my kids more, but they will survive without it. That life I had is over. It's been hard letting go, but I can. I just need something to look forward to. I just need you to give me something—"

"I can't. Not when I know you still love him."

"I sent him away."

"This time. You sent him away *this* time. But he isn't going to give up that easily, is he?"

He brushed his thumbs over her cheeks when tears fell from her eyes.

"We've been here for each other. We've picked each other up

and brushed each other off. But we've done that because the people we love hurt us. Everything we are to each other, we are because of them. I care about you, more than you know, but your heart is still broken over someone else. If you choose to be with me, it has to be because you're ready, not because I'm here to stand in his place."

"My God, Paul, I *never* wanted you to replace him." She frowned as she looked into his eyes. "Is that all I ever was to you? Michelle's replacement? Someone to…to fill a void?"

"Of course not," he whispered.

She stepped away and turned her back to him. "At least not intentionally, right?"

Paul lowered his face. He didn't mean to imply that either of them had been a stand-in for their spouses, but maybe that was the reality of it. Maybe they'd spent these last few months taking up space that had been left vacant simply because it was comfortable. Maybe Matt and Annie had been right all along.

He sighed. "We've always known our feelings for Mitch and Michelle were there. We've never denied how we felt about them. I know you love him, Dianna."

"Do you still love her?"

He didn't know how to answer that. He didn't think he did. He thought he loved Dianna, but if he were honest with himself, he'd never had a very good head for relationships. Doubt was pulling at him. "He's offering what you've wanted."

She faced him and looked as hurt as he'd ever seen. "What if that's not what I want anymore? Yes, there's a part of me that still loves Mitch. Part of me always will—he's the father of my children, the first man I ever loved—but there's a bigger part of me that has been missing you. I know we're not ready. I do. But if we can just...just go back to where we were before New Year's, just take a step back, we'll get to a place where we are ready, and we'll get there in our own time. We just have to take a step back."

He took her hands and looked at them for a moment before lifting her right hand and kissing it. "You're right. We do have to step back. If...if there comes a time when we can be together, as more than friends, it does have to come in its own time. When we've healed and let go of the past. We can't do that, Dianna, if we keep dancing around the things that have hurt us. You need to take time and figure this out without me here. You have to give yourself some time to know what is right. Because even though he hurt you, maybe letting him come back is the right thing. And maybe you can't see that because I'm here, reminding you of what he did. Maybe...maybe the best thing for you—for both of us—is to...take time and figure out what's right."

Disappointment rolled across her face like a storm. Her lip quivered, and tears welled in her eyes. "You're leaving me?"

He hated that he was the one causing her so much pain this time, but he nodded slowly. "We need time."

"Please," she whispered. She started to reach for him but then stopped. "I'm sorry. I'm sorry that I pushed. I won't—"

"Don't. You didn't do anything wrong. We've just come to a crossroads, Dianna. If we move forward into a relationship we aren't ready for, we're going to hurt each other. If we try to remain friends, we're going to be dancing around this thing, and we're going to hurt each other. This has been coming to a head ever since New Year's—probably even longer. We've been ignoring it, but eventually we were going to have to face the reality that we are in over our heads with each other."

Silence hung in the air for a long, uncomfortable moment. For a moment, he wanted to take it all back, everything he'd said.

"Do you..." Her brow furrowed. "Do you want her back?"

Paul sighed. He didn't. He didn't want Michelle back. But he didn't want his feelings to cloud Dianna's. She must have taken his silence as his answer. She sobbed, just one choking sound, as she turned her back on him.

"If you need anything, anything at all..." He stopped when she nodded. "I'm going to go."

He hesitated, but she didn't face him. He started to put his hand on her shoulder but stopped. Time. They needed time. He left her there, ignoring the sounds of her crying as he slid into his coat and shoes. He closed the door behind him, torn between regret and a sense that he had done what was best for both of them.

CHAPTER SEVENTEEN

Saturday was supposed to be family game night. Paul and his siblings used to get together on a regular basis. That had ended when Michelle came into the picture, but at Dianna's insistence, Paul had invited Annie, Matt, and Donna to his house.

Annie had already gathered something was wrong. She'd called him the morning after he'd left Dianna crying in her living room to demand to know what was wrong with her receptionist. He'd acted like he didn't know, but he couldn't deny it now. Sitting at the head of his dining room table with Matt and Donna to his right and Annie to his left, all looking at him with curious eyes, he'd had no choice but to tell them everything.

"How can you be sure she wants him back?" Donna asked.

"I can't," Paul said. "But I also can't be sure she doesn't."

"She's been on edge this week," Annie said. "She looks terrible."

Paul turned his attention from the beer in his hand. "Thanks. I needed to feel worse about walking out on her."

Annie frowned. "I'm just saying, I don't think she's as torn as *you* think she is."

"She doesn't want to sell her house. She can't keep up with her bills. Her kids are making sacrifices she feels responsible for. She's been juggling her finances since he left her, Annie. If he comes back, she won't have all these problems."

"He left her once," Donna said. "Who's to say he won't leave her again?"

Paul nodded. "Trust me, I considered that. I hope to hell that if she gives him a second chance, he doesn't blow it. But I just can't put myself out there when I don't know for sure how she feels."

"Did you ask her how she feels?" Matt asked.

Paul frowned at his brother. "If it were that cut and dry, would I be sitting here?"

"Why isn't it that cut and dry?" Annie asked.

He sighed. "New Year's Eve. She was upset because we thought Mitch and Michelle were getting married. She was crying, and I...tried to comfort her."

Donna gasped. "Did you...you know?"

Paul focused on his drink. "No. But only because at the very last minute we realized it was a bad idea. We talked it out and agreed we weren't ready to have a relationship. That was just a few weeks ago. The only thing that has changed between then and now is Mitch wants her to take him back. She loved him then, and she loves him now. I can't be with someone who loves someone else."

Silence hung over the table.

Finally, Annie reached out and took his hand in a rare show of affection. "Do you think she'll take him back?"

"She's feeling vulnerable right now. If he pushes her..." He swallowed. "If he pushes her, then yes, I think she'll take him back."

"And you're okay with that?" Matt asked.

"It's her choice. Not mine."

"The hell it isn't."

"I can't compete with twenty-two years of marriage, Matt. Even if I could, she's losing her home. She can't pay her bills or provide for her kids unless she gives up something that means the world to her. How the hell am I supposed to make that better for her? Unless I moved in with her—which we *definitely* aren't ready for—I can't."

"So this is about a house? You're giving her up because of a fucking house?"

"I'm giving her up because he can take care of her in ways that I can't."

Annie lifted her hand to stop Matt when he started to challenge Paul's reasoning. "If he leaves Michelle to go back to Dianna," Annie said, "where does that leave Michelle? Probably coming back to you, at least until she finds someone else, right? How much of this is about Michelle?"

Paul shook his head. "I feel like...like something broke New

Year's Eve. Thinking that she was marrying another man, knowing that she'd just erased me from her life like I was nothing—it was the final straw for me. I don't want her back. Not when—"

"Not when you're in love with Dianna," Donna finished.

Paul didn't deny her accusation. He couldn't.

"Tell her you want to be with her," Matt said. "Don't leave her hanging there all alone, waiting for him to come along and pick her up. If you leave her when you know she's vulnerable, you're just giving him an in, and you know damn well he'll take it."

"That's not the point, Matt."

"Nor is saving her the pain of leaving her house," Annie said. "The point is that you don't trust what she's feeling any more than you trust what you're feeling. You're both confused, and you don't want to get hurt again. The problem with that," she said, "is that you're both hurting right now anyway."

"Goddamn it." Paul sighed. "I didn't want this to get complicated."

"Well, guess what, little brother," she said. "It is."

Dianna stood in the doorway of her living room taking in the way the room looked for several minutes before packing away her belongings. She started with the bookshelf, tucking away novels and photo albums along with carefully wrapped photo frames, trinkets, and statuettes. By the time the evening ended, she'd packed all the nonessentials in the room, leaving it nearly empty. Seeing it so bare broke her heart.

She was distracted when headlights flashed through the window as a car pulled into her driveway. She checked the time on her phone. It was too early for it to be Sam coming home from work, but she wasn't expecting anyone else. She couldn't think of anyone who would show up unexpected, except...

"Paul." She was rushing from the room when the doorbell rang, reminding her she needed to fix the chime before new owners took over. She didn't want to leave them with a sad, drawn-out ringer. She rounded the corner into the entry, and as she looked through the glass door, her heart sank. The excitement she felt fell through the floor, and the first real smile she'd managed for days went with it.

She opened the door. "What are you doing here, Mitch?"

"I'm sorry. I know I should have called first. Is Sam here?"

"No, he's at work."

"May I come in?"

She closed her eyes and leaned her head against the door. "I'm tired and—"

"Five minutes. Please. Just give me five minutes."

She hesitated before gesturing for him to enter. He stepped in and took a long time to wipe his feet before moving into the living room. He stopped and stared at the boxes, taking in the almost empty room before looking at her.

"You're really doing it, huh?"

Dianna moved around him. "I don't have a choice." She picked up two books she'd set aside and showed them to him. "I wasn't sure what to do with these. What's the post-divorce protocol for wedding albums?"

He stared at her. The silence was thick and heavy, and Dianna almost told him to leave if he didn't have anything to say.

But then he did say something. "I'm sorry."

Her lip trembled. "Your apology is *way* too late."

He lowered his face. "I'm not proud of what I did."

"Oh, well, that's a shame because you did it so well."

"I left her. I couldn't be with her anymore."

She thought her heart stopped beating for a moment. Part of her wanted to sigh with relief. The other wanted to laugh in his face. She did neither. She dropped the albums carelessly on the floor. "If you came here looking for a place to sleep, you need to leave."

"Mom's getting her guest room ready for me. I just wanted you to know that it's over. It's done."

"Why do you think I care?"

He looked at the wedding albums on the floor. The photos that she'd so carelessly tossed aside, just as he'd done to her. She suspected what he was going to say before he even said it. They may have been apart for the better part of a year, but she still knew him, still knew how his mind worked.

"I don't know what I've been doing. It's like I lost my mind. Seeing Sam hurt, seeing you suffering… It snapped me out of whatever daze I've been living in. I love you, Dianna. I love you, and I'm so sorry that I hurt you."

She hated that he could still stir so much emotion in her. His sad eyes, his pleading face, his pathetic words—they all tugged at her and made her feel weak inside. She had to take a moment to steel herself against him. "Well, you did, Mitch. You tore me apart, and you walked away without a care in the world."

"I regret everything I said and did. I wish I could take it back. All of it."

"But you can't."

"She made me feel wanted," he said after a minute. "It's stupid and selfish."

"It's stereotypical," Dianna spat. "You poor, poor man with your little midlife crisis. How difficult your life must have been living in this beautiful house with your devoted wife and children."

"Maybe it is stereotypical, Di, but it's what I was going through. I made a mistake, but I can fix it."

"What do you expect me to do, Mitch? Pretend you didn't leave me?"

"No, but you could try to forgive me. We could get our lives back."

She walked away from him, suddenly feeling deflated. "Even if I did forgive you, I'd still remember. How could I possibly be with you without remembering where you've been? I saw you with her. I can't forget that. Believe me. I've tried."

"Couples *can* move on after adultery."

She sat on the sofa and shook her head. "I can't trust you."

"We could see a counselor. We could get help. Whatever it took."

"Why didn't you do *whatever it took* before you divorced me?"

"Because I was an idiot."

Dianna grabbed the wineglass she'd been sipping from earlier, gulped what was left in it, and then set it down. As she did, he dropped a photo of their wedding day onto the coffee table. Their wedding had been a lavish event, despite the fact that she was pregnant. She was barely showing, just a slight paunch.

"Do you remember that day?" he asked.

"Of course."

"I sneaked into the room where you were getting dressed, and you almost started crying because you said we didn't need any more bad luck."

She smiled slightly. "You told me you got the job at the investment agency."

"I said I could afford to take care of us and you could stop worrying about how we were going to afford the baby."

"We moved into that horrible apartment building."

"Then we bought this place. Just two years later. We started a life here. Here in our home."

She lowered her face and covered it with her hands. She didn't want him to see her cry, but damned if she could stop her tears these days.

He brushed his hand over her hair, and she pulled away. It didn't feel right for anyone but Paul to touch her like that.

"Dianna," Mitch whispered, "we've had such a great life here. I know I ruined it. I know you're hurt and angry. I wish I'd come to my senses sooner. I wish I'd realized my mistake sooner. But I *did* realize my mistake. Take the house off the market. Give me a chance. We can rebuild our life here, just like we built it before. It's not too late."

"You hurt me so much."

"I know. And I promised on our wedding day that I wouldn't. I swore that I'd always take care of you, and I didn't. I let you down, but I'll never let you down again."

She thought about his words for a moment before she grabbed her wineglass and walked around the coffee table. Without a word to him, she headed for the kitchen. She was refilling her glass, thinking of how stupid she'd be to take him back, when he put his hands on her shoulders.

"Why did you leave her?" she demanded.

"Because I missed you."

She turned and held his gaze. "If you want another chance with me, you damned well better be honest when I ask you a question."

He sighed and shoved his hands into his pockets. "She wasn't what I thought she was. When we were..."

"Committing adultery?"

"She thought I was great. Then we started planning a life

together, and it was so far from what I wanted. It was like she didn't care about me. She just cared about..."

"Your money so she could live the life she wanted?"

"Yeah."

"And now that you see that...what? You realize that things weren't so bad here, so you might as well come back?"

"No." He took her left hand and rubbed his thumb over her bare ring finger. "I realize that nobody will ever be better suited for me than you. I should have told you what I was feeling. I should have given our marriage a chance. I can't begin to tell you how sorry I am that I didn't."

"And how do I know you won't do it again?"

"Because I know what life is like without you. It was horrible. *She* was horrible."

Dianna couldn't stop the soft laugh that left her. "I've heard."

"Oh, right. Paul."

She looked up at him, and her smile faded as she took in his. He was discounting her. Paul. Their relationship. She pulled her hand from him. "Yeah. Paul."

"I guess that's another thing I should apologize for. Bringing him into your life."

She creased her brow. "What?"

"Michelle told me how clingy he is. You won't have to worry about that now." He brushed her hair back, tucking it behind her ear. "I'm sure she'll go running back to him. She needs someone to pay for her manicures."

His words stabbed at her heart. She had done her best not to think of Michelle standing on Paul's porch, begging him to take her back. He'd stopped short of telling Dianna he'd take her back. "He's not clingy." She pushed Mitch's hands from her. "He's considerate. There's a difference."

"Right. It doesn't matter. It doesn't concern us." He put his finger under her chin and tilted her head back. "All that matters now"—he dipped his head—"is us."

Dianna turned her face, and his breath fell on her cheek. He sighed as she turned her back on him and refilled her wineglass.

"What did you do when you found out our divorce was final?" she asked.

He was quiet.

Finally, she faced him. "What did you do when you found out you were no longer married to me?"

"I took Michelle out for dinner."

"To celebrate?"

He nodded. "We decided that if her divorce was final in time, we'd get married New Year's Eve."

"Did you feel any remorse?"

"Of course I did. I just didn't want to think about it."

"You didn't want to think about it?" She laughed softly, walked back to the living room, and looked out the window again. When she saw his reflection, she spun. "I sat right there"— she pointed at the couch—"and cried. For hours. Sam was so concerned about me that he called Paul. He dried my tears and gave Sam money to go buy us dinner because I couldn't even get off the couch to feed our son."

"I'm sorry."

"You keep saying that!"

"It's true."

"I'm sure it is, but I don't know *why* you're sorry. Are you sorry for the pain you caused me and your children, or are you sorry that your relationship with Michelle didn't work out and now you're all alone?"

"I never meant to hurt you."

"Don't you dare say that. You cheated on me. You divorced me. You can't do those things to a person without hurting them, so, yes, you *did* mean to hurt me."

"We were so unhappy, Dianna."

Tears burned her eyes and spilled down her cheeks. "Maybe we were complacent. Maybe we were content. Maybe we were even boring, but that was our life. That was the life we had built together. If you hated it so much, you should have told me. You should have tried to make it better."

"I didn't know."

"You didn't know what?"

He took a breath, and when he spoke again it was calmer. "I was selfish. I was only thinking of myself and what I thought would make me happy. I guess I thought that you'd just...be okay. In my mind, you were carrying on as you always had."

"I've been going through hell." She didn't want to admit that to him, but she couldn't keep it in any longer. "*You* put me through hell. There were times I couldn't pay the bills. I couldn't put gas in my car. I'd see our old friends, and they'd turn the other way, like they didn't even know me. Do you know how degrading that is?"

"I'd like to try to make it up to you."

"How?"

He took her hands and pulled her onto the couch next to him. "You could keep the house, Di. You wouldn't have to move."

"Mitch—"

"I know you're not ready for me to come home. That's not what I'm saying." He grasped her hands when she started to pull away. "Take the house off the market. I'll pay the mortgage, the utilities, whatever you need while we work through this."

"I don't—"

"I can't stand the thought of you selling our home. I know it will take time for us to work through this, but I will take care of you and the boys. All I want you to worry about is helping me fix us so we can get our life back."

"Mitch—"

"You don't even have to work if you don't want to. I'll take care of everything, Dianna. I owe you that much."

"May I speak?"

He grinned slightly. "Sorry."

"The money is a huge issue, I'm not going to deny it. But that isn't the only problem here. The trust is gone. I don't even know how I feel about you anymore. I don't know that a few weeks or months will change anything. And what if it doesn't work out? I'm right back where I am now, with a house that I can't afford."

"If it doesn't work out, what have you lost? Besides a few months of living in the house that you love? I know we have a lot to work on, but can we try? Please."

She pulled her hands from him. "You have to give me time to think."

"Honey, we don't have time. You have people lined up to buy the house. You have to pull it before they accept your counteroffer."

She exhaled and pushed herself up so she could pace for a moment. She didn't have to commit to anything. She just had to agree to consider it. She just had to take some time to think. Time. Just like Paul had told her. She needed time—time to think, to breathe, to find her balance again.

Mitch crossed the room to her. "Three months, Di. Let's just take three months to think about things, to figure out where we stand and what we want. We're already divorced, so if we decide it isn't going to work, all we have to do is walk away. And during that time, you'll have your home, Sam can finish high school in his house, and we'll all have time to let the dust settle and see where we stand."

She closed her eyes, thinking of how much she had wanted Sam to finish school here. To have the security of his home for what was left of his childhood. That had always been her goal. From the time Mitch left, she had been determined to keep Sam here so he would have one less disruption in his life.

"Even if I did decide to give you this time," she said quietly, "we couldn't just pick up where we left off. Don't think I'm just going to automatically forgive and forget. You have to earn my trust."

"I can do that. I *will* do that. I'll bring you a check tomorrow," he said softly. "Enough to pay the mortgage and utilities."

She rubbed her forehead, trying to get her thoughts to stop swirling like an emotional tornado through her mind. "Not so fast. Give me some time to think. We'll talk tomorrow."

"Di—"

"We'll talk tomorrow."

"Okay. Just...the longer you wait, the more time the buyer will have to close the deal."

"I know. You should go."

He left her alone, and she pressed her palms against her eyes, not quite certain what had just happened.

Paul wasn't surprised when he opened the door to find Michelle standing on his porch. He'd been expecting her ever since Dianna told him that Mitch wanted to come home. If anything, he was surprised it had taken her until Saturday morning to show up. He sighed as she batted her eyes and let her tears flow freely down her cheeks.

She sniffed dramatically. "May I come in?"

He frowned and stepped aside.

She walked in and gasped as she looked around. "Wh-What have you done?"

"I redecorated."

She stopped at the entry to the living room. "Why?"

"Because I hated the way it looked."

"Since when?"

"Since the day you did it."

Her brow creased. "You never told me that."

"I wanted you to be happy."

Her face softened and she smiled. "I've missed that, you know? How you always put me first."

Paul didn't answer. He didn't have anything nice to say. Anger bubbled just below the surface as she pouted—a look that used to wrap him around her finger. Now it just pissed him off. He was certain she'd used that look on Mitch, too. Probably as she convinced him to leave Dianna and drove a wedge between him and his kids. Michelle hadn't just hurt Paul—that he could get over. She'd hurt Dianna, Sam, and Jason. And that didn't sit well with him.

"I like this." Michelle picked up a newly framed photo of Paul and his siblings. "This is a great photo. When was this?"

"Christmas."

"You look happy in that picture."

Dianna had teased the siblings until they gave in, huddled close together, and smiled wide for her to take the photo. He couldn't help but smile. It faded quickly, however.

"It was a good day," he said.

"I'm sorry I missed it."

He wasn't sorry she'd missed it. That had been the best Christmas he'd had in years, and he knew why. Because Michelle wasn't there. Dianna had walked into his family gathering, and it had been smooth and peaceful and free of the tension Michelle had a way of bringing out. He had truly enjoyed the day. Dianna had made the day perfect, and she hadn't even tried. She'd done it just by being there.

Paul didn't snap out of his thoughts until Michelle put her hand on his arm.

"Did you hear me?" she asked.

He shook his head slightly. "Sorry. What?"

She gave him a sad smile. "I said I left him."

"*You* left him?"

"He just wasn't you."

He scoffed. "Wasn't that the point? He was so strong and independent and didn't smother you?"

She pouted for him again. "I didn't mean those things. I was angry."

"*You* were angry? You were leaving me for a man I didn't even know you were having an affair with, but *you* were angry?"

"He manipulated me. You have to know that he used me."

Paul cleared his throat. "What, uh, what led to this tragic breakup of yours?"

"He just didn't take care of me like you did."

"Hmm. Are you sure he didn't leave you?" He smiled at the surprise on her face. "Mitch was at his ex-wife's house a few nights ago, cooking her dinner and asking her to take him back."

Her eyes widened. "He did what?"

Paul nodded.

"That goddamned liar. He told me he was working late."

He smirked. "That's what he used to tell her when he was with you. Ironic, isn't it?"

Michelle exhaled slowly, and then she stuck her lip out once more. "Do you see? Do you see how he treated me?"

"You had an affair with a married man. A man who had been with his wife for half his life. What did you think was going to happen, Michelle?"

"He said he loved me."

"Do you know who loved you?" he asked softly. "*I* loved you. Even though everything was always about you. Even though you always took and never gave back."

"I didn't—"

"You did. You did, but I still loved you. Because on the rare occasion that you actually appreciated what I did for you, you made me feel like I'd given you the moon. I've thought a lot about this moment, you know. About you coming home, about what I would say to you."

"You have every right to be upset."

"But I'm not. Not anymore. I was for a long time. New Year's Eve was tough. We knew, or we thought—"

"*We?*"

"Dianna and me."

"*Dianna?*"

"Yes."

"Mitch told me you guys were together, but I didn't believe him. I mean, what could you possibly see in *her*?"

Paul lifted a brow. "You mean beyond the fact that she's kind and generous and beautiful?"

Michelle snorted. "Please, Paul. I've seen her."

"Excuse me?"

"She might be kind and generous and all that, but she looks like an old pair of boots. Tired and worn down."

Rage rolled through Paul. He clenched his jaw and took a slow breath to contain his anger. "Maybe that's because she's always taking care of everyone else while that worthless husband of hers was too busy screwing you to notice no one was taking care of her. Maybe if he'd put half the effort into his wife as he did his mistress, she wouldn't look so tired and worn down. You may think I smothered you, but did you ever want for anything? Was there ever a time when I didn't take care of you? She doesn't have that. She's never had that because he's too goddamned selfish to even notice her."

Michelle leaned back a bit but didn't speak.

"She may not dye her hair every other week or put her makeup on with a trowel, but she *is* beautiful. Inside and out, which is more than I can say for you. While you've been living the high life with *her* husband, she's taught me a thing or two about myself. All those things you hated, Michelle—the flowers and the attention—those are things that most women appreciate.

The only reason you didn't was because you wanted them on your terms. You want everything on your terms. But my terms have changed, and there's no way in hell you can live up to what *I* want, so you might as well turn your ass around and leave."

She stared at him for a long moment. "You're in love with her, aren't you?"

"That's not your business."

She rotated her jaw, and her eyes turned cold as she narrowed them to glare at him. "She's going to take him back, you know. She's pathetic. She has no way of surviving without him."

"Actually, she's been doing pretty amazing."

She turned toward the door and then stopped. "He's probably there right now, Paul. Crawling into her bed. Telling her all those sweet things a weakling like her needs to hear. She's probably already forgotten about you."

He didn't move as Michelle walked away. But every footstep made his heart feel heavy. Not because she was leaving him but because she was right. Mitch was going to beg Dianna to take him back. And because Paul had walked away from her, because Paul had left her, she was going to listen to Mitch. She was going to take Mitch back because Paul was too stupid to recognize what everyone else could. He was in love with Dianna.

CHAPTER EIGHTEEN

*B*y the next afternoon, Dianna was tied in knots. She couldn't even see straight. She'd spent all night thinking, re-thinking, and thinking again. The one person she wanted to talk to about all her problems was the one person she couldn't. Paul had closed the door, at least for now, on their relationship. It didn't help that she kept waiting for Annie to say something about her relationship, or lack thereof, with Paul.

As if they sensed that she was on the verge of breaking, her co-workers left her alone. Which, honestly, only added to her apprehension. It wasn't like Annie to avoid her.

Dianna didn't look up until the front door opened and a delivery man walked in carrying a vase holding a huge bouquet of brightly colored flowers. They were beautiful, but she didn't smile when he said the delivery was for her.

She signed for it and then opened the card.

I love you! Mitch

Disappointment seized her. Had she actually thought they'd be from Paul? Yes, part of her had. Or at least had hoped. She tucked the card back in the envelope and set the vase out of the way without so much as smelling the flowers. She focused on her work, ignoring the delivery—ignoring the world until Annie tapped on the counter.

She looked at the flowers looming over Dianna's desk, but Dianna pretended not to notice.

"They've come back with a really nice counteroffer. You want to talk about it?"

She nodded and followed Annie into her office. She sat across from Annie, who pushed papers across to her.

"They've come up three thousand and are willing to cover their closing costs. That's a pretty good jump. I think you should accept."

Dianna stared at the papers, and a tear rolled down the side of her nose. She swiped it away, hoping that Annie hadn't seen it. "Can, uh, can I have some time to think about it?"

"Yeah. Of course."

"I'm sorry. I don't mean to yo-yo on this."

"This is a big decision. You have to do what feels right."

"I just wish I knew what that was." She pushed herself up.

"Di," Annie called. "If you need some time off—"

"I don't. I'm fine."

"If you do, just ask."

"Thanks." She left Annie's office and collapsed behind her desk. Turning her chair, she looked at the brightly colored flowers. She wished things could be simple, that she had a sign directing her toward what she should do. Her thoughts were interrupted by the phone. She tried to sound happy as she answered. "Thank you for calling O'Connell Realty."

"Good afternoon."

Dianna closed her eyes at the cheery voice. "Hi, Mitch. Thank you for the flowers."

"I wanted you to know I was thinking about you. Have you had lunch yet?"

"Um, no. Actually, I haven't."

"May I pick you up? We could talk some more about taking the house off the market."

She looked at her bouquet. Was this the sign she'd been wishing for? Was this the universe's way of telling her what she should do? "Sure," she said weakly.

Within the hour, Dianna climbed into Mitch's truck and fastened her seat belt.

He touched her forehead. "Are you okay? You look sick."

She closed her eyes and pulled away. "I'm stressed."

"Because of me?"

"Because of everything. They came back with a counteroffer. A good one. I'd be an idiot not to take it." She looked out the window as he backed out of his parking spot. "I am so mad at you right now. I can't believe what you are putting me through."

"I'm sorry. I'm trying to make up for it, Di."

"Well, you shouldn't have done it in the first place."

They didn't speak again until he pulled into a drive-through. She ordered a sandwich and a water and then sat back in more tense silence until he parked his truck overlooking a pond near their neighborhood. She thanked him when he handed her a foil-wrapped sandwich and unwrapped it before covering it back up and tossing it aside.

"They put mustard on it." She leaned her head back and closed her eyes. Of course they'd put mustard on it. She'd specifically asked them *not* to, and it was just her luck these days for everything that could go wrong to go wrong, including her fucking hamburger.

"I can't stand seeing you like this," Mitch said softly. "All this stress isn't good for you."

She scoffed and looked out at the ice-covered water.

"Let me ease some of that for you," he said. "I owe you that much."

"And all I have to do is give you another chance to put me through this hell again, right?"

"If you decide to give me another chance, I know I would do better. Come on, Di. I can't stand to see you this torn up. You look like you're about to break."

She laughed softly. "I think I've already broken. I think I broke the night..." She stopped herself from saying the night Paul left.

"I know."

She shook her head, letting him think he was the one who

cut away her final bit of strength. She didn't care enough to correct him.

"The house sold quickly this time," he said. "It will sell quickly again if you decide to put it on the market. But at least it will be because you are ready and not because you are desperately trying to keep your head above water."

"I don't trust you enough to count on you for that long. What if you work things out with her and leave me high and dry again?"

"We can go to the bank right now. I'll transfer enough to cover three months' mortgage plus a cushion for your utilities and expenses. Three months without the financial noose around your neck would clear your mind enough to think about us and where we stand. And I'm *not* going back to Michelle. She was the single biggest mistake of my life. I know that now."

Dianna closed her eyes and sank down in the passenger seat. She'd been tossing his offer around since he'd made it. Three months of not worrying about money would be heaven. It would be all she had been asking for. But at what cost? She'd feel obligated to give Mitch a chance. Was that fair to him? To her? When she was so torn over how she felt about Paul?

"Three months of not worrying. Can you really turn that down?" Mitch pressed.

"But the offer on the house—"

"There'll be another offer if you decide to sell later. This isn't a onetime shot, honey. There're always people looking to buy houses, and you've made our home beautiful. Someone will want it."

"I can't imagine not living in that house," she whispered.

"You don't have to. At least not for the next three months."

She looked at him, and he smiled as he started the truck.

sh

Paul parked next to Dianna's car and took a deep breath, steadying his nerves. He probably should have called first, but he'd been working up the nerve to face her. He didn't want to give her the chance to tell him she needed time—the very excuse he'd given her. He grabbed the bouquet of roses he'd picked up on his way and hurried into the lobby of his sister's business.

His smile fell when Dianna wasn't sitting behind her desk.

Annie stepped into the lobby. "She's out to lunch."

"Oh. Her car is still here."

Annie shrugged. "She didn't say who picked her up, but I'm fairly certain it was Mitch."

Paul's heart dropped to his stomach, and then his stomach bottomed out. "How can you be so sure?"

She nodded toward Dianna's desk. There was a huge bouquet of flowers. "She was barely out the door before I snooped at the card. They're from him."

Paul sat heavily on a bench in the waiting area. "I blew it, didn't I?"

"I don't think so." Annie sat next to him. "She hasn't exactly looked happy the last few days. I don't think she's thrilled that he's back in her life."

"She isn't thrilled about anything happening in her life right now. She all but begged me to be there for her, and I turned my back on her. I'm such an idiot."

"No. You were trying to do what is right for everyone involved."

"Was I? Or was I just too damn scared to go after what I wanted?"

"You've both been hurt. It makes sense to take your time and be sure."

"What if doing what made sense cost me Dianna? I pushed her away, Annie. I told her to forgive him."

"You told her to consider everything that was going on before making a choice."

"I should've...I should have told her how I feel. I should have shown her all the cards before telling her to make a choice."

Annie's phone rang. She showed the screen to Paul. It was Dianna. "Hello?"

Paul leaned close so he could hear.

"Annie, it's Dianna. I, um, I'm sorry, but I'm going to pull the house from the market."

Paul's heart dropped. There was only one way she could afford to do that—if Mitch was going home. He fell back and looked up at the ceiling.

He was too late.

8h

Paul sat in his dark living room, nursing his second glass of vodka. His feet were propped up on the coffee table as he slouched on the sofa staring into the darkness. When he'd sat down, the sun was still shining, but he hadn't bothered to get up once it set to turn on a light. He sighed when his phone rang. He'd ignored two calls from Annie already. He expected this one to be from Matt. But when he looked at his phone, his heart grew heavy. It was Dianna. He knew why she was calling. To tell him she was back with Mitch. He smiled slightly. At least she had enough respect for him to let him know what was going on.

His smile faded, and he ignored the call. Once the caller ID screen faded, he was met with a picture of them on his phone's wallpaper. Her face was pressed against his as he snapped the photo on New Year's Eve. It was taken well before midnight, well before they had kissed, before things had fallen apart. He sighed when the phone beeped to let him know he had a voice mail. He wanted to listen to it to hear her voice, but he didn't want to hear her words.

He downed what was left in his glass and looked at the bottle of liquor tempting him to have another. Instead, he picked up his phone again. He ignored the message that he had a voice mail and opened his Facebook app. He scrolled through his history. Almost everything had something to do with Dianna—a check-in from someplace they ate, a comment about something they'd done, a photo of them together on Christmas. Milestones of the relationship that they both insisted they didn't have. Sighing, he closed the application and called his voice mail. He put the phone to his ear and held his breath as her voice came to him.

"Hey." She sounded nervous. "I don't know if you want to hear from me right now or not. I kind of made a mess of things the other night. I'm sorry about that. I just wanted to let you know that I took the house off the market. Mitch is going to help me out for a few months. We're not back together," she added quickly. "He wants me to think about things. And to not sell the house until I decide, so...I don't know what that means for us... Mitch and me, I mean...I just..."

Paul imagined her biting her lip in that way she did when unsure of herself.

"I can't keep going on like this. I need things to settle down for a while, and he's giving me that. So, I guess I'm taking the coward's way out of this mess, at least for a few months. I hope you understand and...I guess I thought you should hear it from me. Take care of yourself, Paul."

The message ended, and he let out the breath he'd been holding. She wasn't the one who'd made a mess of things the other night. He was the one who screwed everything up. She sounded miserable—broken and defeated. He wanted to go to her, to hold her and tell her to forget Mitch. He'd take care of her. He'd take care of everything.

He even started to stand before the vodka rushed to his head and he fell back down. He put his elbows to his knees and held his head as the room spun around him. When it slowed, he exhaled slowly and swallowed the dread that had been clouding his heart.

He couldn't go to her. Not now. She'd made her choice. She'd taken her house off the market, turned down the offer she had on it. Mitch had stepped in to save her, and she'd accepted him.

"What did I do?"

CHAPTER NINETEEN

*T*he realization that he was an idiot came over Paul yet again as he drove home Monday—Valentine's Day. He'd called the florist and canceled the flower delivery he'd scheduled weeks ago for Dianna. They'd offered to alter the delivery address, but he'd declined. He didn't have anyone to give them to.

And why didn't he have someone to give them to? Because he was a chicken shit. He'd had a woman he cared about—*loved*—standing in front of him asking him to take her, and he'd said no.

He flipped off the radio, tired of hearing slow songs and commercials about jewelry and flowers.

"Come on," he yelled at the car in front of him. He pressed his hand against the horn when the car didn't move the moment the light turned green. He cursed the drivers around him as he made his way home. Once inside, he dropped his briefcase, kicked off his shoes, and hung up his coat, but as soon as he turned around and noticed the blue walls, he was instantly reminded of Dianna. Just as he had always been reminded of Michelle when the room was that hideous red-orange color she'd loved so much. He'd hated his home for so long because it reminded him of his wife. Now he hated it because it reminded him of Dianna.

He couldn't win for losing.

The only room untouched by Dianna, as had been with Michelle, was his office. He reheated leftover pizza while he changed into house pants and a T-shirt, and then he carried his dinner and a beer into his office and sank into the chair as he waited for his computer to boot up. He'd spent the better part of the weekend in that room and was content to spend his evening there as well, but then Annie called out to him. He dropped his pizza on the plate and set it on the desk.

"Back here!"

She walked into the office and leaned against the door, frowning at him. "Come to dinner with me."

"No."

"Pauly, get your ass up and come with me. I'll be damned if I spend yet another Valentine's Day home watching *CSI* reruns by myself."

"Why don't you have dinner with Marcus?"

Annie glared at him. "I don't date my employees."

"Too bad. He likes you."

"Which proves that he's an idiot. I don't date those either."

Annie actually didn't date anyone. She had an almost twenty-year-old daughter but had never been married. She'd said she didn't like the girl's father enough to commit to him, and he didn't like her enough to stick around.

Paul looked at the dried-out pizza slice on his desk. "How was she today?"

"Better. She looked like she actually got some rest this weekend."

"Did he send her flowers today?" He heard the clip in his tone, but he needed to know. If Mitch couldn't be bothered to send her flowers for Valentine's Day, then maybe Paul could justify going against his better instinct and calling her.

"He did, and I heard her saying she had dinner plans, so I expect he's taking her out somewhere."

Paul nodded. "He damn well better."

"Come on. Take me to dinner so I can pretend people like me."

Paul chuckled as he got up. "Plenty of people like you. You just don't like them."

She grabbed his arm as he started past her. "She's going to be okay. What about you?"

He nodded. "I'm okay. Or at least I will be."

Dianna looked at her reflection in the mirror and debated if she should change. She didn't want to give Mitch the wrong idea. The dress she'd bought—tight-fitted, red, knee-length, and ruched in all the right places to hide her self-perceived flaws—had been for Paul's benefit. She'd found it in a consignment shop while looking for new work clothes and had fallen in love with it. It would have been perfect for their first Valentine's Day, and she'd so been looking forward to him seeing her in it. He'd complimented her profusely on her dress New Year's Eve, and she'd noticed how he liked looking at her legs, so she'd happily gotten something with a higher-than-normal hemline.

She'd bought this dress with Paul in mind. Wearing it for Mitch felt wrong.

She glanced at the clock next to her bed and sighed. Mitch would be there soon. She didn't really have time to change. Even so, she gripped the hidden zipper and slid it down her back. She returned the dress to the closet and pulled out beige slacks, pairing them with a dark pink blouse. She looked nice, but not... whatever it was she had been going for when buying that dress. Slipping on a pair of flats, she put back on the jewelry she'd worn to work: a silver bracelet—a gift from Mitch that she'd worn for the first time since he'd left her, a silver necklace, and a pair of hoop earrings. She touched up her makeup, brushed out her long hair, and frowned at herself in the mirror.

Maybe she was underdressed now. But it wasn't a date. It was *not* a date, and she didn't want him to get the impression that it was, so maybe slacks and a blouse were the perfect choices. She chewed her lip when the doorbell rang. That dreadful noise surrounded her, and she had to close her eyes.

With her eyes closed, she gave herself a moment to entertain the thought of Paul standing at the door. He'd be holding a bouquet of roses and smiling at her like there was no place else he'd rather be. He'd hug her, kiss her cheek, and tell her that she looked beautiful. Then they'd go to the sushi restaurant, and he'd laugh as he gently coaxed her into expanding her culinary tastes. She'd probably hate it, but she'd try it. For him.

She would have tried it for him.

"Stop it," she whispered.

She turned the light off as she walked out of the room. She didn't hurry as she walked down the stairs, still clearing her mind. Mitch smiled at her through the front door glass, and she smiled back as she let him in.

"I still need to replace that doorbell, don't I?" he asked.

"I keep telling myself I'll get around to that, but it seems the only time I think about it is when it's ringing."

"Well, I'll put it on my to-do list for next weekend."

She wanted to tell him not to do that. This was her house now, and fixing the doorbell was her responsibility, but he pushed a box of chocolate-covered hazelnuts toward her.

"I know you like these."

"I do. Thank you." She took the box and looked at it. "You didn't have to do that. I mean, I didn't—"

"I wanted to," he said before she could finish. "I want you to know that I'm trying to be more aware of you, and... I'm just trying."

"I know you are." She set the candy down and reached for her coat.

He took it from her and opened it so she could slip her arms in. He pulled it up and then put his hands on her shoulders and pressed a kiss to the back of her head. He'd quit doing things like that years ago. He didn't kiss her head like that anymore. Paul did.

Dianna swallowed the surge of emotion—was it guilt?—as she leaned from his kiss and reached for her purse. She turned and noticed the hurt on his face. "I didn't mean to pull away like that."

"It's okay." He opened the door and gave her plenty of space while she walked out. He waited by the stairs while she locked the door, and then he walked behind her to his truck and held the door open while she climbed in. "I made reservations at that Italian restaurant you like so much."

Her heart seized for a moment as memories of dinners with Paul flooded her. It was their wine that Paul had gotten drunk on the night that his divorce had been finalized. She'd held him that night, after he'd gotten sick. When she woke in the morning, he was curled around her, surrounding her in his warmth.

Mitch cleared his throat, pulling her mind from Paul.

"Um, I want to thank you. I feel like tonight's the first step to getting back what we had."

She looked out the window. And there it was, exactly as she

expected. Brushing their divorce under the rug. That's how he dealt with things: ignore them, and they no longer exist.

"Do you miss her?" She hated the question the moment she said the words. She hadn't thought about them, hadn't even considered what his answer may be. Her question surprised her as much as it seemed to have surprised him.

He glanced at her. "No."

She waited, expecting more, but that was the end of it. No. No, he didn't miss the woman he'd left her for after twenty-plus years of marriage. No, he didn't miss the woman he'd planned to marry.

Dianna didn't believe him. He couldn't have done those things without feeling something for Michelle. And he couldn't just walk away from that without missing her. Maybe he just didn't miss her as much as he'd missed his old life, but he still missed her. He had to. Otherwise, everything Dianna had been through, everything he'd put her through to be with Michelle, seemed so...pointless. And it couldn't have been pointless.

"How did you meet her?"

"Di, can we not—not tonight. I'll tell you whatever you need to know, but can tonight just be about us?"

She looked out the passenger window again, and he let out a long, slow breath.

"I was buying you a birthday present at that little boutique you like. She was there."

She spun her head to him. "You met your mistress while you were buying me a gift?"

He didn't respond.

"Did she know why you were there? That you were married?"

"Yes. She…she helped me pick it out."

Dianna looked at the bracelet on her wrist. The last birthday present she'd gotten from her husband. "Well. I wore it for you tonight." Her voice was flat, void of all emotion. No anger, no shock or upset. Just flat. She stared at the silver for a moment before unhooking it. She dropped it into the cup holder of his console, no longer feeling like she'd done something special for him.

She watched the scenery passing as this latest feeling of betrayal sank in. She should be over it by now. Shouldn't she? Shouldn't this pain be less sharp? Less emotionally debilitating? But it wasn't. She was right back in that spot, right back to feeling the humiliation, the degradation of having been the last to know. She was such a fool. Such an idiot.

"I'm sorry, Dianna."

"Can you take me home? This isn't a good idea tonight."

She anticipated that he would argue, make excuses as he'd always done, but he turned right at the next stop sign and drove around the block. Apparently he understood there was no point in debating with her.

He parked in her driveway. "Would you be willing to see a counselor?"

"I don't know. Is there anything else I need to know? Any

other secrets or lies or *omissions* that you need to share with me?"

"You know those business trips I had to take?" he asked after a few tense moments of silence.

She closed her eyes. She'd suspected he'd lied about those.

"I was with Michelle. But it wasn't just... I mean, obviously I was with her. But..."

"For God's sake, just spit it out."

Mitch looked at her. "I took her to that resort on the lake that you wanted to go to. I wanted to do something special with her, and I remembered that you had gone on and on about how much you wanted to go there for our anniversary because it looked so romantic."

Dianna's breath caught. "So you took your mistress instead? After lecturing me about how expensive it was and how we were saving for our retirement, after making me feel like I was asking for too much from you to take the time off work to be with me, you took *her*?"

Mitch sat quietly for a moment. "Twice."

"You are such an unbelievable asshole."

He focused out his window. "I'm not proud of what I've done. I know I hurt you. I'm ashamed of that. I'm ashamed of myself. I hate what I did. But I can't change it."

"And I can't change how much it still hurts." She climbed out of the truck and walked to the house without looking back.

sh

Paul hesitated when he saw Dianna sitting in what had somehow become their booth at the café. He hadn't stepped foot inside since the last time he'd come with her, but after Annie left, he'd felt too restless to be at home. He hadn't intended to stop at the café, but when he saw it was still open as he drove by, he decided to stop for dessert. He started to leave, but Dianna grabbed a napkin and wiped her face, and he realized she was crying. Then he remembered that she was supposed to be out to dinner with Mitch.

Something had happened that led her to be sitting there alone on Valentine's Day instead of with her...whatever Mitch was. Paul crossed the café and put his hand on her shoulder.

"I didn't mean to startle you," he said when she jolted and looked up at him with wide, red eyes.

She creased her brow as if she weren't sure what she was supposed to say.

"May I sit?"

She nodded, and he slid into the booth across from her.

"What happened?" he asked.

She tucked a strand of hair behind her ear and turned her coffee mug a few times. "We were on our way to dinner, and I just... I guess, to be honest, I didn't want to be there, and I think I just..."

"You fought?"

"I asked questions I shouldn't have." She closed her eyes and rested her forehead in the palm of her hand. "Did you know they went on vacations together?"

"After I found out she'd been cheating, I guessed she hadn't been visiting her sister as frequently as she'd told me."

"I had asked him to take me to a lakeside resort for our anniversary. I'd found this beautiful hotel that sounded so amazing. He said we couldn't afford it. Then he took her. *Twice*."

Paul sighed as he lowered his face. Even without the tears in her eyes, he could imagine how much it had to have hurt her to hear that. "I'm sorry."

She nodded numbly. "She picked out my birthday present last year. That's how they met. Buying me jewelry. Isn't that romantic?"

She wiped her eyes, and Paul had that familiar mixed emotion of wanting to hug her and wanting to punch Mitch at the same time.

"She selected a beautiful silver bracelet. I used to wear it all the time and tell him how much I loved it. For months, I literally wore evidence of his deceit and it made me feel loved. He let me do that," she said quietly. "He let me show her bracelet off like it was a token of his affection rather than what it was—proof of his betrayal. It makes my stomach turn when I think about it."

Her face scrunched for a moment before she drew a quivering breath. She turned away when the waitress approached with a coffee mug for him and a pot in her hand to top off Dianna's drink. He shook his head when the waitress asked if he wanted anything else.

"I'm sorry," Dianna said when they were alone again. "I guess you don't want to hear all that."

"I'd guess you didn't really want to hear it either."

"I thought I needed to know, but now that I do…"

"It hurts all over again."

"It hurts so much I can't breathe," she whispered. "I feel so used and…insignificant. Why did I do this? Why did I let him tear me apart again? I just… I'm sorry." She exhaled loudly.

Paul rested his hand on her arm. "Don't apologize. You can always talk to me."

"But I'm talking about things you don't care to know."

He shook his head. "You can *always* talk to me. About *anything*."

She chewed her lip for a moment, as if she were debating what she should say. Finally, she asked, "How are you, Paul?"

"We'll get to that in a minute. Right now we're talking about you."

Dianna frowned. "I thought I was doing the right thing. He offered to pay the mortgage for a few months, and all I had to do was stop worrying so I could clear my head. It seemed like the answer. I got to stay in the house, I didn't have to worry about the boys, and…"

"And you didn't have to take on everything alone anymore."

She nodded. "I felt relieved at first, but then it all just came crashing down."

"It's going to take time, Dianna."

She nodded. "He wants us to go to counseling."

Paul considered his words as silence lingered between them. He could do it, he was certain. He could tell her right now to walk away from Mitch, and he suspected she would. But that damned logical side of him knew that wasn't the answer. She had to process this pain she was going through, and she had to do it without his interference. He'd distracted her from it long enough. They'd distracted each other for months, and all it left them was more problems. But she was there now, facing her broken heart, and he had to let her do it on her own.

"Even if you get through this and decide you can't be with him, going through counseling will help you resolve all the damage he did. You have to do that, Di."

"Did—" she started but stopped.

"What?"

She flicked her gaze at him. "Did she come home?"

He nodded. "I told her to go to hell, though. There has to be something better out there than someone who would paint my walls such ugly colors."

Dianna laughed a sad, congested sound.

Paul smiled, glad that, even if for just a moment, he'd eased some of her misery. "I'm sorry you're going through this again, but you buried your pain for so long, it was bound to resurface sometime. It's better to deal with it now than to have it sneak up on you in a year or two."

"Have you dealt with it? Have you coped with all the damage she did?"

"I only had three years of a fairly one-sided marriage to deal with. You had a lifetime of family and memories. We have completely different levels of coping."

"She still hurt you."

He nodded. "And I still have some work to do, but I can honestly say I'm getting better." He hesitated for a moment but then brushed her hair behind her ear and then rested his palm to her face. His heart tripped when she covered his hand with hers. "I shouldn't say this, but I've missed you," he whispered. "I've missed you like crazy."

She smiled. "I've missed you, too."

He held her gaze for what seemed like an eternity. "I'm sorry for leaving like I did."

Dianna shook her head. "I shouldn't have pushed."

Paul put his hand on hers on the table and watched as he trailed his finger over hers. "You didn't. Like I said, we were coming to a head one way or another. You have to work through this. You can't move on, with Mitch or anyone else, until you do."

She drew a deep breath and then let it out slowly. "I don't know that I did this for the right reasons, Paul. He kept telling me I wouldn't have to sell the house and I wouldn't have to worry about the bills. That had been weighing so heavily on my mind that I think I just... I gave in to him because I was so tired."

"Whatever the reason, it was the right decision. You have to resolve all the pain he caused you, and you couldn't do that when you were drowning in so many other problems. Whatever the outcome, you needed this reprieve so you could stand back and focus on mending your heart."

"It just hurts so much."

"I know it does." He entwined his fingers with hers and stared at their interlocked hands. "I want you to know that if you need me, you can call me. Anytime. I know things between us are...whatever...but I care about you, Dianna. Very much. I don't want you to feel like you are alone. You're not. I'm always here."

She nodded. "Thank you. That means a lot to me." Taking another deep breath, she sighed loudly. "What are you doing here this time of night?"

"I had dinner with Annie. After she left, I just... I was restless. I thought maybe some pie would help."

She smiled and lowered her gaze. "We were on our way to dinner when I made him take me home. I got inside and... My mind was racing. I thought getting out would help."

"Did it?"

"Nope. Instead of sitting on the couch crying, I sat here. At least here I couldn't throw my coffee mug."

He laughed, recalling the first day they met and how he'd cleaned up the shattered cup and spilled coffee from her kitchen floor. "Did you eat?"

She shook her head, and he gestured to the waitress.

"Can we get a couple menus, please?"

"Paul, you just had dinner with your sister."

"And now I'm having dinner with you." He opened the menu that was put in front of him and scanned the selections. She hesitated before finally doing the same. His heart warmed when she glanced up at the same time and smiled.

Her eyes were red-lined and puffy, her nose bright from her

wiping it, and her cheeks were pale. Her hair was flat from running her hands through it the way she did when she was stressed, but in that moment Paul thought he'd never seen her look more beautiful. He couldn't stop himself. Reaching across the table, he took her hand in his and squeezed it.

"Happy Valentine's Day, Di."

"Happy Valentine's Day, Paul."

CHAPTER TWENTY

*M*itch cleared his throat as he pushed his dinner around on his plate. "Have you started making plans for Sam's graduation party?"

Dianna lifted her gaze from the lasagna on her plate and glanced at him. "Um, I'll probably just get a few trays from the deli."

"No. Don't do that. Call that barbeque place he likes. Get them to cater it."

"That's going to be really expensive. I can't—"

"You don't have to worry about that."

She frowned. He was constantly telling her not to worry about money. He was *paying* for everything. Their meals, their counseling. Her bills, her mortgage. He was creeping further and further into her life, and she was starting to resent it. "I can't afford catering, not even half of it."

"Sam would like it if we had barbeque. I'll pay for it."

"We're divorced. We have to split things now."

He lowered the fork that was halfway to his mouth. "When are you going to stop reminding me that we're divorced?"

Dianna lifted her brow at him. "I don't know. When are you going to stop acting like we can just pick up and keep going like you never walked out on me?"

"I don't want to fight," he said firmly but quietly so the tables around them wouldn't hear.

"Stop treating me like I'm a child."

"I'm not treating you like a child."

"You've *always* treated me like some *thing* to be taken care of and tolerated. I'm sick of it, Mitch."

"Well, it didn't bother you before, did it? You were perfectly happy letting me take care of you for the last twenty years."

Dianna glared across the table. "I cannot believe you just said that."

"What? You deny it? You never had to work a day in your life."

"You think raising our sons wasn't work?" she demanded just above a whisper. "Taking care of you wasn't work? Making sure you had a clean home and clothes and dinner every night and everything else I did for you wasn't work? You may have made the money, but I made your *life*." She ground her teeth together as she dropped her fork on the table and yanked the napkin from her lap. "Take me home."

"No."

"Take me home, Mitch."

"*No.*"

He took her hand before she could stand. He glanced at the table next to them. She followed his gaze and sank back into her seat when she noticed them watching.

"I don't want to be around you right now," she said.

"You can't keep pushing me away, Dianna."

"I don't like how I feel when I'm with you."

"How's that?"

"Angry. Defensive."

He sagged a bit and pulled his hand away. "I'm sorry. I don't want you to feel that way. I didn't mean to lose my temper. I know this isn't easy. I hurt you deeper than I could ever know, and I deserve your anger and your defensiveness. I know you worked hard to take care of us," he continued. "I didn't mean what I said. It was a jerk move. I apologize. Sincerely. I am sorry. The bad thing about knowing each other so well is knowing what buttons to push to get the biggest reaction."

She closed her eyes and nodded. "Yeah. I'm sorry, too. Sam would love having barbeque at his party. If you pay for the catering, I'll take care of everything else."

"That sounds fair."

She put her napkin back on her lap and picked up her fork just as someone called out to Mitch. Dianna lifted her head and smiled at the elderly couple who had stopped at their table. She was used to him running into clients on occasion. It was nothing new. His reaction, however, made her crease her brow in confusion.

He was always so friendly with his clients. He had to be since he worked with their money. His greetings were usually warm, but he gave the couple a curt hello and glanced at Dianna. He cleared his throat nervously, and she tilted her head, curious about his uneasiness.

"You must be his new wife," the woman said as she gave Dianna a wide smile.

The world shifted beneath Dianna. Her breath rushed from her as if she'd been crushed. Her heart dropped like a boulder falling off a cliff, and the food in her stomach lurched upward as the muscles in her abdomen tightened. Every nerve in her body tensed, and a cold sweat instantly broke out on her skin, causing a clamminess to rush over her. Her hands started to tremble. She was certain that everyone around them had heard the woman and somehow knew that, no, she wasn't his new wife.

"Melissa?" the old woman asked.

"Michelle." Her husband spoke at the same high volume.

"Oh, Michelle. That's right. It's nice to meet you, dear. Congratulations on the marriage. You've got a good man."

Dianna tried to smile to be polite, but she didn't think she quite managed it because the couple looked confused before turning to Mitch.

"Enjoy your dinner," Mitch said stiffly, and the couple moved on. "Dianna, I'm sorry. They don't know…"

The feeling engulfing her was so familiar, she realized. The humiliation, the hurt, the betrayal, the knife cutting at her heart and soul and pride. The feeling of inadequacy and gullibility. The feeling of being completely and utterly mortified. This was how she'd felt so often over the last year. And every time she felt this way, it was because of Mitch.

Mitch and Michelle.

She took a breath, which must have been the first one for some time because her inhalation was gasping, her body desperate for oxygen. The air quivered as it rushed back out. She closed her eyes, wishing the earth would open up and swallow her.

"Excuse me."

"Dianna."

"I need a minute." She pushed herself from the table and rushed into the ladies' room. The face staring back in the mirror was one she hadn't seen in some time. Pale and tense and full of pain. Her eyes burned with anger to the point they looked hateful. Her lips trembled, and her jaw muscles worked as she ground her teeth.

She looked like she was on the verge of breaking. And she was.

There should never have been a question as to who Dianna was to Mitch. Ever.

You must be his new wife.

They had thought she was Michelle, the woman he loved. The woman he had planned to marry. His future. They thought she was his future, not his past. They thought she was his wife.

And she used to be. She used to be his wife. Not his *new* wife. Just his wife.

Taking a few breaths, Dianna pushed herself from the counter and walked out of the bathroom. She ignored Mitch when he called out to her. She didn't look back as she marched out onto the street. She just moved forward.

Finally, she stopped. Mitch was nowhere to be seen. Collapsing onto a bench, she dropped her head into her hands and finally let the pain she'd been fighting sink in.

You must be his new wife.

No. No, she wasn't. She was his old wife. The one he didn't want anymore. The one he tossed away. She was the old wife. The one who was forgotten.

She pulled her phone from her purse and dialed Kara, but it immediately went to voice mail, and Dianna swallowed the sob that welled in her chest. She wanted to go home. She just wanted to go home. She tried another friend, but the phone sang out an old Madonna tune before an automated voice told her to leave a message. The third name she selected from her contact list was one who always took her call.

As soon as Annie answered, Dianna choked out a horrid sound that even she didn't understand.

"Dianna? What's wrong?" Annie asked, sounding panicked.

"Can you," she gasped, "please come get me?" She heaved again. "I was with Mitch, and... They thought... I can't..." She lowered her face when a couple walking by looked at her.

"Where are you?"

"At the park. Near the fountain."

"Don't leave. I'll be there in a few minutes."

Dianna dropped her phone into her purse and slouched back on the bench. She sat staring, ignoring people who walked past her, ignoring her phone when it rang yet again. Ignoring everything as she heard the woman's voice over and over in her mind.

You must be his new wife.

sh

Paul kneeled in front of Dianna. He didn't have to ask if she were okay. She obviously wasn't. She collapsed forward, dropping her head onto his shoulder, and he wrapped his arms around her. He held her in their awkward position for a few moments while she sobbed. Finally, he stood, pulling her with him. He walked her to where Annie's car was pulled up to the curb and opened the back door. Dianna slid in, and he followed her. He put his arm around her, and she leaned into him as Annie drove away.

Paul caught Annie's gaze in the rearview mirror. Her eyes held the same amount of concern he felt. He'd seen Dianna have her fair share of crying fits, but nothing like this. He ran his hand over her hair, soothing her as much as he could.

Her phone rang, but she didn't move. After the second time, she pulled her phone from her purse and answered. "I don't want to talk to you right now." She listened for a second. "No. Don't call me again." She hung up and looked out the window. "Our counselor wanted us to go on a date. It was actually going okay. We'd only had one fight all night."

She sniffed deeply and then exhaled slowly. Paul squeezed her shoulder for reassurance.

"We ran into some of his clients. They thought I was Michelle. They congratulated me on our marriage and told me he was a good man." She laughed softly. "It was like...being punched in the gut and slapped in the face and pushed through a meat grinder all at the same time."

Paul pulled her to him, and she rolled into his chest, burying her face against him. He kissed her head and soothed her until Annie pulled into his driveway and parked next to Matt's car.

Dianna looked up at the house. "You were having game night?"

"Yeah."

"I guess that explains why you're here."

He gave her a weak smile. "I was there when Annie answered the phone. She didn't want me to come, but I'm stubborn sometimes."

"You should take me home."

"Fat chance of that." Annie shut off the car and turned around. "You okay?"

Dianna shook her head. "No, I'm not. I'm really not."

"Come on." Paul helped her out and put his arm around her as they walked to the house.

Donna and Matt met them at the door. Donna's mouth fell open, and Annie shook her head, silencing the questions before they could be asked.

"Fix her a drink," Paul instructed whoever wanted to listen.

"And bring her some aspirin."

He led her into his room and straight to the bed. Sitting her down, he kneeled before her and eased her shoes off. He was piling pillows against the headboard when Donna came in with a glass and a bottle of pills.

"Did you eat?" she asked.

Dianna nodded.

"Do you want us to stay?" she whispered to Paul, as if Dianna wouldn't hear her.

He shook his head and took the drink and pills from her. "I'll call you."

When she was gone, he handed Dianna the glass and opened the bottle. He tapped out two pills and set the bottle aside as she swallowed them.

"Jesus," she hissed. "That's straight whiskey."

He couldn't help but chuckle. "Matt poured that, then."

"I'm sorry. I didn't mean to ruin your night."

"Don't apologize." He took the glass. "I want you here. I want to help you through this. Come on. Lean back and stretch out."

She turned on the bed and sat back on the pillows. He ran his hand over her leg and determined she was cold. Grabbing the comforter, he pulled it from the other side and covered her.

She closed her eyes and sighed when she heard Mitch's ringtone coming from her purse. "He won't stop calling."

"I'm sure he's concerned."

"It wasn't his fault. They were clients. They didn't know. But it was like... 'You must be his new wife.' That's what she said.

'You must be his new wife.' And he just sat there looking as stunned as I felt." She scoffed and rubbed her forehead. "I'm such an idiot."

He ran his hand soothingly over her thigh. "Why were you fighting?"

"Because I insisted on paying half of the cost of Sam's graduation party, which meant not getting the caterer that Mitch wanted."

"You fought about money?"

"He said I never used to mind taking his money before."

"That was out of line, huh?"

"Yeah." Dianna gulped down some of the whiskey in her glass and then closed her eyes when Mitch called again. Paul handed her purse to her, and she pulled out her phone.

"What?" she asked as she put the phone to her ear. She closed her eyes. "I just need some time, okay?"

She drew a shaky breath, and Paul squeezed her thigh.

"But it was you, Mitch. You did this. You did all of this. I can't talk to you right now."

She hung up and carelessly tossed her phone onto the bed. She dropped her face into her hands and took several deep breaths while Paul sat quietly beside her, waiting for her to talk to him.

"Relationships shouldn't be this hurtful. Being with someone shouldn't cut so deep. I shouldn't feel like this all the damn time. But I do. Whenever I'm with him, I feel small and defeated. I don't want to feel like that anymore."

Silence fell between them that wasn't broken until his phone rang.

"Hey, Annie," he said quietly. "No, she's going to stay here. I don't want her to be alone. She's pretty upset." He brushed Dianna's hair from her face. "Yeah, that'd be great. Pancakes would be perfect. See you then." He hung up and smiled. "They're going to be here at nine in true mother hen fashion: with all the fixings for a huge family breakfast. I hope that's okay."

"It'll be nice."

He looked down at his phone nervously. "Um, I need to make up the guest room—"

"No, you don't," she whispered.

His gaze darted to hers, surprised, but then he smiled. He pushed himself up. "I'll get you something to sleep in."

She reached for her phone. "I need to text Sam." She typed out a message while Paul pulled out a T-shirt and a pair of house pants for her.

"There's an extra toothbrush in the drawer."

She disappeared into the bathroom, and Paul ran his hand over his hair as he looked at the bed. It wasn't a good idea to stay here with her. Noble as he was trying to be, having her body against his all night seemed to be mocking fate. She was hurting and upset, and he had nearly lost his mind from missing her. That was a bad combination for a man who was trying to do right by the woman he wanted.

He looked at the bathroom door when the water started.

Changing quickly, he waited for her to emerge and smiled at her body swimming in his clothes. Dianna crawled into what was her side of the bed and fluffed the pillow. She sighed as she put her head down and closed her eyes. He brushed his teeth, readied for bed, and then went to double check the doors.

By the time he returned, she was breathing softly, and he thought she may have been asleep. As soon as he got into the bed beside her, though, her hand found his, and he squeezed her fingers.

"I wanted to call you," she said, "but it didn't seem right to pull you into this. I tried a few other people first, but I couldn't get through. I knew Annie would answer, but I didn't know she was here."

"Are you sorry she was?"

"No. I needed you."

She moved closer, and he lifted his arm so she could rest her cheek to his chest. She lay still for a few moments and then moved her hand down his chest, over his stomach. His heart started pounding as she slipped her fingers under his shirt and her cool palm rested on his hot skin and then inched around his waist, making breathing difficult.

A trembling sigh left her in the dark, and he tightened his hold on her. He tried to fight his body, but he couldn't stop the way he tensed into an erection as her fingers danced lightly over his skin.

He rubbed his palm up her back. "I'm sorry, Dianna."

"For what?"

"When I saw you at the café, I should have told you it was okay to walk away from him instead of pushing you to keep trying. I was just concerned that…"

"What?"

He inhaled the sweet vanilla scent of her hair. "You still love him, don't you?"

Her fingers stilled, but her thumb moved back and forth, sending lightning bolts of desire through him. "Not like before. No. And no matter how I play this out in my mind, it always ends the same. With me telling him that we can't work this out." She sighed. "I'm starting to feel like I'm deceiving him, and I don't want that. I don't want to feel like the betrayer here. I really thought, or at least I *wanted* to think, that we could somehow start over. But it isn't going to happen. I'd like for us to be friends, parents, but I don't see how we're ever going to be a couple again."

His lip curved into a smile as hope lightened his heart. He moved his thumb over her shoulder. "You've had a rough night. It's not a good time to make that decision."

She shifted her body, sliding her leg up his, and tightening her hold on his side. His hand was on her thigh before he realized what he was doing.

"The thing is," she whispered, "I didn't come to that decision tonight. Or lightly. I've been considering it for weeks. Tonight, I just realized…"

"What?"

"I see him differently. He may be sorry, and he may have

realized his mistake, but he can't change the fact that there is a side to him that I never knew. A side I don't want to know. That sounds awful, doesn't it?"

"No, it doesn't."

"I agreed to counseling, I told him I'd try, but I feel like the best I can do is maybe not be so angry at him anymore. I can't forgive him. And I can't be with someone I can't forgive." She moved her hand to his chest as she pushed herself up, just enough that her breath kissed his face "And I don't want to be with someone who only treats me well when he's trying to earn my forgiveness."

"You deserve better."

"I'm glad you think so." She kissed his cheek lightly. "I think I should sleep on the couch."

He rolled her beneath him. As he looked down at her face in the darkness, temptation nearly won out. She wouldn't stop him if he kissed her, of that he was certain, but he could wait. If she ended things with Mitch, as she said she intended, she would be his in time. He would wait.

"You stay." He pressed his lips to her forehead. "Get some sleep."

He pulled away before she could protest. In the living room, he grabbed the blanket off the back of his couch and stretched out. He stared at the ceiling, thinking of how perfectly her body fit to his as he drifted to sleep.

CHAPTER TWENTY-ONE

*P*aul ignored how his siblings smirked as he ran his hand over Dianna's hair and kissed her forehead. "Call me later."

"I will."

He opened the door, and she walked out with Annie and Donna—both grinning like know-it-alls—trailing behind her. She didn't think it was a good idea for Sam to know she'd stayed with Paul, and he had to agree. The kid was getting enough mixed signals from his parents already.

Paul turned and found Matt grinning.

"Shut up," he told his younger brother.

"What?" Matt asked.

"Whatever you're going to say. Don't."

"I wasn't going to say anything."

"Right." Paul moved past him toward the kitchen. The women had cleaned up from their big family breakfast, but he needed something to do to avoid looking at Matt. He wiped the counter and poured another cup of coffee.

"She looked a lot better this morning."

"Getting a good night's sleep will do that."

"Did you tell her?"

"Tell her what?"

Matt sat at the bar. "That you love her."

Paul stopped stirring his drink and looked at his brother. "No. And I'm not going to until the time is right. If it's ever right."

"What do you mean, if? She stood right here and told Annie and Donna that she's done with him."

"That doesn't mean she's ready for me to pile more bullshit on top of her."

"Being in love with her is bullshit?"

"It is if she isn't ready for it. She's still got a lot to work through, Matty. She's going to have to sell her house. That's going to be hard for her."

"So be there for her. Help her."

"I'm going to. But I don't want..."

"What?"

"You know how I am. You told me a hundred times when I was with Michelle. I jump in and rescue these women, and things get complicated. I don't want to be that guy anymore. And I don't think Dianna wants to be the damsel in distress."

"There's a world of difference between Michelle and Dianna. You know that, right?"

"I know."

"Helping Dianna is a far cry from letting Michelle bend you to her will. Dianna wouldn't do that. She respects you."

"I know." He smiled again. "Do you see how this conversation has turned? A few months ago, you were warning me to be careful about getting involved with Dianna. Now you're telling me I should just suck it up and jump in. You, little brother, are just as screwed up as your big sister."

"*Our* big sister. And Dianna's good for you, Paul. She genuinely cares about you."

He nodded. "I think so, too."

"So don't let her slip away."

Paul pushed himself up. "I won't. Not this time."

8h

Dianna was glad she had asked Annie and Donna to take her home. Mitch's truck was in the driveway, and Dianna suspected he had been there all morning, waiting for her to get home.

"You okay?" Donna asked.

"Yeah. Thanks, girls. I appreciate the lovely breakfast and knowing glances every time Paul spoke to me."

Donna giggled, but Annie opened her mouth as if offended. After a moment, she clamped her lips shut and grinned.

"Call me later," Annie instructed as Dianna climbed out of the back seat.

Dianna was on the porch when the front door opened, and

Mitch looked at her with sorrowful eyes. She lifted her hand to stop him. She wasn't ready for his barrage of explanations and apologies. "I'd like to change."

"Can I make coffee or anything?"

She shook her head and walked upstairs, leaving him looking helpless in the entryway. She plugged in her phone, which had died sometime during the night, and slipped out of her dress. She pulled on a pair of yoga pants and a T-shirt and then pulled her hair back in a ponytail and took a few breaths before going downstairs.

Mitch was standing where she'd left him, and she almost laughed. He looked like a lost but devoted puppy standing there. She walked by him and into the living room, where she dropped onto the couch and pulled her legs beneath her. He sat, much more tentatively, on the other end of the sofa, and she realized he was still in the same slacks and dress shirt as the night before. The blanket that was usually neatly folded on the back of the couch was in disarray.

"You slept here?"

"I didn't think Sam should be here alone."

"I let him know I wouldn't be home. He's seventeen, Mitch. He's perfectly capable of being home alone."

"I know. He told me." He lowered his face. "He asked me what happened. He was pissed at me, too. He's gotten to be pretty protective of you, hasn't he?"

She smiled. "Yeah, I guess."

"I'm so sorry, Dianna. As soon as I saw them, I knew what

was going to happen. I just didn't know how to stop it. They're newer clients. They didn't know about...us."

She shook her head as she lowered her gaze. "Even if they had, why would they think you'd be out to dinner with your ex-wife?"

He lowered his face.

"I don't mean it to sound like I'm mad," she said. "That's just the truth. Why wouldn't they have thought I was her?"

He ran his hand over his hair. "I really blew it, huh?"

"I shouldn't have left like that."

"I don't blame you. I probably would have run out of there, too."

"It was humiliating."

"I know."

She bit her lip. "It was also a really strong reminder that no matter what we do, we can't pretend she didn't happen to us. She's part of us now, and we can't ignore that."

Mitch closed his eyes and nodded.

"I don't know if I can live with that. I don't know if I *want* to."

"Don't give up on me, Di. Please. Not because of this. This wasn't something I could control."

"No, you couldn't control it, but you certainly set the ball in motion. These are the consequences of your actions, and I'm so tired of being the one who pays the price. You had the affair, but I'm the one who is constantly being trampled on because of it. I can't take any more."

"No, please." He slid to her and grasped her hands. "Please, don't say that. We just need more time."

"More time for what? To fight? To push each other's buttons? To feel used and disgraced? This can't be any easier on you than it is on me. Aren't you tired of begging for my forgiveness?"

He kneeled in front of her. "I will beg for your forgiveness every single day for the rest of my life if I have to."

"Come on. At some point we have to accept this isn't working and move on."

"Maybe, but this isn't the time. Not because of this, Dianna."

"I called Annie last night. I didn't know she was with Paul, but he came with her when she came to pick me up."

Mitch's face sagged.

"I was with him last night. Not like that," she said when anger lit in his eyes. "He stayed in another room, but we talked quite a bit. I just wanted you to know because I didn't want to feel like I'd lied to you."

"Does he want you to leave me?"

His eyes were hard, angry, untrusting, and she almost laughed. He was jealous? Really? That was rich.

"He's the reason I gave you a second chance, Mitch. I didn't want to, but he knew if I didn't, I'd always wonder if I'd done the right thing. He's done nothing but take care of me."

He pushed himself up. "Yeah, he's some kind of hero, huh?"

She shook her head. "I'm not going to fight with you about

Paul. And if you're smart, you won't start a fight about Paul. You won't like how it ends."

He looked down at her but didn't say another word. Instead he paced for a moment and then sat beside her again. "Will you come to counseling Monday so we can talk about this more?"

"No. I'm not doing this anymore."

"Because of Paul?"

"Because of how being with you makes me feel."

"Angry," he said, repeating the word she'd said the night before.

"I'm sorry, but this isn't going to work."

"You can't say that yet. We've barely gotten started on fixing things."

She bit her lip. "After you left me," she said quietly, "I kind of went into survival mode. Everything I did was just to get by financially. I ignored everything else. I buried my hurt and focused on that one thing so I didn't fall apart. And then one day Paul showed up at the door, asking me to testify—"

"If you tell me that you are in love with that prick—"

Dianna lifted a brow at him. "*You* walked away with *his* wife. How does that make him the prick? If you care at all about me and your children, you should be thanking Paul. He bent over backward to help us out while you were off living your midlife crisis. I'm not saying I'm in love with him. I don't know what I feel for him because I've been so busy trying to figure out how to get by. I'm trying to explain to you how I got to where I am right now, and I can't do that without talking about Paul because, like it or not, he is a huge part of my life now."

"Okay," he said, still sounding irritated. "Paul showed up. Then what?"

"I called him when I found out you were getting married. I was inconsolable. I completely fell apart, and he was so kind and patient, even though he was hurting as well. He took care of me that night, and then he helped me pawn my wedding rings—"

He creased his brow. "You sold your rings?"

"So I could buy the boys Christmas presents, Mitch. I didn't have money to buy them presents. And then when our divorce was final I was so broken, and Paul once again put me back together. We didn't even realize it, but we were in this cycle of picking each other up and dusting each other off. We became dependent on each other. Everyone kept saying we needed to stop, to step back, but it wasn't until you asked to come home that we realized just how deep we'd gotten."

"So you do love him?"

Dianna sighed. "I used him so that I didn't have to figure this out on my own. Every time I fell, he was there. He became the safety net that I lost when you left. I knew, no matter what happened, Paul would be there. But then you showed up, asking to come home, and he ran as fast as he could. And I don't blame him. Everything we were to each other, we were because I loved you and missed *you*."

Mitch ran his hand over his face. "I don't get what you're saying, Dianna."

"He left, and I lost my safety net again. I was alone and scared and selling my home, and I grabbed whatever I could to survive." She bit her lips. "I didn't give you a second chance for the right reasons, Mitch, and no matter how many times you say that is okay, it isn't."

He sighed. "It is because whatever the reason, we're here. We're trying to make things better."

She frowned. "You're trying to make things better. I'm just trying to make sense of my life. And when I stand back and look at everything that has happened, being with you doesn't make sense anymore."

He looked at her like she'd slapped him. "You haven't given it enough time."

"When you asked me to let you help me with the mortgage, you said once I didn't have to worry about the money, I could focus on fixing other things. You were right. Without the stress of keeping a roof over Sam's head, I was able to see things more clearly. I may have been a mess all these months, Mitch, but even so, I've found new friends and a new life. It's been confusing and frustrating, but I like it. I love my job and my co-workers. I love my friends and going to yoga every Saturday. It's not what I expected, not what I would have chosen, but it's what I have, and I want it."

"So you're picking yoga class over our marriage?"

She shrugged. "I guess so."

He scoffed and shook his head. "That's nice, Di. That's real *fucking* nice."

"Hey," she said, harshly enough for him to look at her. "You chose perky tits and bleached hair over me, so don't act like I owe you anything more than what I've given you."

He clenched his jaw, and she rubbed her hand over her forehead as she took a few cleansing breaths.

"I don't want us to hate each other," she said. "You mean too much to me for that. We have two great kids. We need to get along for them. We're family, Mitch, no matter what, and we need to be able to act like it. Be angry if you want, but please don't hate me."

"I don't hate you, Di. I just..." He lowered his face and shrugged. "I somehow thought that you'd be here waiting for me to come back to you. I thought you'd be so happy to have me come back that you'd just open your arms and we'd go on like I'd never been gone."

"I know you did. And I probably would have if Paul hadn't helped me. I probably would have been angry, and I probably would have screamed and yelled, and then I would have forgiven you because I wouldn't have thought that I had any other choice."

A hint of a smile touched his lips. "I don't know if I should thank him or punch him in the face."

"You should thank him. You said yourself seeing him made you realize what you'd lost. And I don't mean me. I mean Sam and Jason. Seeing Sam turn to Paul when he needed a father cut you. I saw it. You turned it around, and you never would have done that without Paul."

Mitch nodded. "I wish I'd turned it around sooner. I wish I'd walked away from Michelle the day I met her."

"But you didn't."

"So what are you going to do?"

She drew a breath before looking at him with a conviction she didn't quite feel. "I'm going to sell the house. I'm going to get something smaller so I don't have to worry about the payments. I'd like to repay you the money you gave me."

He was shaking his head before she finished.

"I can't do it now," she continued, "but with the money from the sale—"

"No. I gave you that money to help you out because I hadn't done right by you, and I know that. I shouldn't have fought child support and alimony. I was the one who left. I should have made sure you were taken care of, and I didn't do that. You don't owe me anything."

She nodded. "Thank you."

They were silent for what seemed an eternity before he finally said, "I don't want to lose you."

"I'm sorry, Mitch," she whispered, "but you already have."

He stared at his hands for a long time. "If you need anything, call me. I'll be here."

"Thanks."

"I love you. I really do."

She offered him a soft smile. "I love you, too. Just not like before."

He hesitated before standing. When he was gone, she drew a

deep breath. Even though it was what she wanted and she didn't regret it for a moment, she had to swallow hard to fight her tears. She closed her eyes and rubbed her temples as a new problem presented itself.

She'd settled her feelings for Mitch. Now she had to figure out how the hell she felt about Paul.

CHAPTER TWENTY-TWO

*A*nnie leaned on the desk in front of Dianna. "Come see me for a minute."

Dianna followed her and dropped into a chair across from Annie. She had been expecting an in-depth Q&A session since arriving that morning. She wasn't sure how much she wanted to divulge. Annie and Donna had subtly been dancing around what they both clearly wanted to know. Where did Paul and Dianna stand with each other? Dianna had avoided discussing that issue because she honestly didn't know the answer.

Before Dianna had met Annie, Paul had complained about her constantly sticking her nose in his relationships. Dianna finally understood exactly where he was coming from. Annie, though much more subtly where Dianna was concerned, seemed determined to know exactly how Dianna was feeling. All Dianna had said when she'd called Annie to let her know she was okay was that she'd broken things off with Mitch and it had gone as well as could be expected. She'd left the questions about Paul unanswered. And she knew that was eating away at Annie.

"How are things going?" Annie asked.

"Hmm?"

"Don't act innocent with me."

Dianna grinned. "I told you. Mitch was disappointed, but we left things amicably."

"How are you feeling? Do you feel like things are getting better? Are you feeling stronger?"

Dianna wasn't sure how to answer that. "Um, I guess."

"I'm not trying to pry—"

Dianna snickered, and Annie narrowed her eyes a bit.

"I'm just trying to get a feel for whether or not you are interested in taking on a bigger role."

"Such as?"

"The market is picking up. I need a new agent."

Dianna stared at her blankly. "I'm not an agent."

"No, but you could be. And a good one. You're smart, people like you, they trust you. You'd make a hell of a lot more money selling houses than managing the office."

"But...don't I have to go to school for that?"

"There are some classes available on the weekends. It only takes a few weeks. You have to take a licensing exam, but it's nothing you can't handle."

She laughed softly. "Um, this is kind of a surprise. I'm not sure."

Annie reached into her desk and pulled out a stack of papers.

"Read this. Let me know what you think. You're an employee here already, so I'll split the cost with you. I can help you study. You've been around here enough to know the basics. All you have to do now is get the finer legal points of closing the deal and the license to back it up."

Dianna took the papers and looked at them for a moment before meeting Annie's gaze again. "You really think I could do this?"

"I wouldn't waste my time asking if I didn't. Think about it and let me know. And do it quick. If you aren't interested, I need to find some other sucker to work here."

Dianna took the papers with her and sank back behind her desk. She spent a good part of the morning looking them over, reading them, and researching classes online. She found a class that was available for the next three weekends that still had openings. If she enrolled and passed the exam, she could be an agent in a month.

She gnawed at her lip. She wasn't certain she wanted to make another change in her life. Then again, this was a change for the positive, a move in the right direction, and it was something she thought she'd enjoy. She glanced at the time on her computer. It was nearly noon. She pulled her phone from her purse and considered for only a moment before dialing.

"Hey, you," Paul answered. "What's up?"

"Do you have lunch plans?"

"No."

"Do you want some?"

8h

Paul had tossed the food he had been eating into the trash as soon as Dianna had suggested they meet. He'd only taken three bites from the sandwich, but that didn't matter. When he got to the café, she was sitting at their table looking at a menu. His heart lifted. He hadn't stopped thinking of her since he'd seen her a few days before. No... He hadn't stopped thinking of her since he'd met her. "Hey."

She turned and smiled brightly. "Hey. They have a turkey and feta panini that sounds great."

He looked over the menu for a moment before deciding she was right, the sandwich sounded delicious. They both ordered the turkey, glasses of water, and coffee.

"How are you?" he asked.

"I'm okay."

"Has, um…" He shifted. "Have you heard from Mitch?"

She shook her head. "No. I don't expect to, either. I think he finally heard me."

"Good."

"It is good. The rest of my weekend was amazingly quiet. It was just what I needed." She took a breath, but the waitress appeared with their drinks. She smiled and waited for the girl to disappear before saying, "Annie asked me to become an agent."

He leaned back, surprised. In all the years that Annie had been operating her business, she'd never asked anyone to become licensed. She wanted experienced salespeople, and that's who she hired. "Really?"

"I'm thinking about it." She bit her lip and took a breath. "I'm a little nervous about the living-on-commission thing. It seems so risky. What do you think?"

He smiled. "What do mean? It's great. Annie has had a few bad stretches now and then, but she's always managed to get by. You just have to remember to budget and keep track of what you're spending. You've already been doing that, so you're ahead of the game."

She pulled out the papers and handed them to him. "There's a class that starts this weekend. They still have openings. I could finish the requirements in three weekends. I could be done in a month or so. Annie said she'd help with the cost. I think I could actually do it."

He took her hands in his. "You have to. You have to try it. If you don't like it, then you do something else. Simple as that."

"That's the thing." Her smile fell a bit. "I like the job I have."

"Honey, you have Annie wrapped around your finger. If you wanted your job back, she'd give you your job back."

She laughed. "Annie is *not* wrapped around my finger, and I couldn't just take my job back if she's already given it to someone new."

"She's never done this for anyone else, Di. *Ever*. She doesn't invest in people unless she really believes in them. If she thinks you have what it takes to be a good agent, then you do. You have to do this. You *have* to. This is a great opportunity. And like I said, if you don't like the job, walk away. Do something else."

The smile that spread across her lips was slow, but it was wide. "I think...I think I want this."

"Then do it."

"Yeah?"

"Yeah."

She squeezed his hands tightly. "Okay. I'm going to do it."

"Call her."

"What?"

"Call Annie right now. Tell her you're going to sign up for classes starting this weekend." When she simply stared at him, her eyes wide and mouth open, he tugged at her hands. "Come on. Call her before you get scared and back out."

She glared at him playfully. "I'm not going to get scared."

"Then call her."

She looked at him with defiance as she reached into her purse and pulled out her phone. "Annie," she said after dialing. "I found some classes that start this weekend. If all goes well, you'll have a new agent this time next month."

She nodded and said goodbye and then dropped her phone back into her purse.

"What'd she say?"

"She said she knew I'd do it."

"Well, she does know everything."

"Kind of like her brother?" Dianna asked softly.

"Just like her brother."

Her smile softened, and she held his gaze for a long moment. His heart started thumping at the look on her face. He wasn't sure what she was thinking, but the affection in her eyes went straight to his heart.

"I wouldn't be here if it weren't for you," she finally said.

"In a rundown café getting ready to make another life-altering change?"

She creased her brow for a moment. "Exactly."

"This will be good for you. I think it will help you stop feeling like things are spiraling out of control."

She rested her chin in her palm as she planted her elbow on the table. "What about you? Have things settled for you?

"I took your advice and reached out to my boys."

"How did it go?"

"They asked about you, about why all of a sudden they weren't seeing pictures and updates about you."

"What'd you tell them?"

His smile faltered. "That I blew it."

Dianna's lips fell as well. "No, you didn't," she said quietly. "You were right. We were in over our heads. I just chose to ignore that because it didn't hurt when I was with you, and that's all I cared about. We went from being emotionally dependent on them to being emotionally dependent on each other. We never resolved anything. I know that now."

"Do you regret us?"

She shook her head. "Not at all. Like you said, it was just the wrong time."

"Maybe the right time will come along."

"I hope so," she whispered. "I think it says a lot about where we are when the first person I want to talk to about a life-altering decision is you. You're the first person I want to run to. It wouldn't be that way if any part of me felt like Mitch and I could work this out."

Paul let out the breath he hadn't even realized he'd been holding. "I'm glad. That you want to call me first." He gave her a slight smile.

She smiled, too, but it didn't last. "Thank you."

"For what?"

"For being so patient."

He didn't look away until the waitress returned to dole out their sandwiches.

Dianna accepted the plate and sat quietly while Paul assured their server they didn't need anything else.

"I hope I've helped you half as much as you've helped me," she said when they were alone.

"You have. You really have."

"Good."

"So, we've covered all the really heavy topics, but there's one more thing I need to ask you."

Dianna stopped lifting her sandwich halfway to her mouth. "What?"

"Exactly what do I have to do to get you to play that piano for me?"

CHAPTER TWENTY-THREE

*B*y the end of the following month, there was a *Sold* notice adorning the *For Sale* sign in Dianna's yard, and she'd contracted the one-and-a-half story that she'd fallen in love with when she first started looking for a new home.

The past weeks had been a whirlwind. She'd barely had time to breathe with her class and work schedules. It had been good, though. It made it impossible for her and Paul to jump back into that co-dependent cycle they tended to get into. While she was busy selling her house, getting her real estate license, and getting her life back on track, Paul had been focusing on rebuilding his relationships with his kids. She and Paul had seen each other for an occasional lunch, but for the most part, they'd been too busy to spend much time together.

That was changing tonight. She'd finished her classes, and Paul wanted to take her out to celebrate. Not just dinner, but they were finally going to use the season passes to the theater he'd bought them for Christmas to attend the opening night of *The Odd Couple*. Dianna had barely made it through the last class, her excitement was so overwhelming.

After rushing through the shower, she rubbed herself down with her favorite scented lotion and slipped into a new black lace bra and panty set. She wasn't exactly planning to seduce Paul, but she wasn't opposed to seeing where the night led them either. She added nude thigh highs and a light application of makeup before she slipped on the red dress she'd bought for Valentine's Day and added a pair of black high heels. She'd just pulled her hair back in a loose bun when the doorbell rang.

"Wow," Paul said when she opened the door. "You look amazing."

She could have said the same about him. She loved seeing him in a suit. His hair was brushed to the side, begging her to run her fingers through it, and he had a slight blush on his cheeks that made him look a bit shy as he held a bouquet of flowers out to her. Her heart sped up as she prepared to go out on her first "official" first date in over twenty-four years.

Exhaling slowly, she took his hand when he held it out to her. He pulled her to him and kissed the corner of her mouth. She slid her arm around him and hugged him closer to her as his breath whispered over her cheek.

"Ready?" he asked.

She sighed. Yes. She was most definitely ready. They talked about their week—her classes, and he skimmed over a case he'd just settled—as they drove to the restaurant. Over dinner, conversation turned to his kids and the sale of her house. Their chatter didn't end until they were sitting in the dark theater. She desperately tried to focus on the play, but Paul rested his hand on her knee, touching just below the hem of her skirt, and the heat from his palm consumed her. Soon after, her hand was on his thigh. Not just resting but gently massaging. She'd never been so bold, but she couldn't seem to stop herself.

Within moments, his hand moved a bit higher, and she was finding it hard to breathe. His touch was far from inappropriate, but he was stirring something inside her that made her heart race with a strange mixture of fear and excitement. Everything in her life was so new right now, everything was so different, and what she was feeling for Paul was no exception.

As she looked at the man next to her, a sense of belonging washed through her. She was supposed to be here, with him. She didn't want to be anywhere else, and for the first time, she realized that she no longer regretted the end of her marriage. She had loved Mitch, and in their time they had been in love, but that had faded long ago. She would always love him, but it wasn't the kind of love she wanted. It was friendly and kind, but it was miles from what she was feeling for Paul. And she *wanted* what she felt for Paul.

The lights rose as the play ended, and then Dianna and Paul shuffled out with the crowd.

"Are you okay?" he asked as they climbed into his car.

"I was just thinking."

"About us?"

"Mm-hmm."

"I know you have a lot going on, Di. I'm not going to push you for something you aren't ready for."

She grinned. "Like what?"

He laughed quietly as he shook his head. She suspected that if the car had been better lit, she would have seen his cheeks blushing. She put her hand back to his thigh, and he put his to hers. He drove the rest of the way to her house in silence, his thumb brushing over her leg. After parking in her driveway, he held her hand as they walked to the door, but as she stepped in, he pulled her to a stop. She looked at him curiously.

He hesitated before looking at her. "It's getting late. Maybe I should go."

"Do you want to go?"

"I want to do this right."

She considered his words for a moment before pulling him with her as she walked inside. She set her purse on the table by the door and led him into the living room. She sat on the edge of the sofa. He sat half a cushion length away. She turned so she could face him, her legs crossed and her elbow resting on the back of the couch as she propped her head up and stared at him. She'd never, not once in her life, felt like any kind of seductress, but as they stared at each other, her insides started to twist and she felt sexier than she ever had.

The intense staring dragged on, not for seconds but for minutes—a long stretch of silence that said so much more than any words they could have whispered. Finally, he lightly cupped her face. His touch, as soft as it was, sent a shockwave through her that took her breath way. She gasped, causing her lips to part, and his attention instantly dropped to them. He was going to kiss her. And it was going to lead to other things. And, more than anything else at the moment, she *wanted* it to lead to other things.

"Are you sure?" he whispered.

She couldn't remember the word she was supposed to say. Couldn't think of how to answer his question. She parted her lips, knowing she should say something, but her phone dinged from the other room, announcing that she had a text message. The tone also let her know who it was from.

"That's Sam." She hesitated before standing and stepping around Paul. She laughed quietly as she read his text. It was like the fates were telling her something. She walked back into the living room. "He's spending the night with a friend."

"Didn't you say he was out with his girlfriend?"

Dianna nodded. "God help me if he gets that girl pregnant."

The intensity of the moment was broken, but her desire was still there. So was his. She could see it as she looked into his eyes. Instead of resuming her seat beside him, she eased down into his lap. His hands were instantly on her, one around her waist, the other on her thigh. She put her arm around his neck and trailed the fingertips of her other hand along his jaw before resting her palm on his chest.

"Do you want to leave?" she whispered.

"No. Do you want me to leave?"

"No."

He captured her mouth with his. They hadn't kissed, not like that, since the night of Sam's accident, and it had been building within her. She clutched his hair in her fist and pushed her mouth to his. He kissed her hard and deep, and she was breathless when she finally pulled back and put her forehead to his.

"I have to tell you something," she whispered.

"What?"

"I...I was nineteen when Mitch and I started dating, and... We were together all that time, and I..." Embarrassment choked her words. She gave up trying to sound dignified and shook her head. She started to climb off his lap, but he pulled her back to him.

"And you never cheated on him."

"No. I've never been with anyone else, and quite frankly, I'm terrified that I've been doing it wrong all these years."

"Well, you couldn't have been doing it *all* wrong. You have two children."

She quietly laughed at his lame joke. "You know what I mean. I want you so much, but I don't want to disappoint you."

He gently touched her chin and lifted her face. He didn't speak until she looked into his eyes. "That could never happen. Ever." He put a soft kiss on the corner of her mouth and brushed a strand of hair behind her ear. "If you aren't ready to take this step, I'm okay with that."

"I know. I'm just nervous. That's all."

"Well, I'm nervous, too. What if *I* disappoint you? Hmm? What if *I've* been doing it wrong all this time?" He laughed and then brushed her chin gently with his finger. "The only person you've been with is the man you committed to be with your entire life. That's nothing to be ashamed of, Dianna. You should be proud of that."

"That I'm in my forties and have less bedroom experience than most twenty-year-olds?"

"Not less experience. Fewer partners. There is a *huge* difference. Women like that may know how to get a man into their beds, but they don't know a damn thing about commitment. That's what matters. That's what's beautiful. You thought you would spend your life with him, and you stood by the promises you made. You should be proud of that."

"I am."

"I'm not asking for, nor expecting, you to do something you aren't ready for."

She traced her fingertips along his jawline. "You wouldn't be here if I thought you were."

"I've been wanting to tell you something for a while now, but I was afraid you weren't ready to hear it."

Her heart dropped at the sudden intensity on his face. She forced a grin to lighten the blow of whatever he was about to say. "Are you about to outdo my confession by telling me you're a virgin?"

He laughed as he slid the tips of his fingers under her hemline and caressed her thigh. "I considered it momentarily, but no. I was going to tell you that I've fallen deeply, madly, insanely in love with you."

Her breath rushed from her, and she stared into his eyes, trying to gauge the truth there. "You don't have to say that just because—"

He tightened his grip on her thigh. "If you discount my profession of love because you think I'm trying to get you into bed, I'm going to be highly offended."

She bit her lip before she could finish that very statement.

"I hated every moment that you spent trying to make things right with Mitch. I hated the thought that you actually *might* make things right. But I couldn't tell you how I felt until I knew you weren't in love with him. And I didn't know that until you decided—on your *own*—you were ready to leave him."

She ran her fingers through his hair. "I'm so sorry if I hurt you."

"No. Don't apologize. We both needed you to be sure, and you couldn't be sure unless you tried to forgive him."

She touched his cheek, caressing the smoothness of his shaved skin and absorbing the heat that she had missed so much. She looked into his eyes and held his gaze as she whispered, "I never could have gone back to him, Paul, because he wasn't you. I don't know the exact moment I fell in love with you, but I know it was long before I should have. I'm sorry we had to go through so much before I could see it."

He opened his mouth, and she put her finger to his lips.

"You don't get to discount my profession, either. I love you. I do. And I've been waiting for us to get to this place for so long. I don't want to wait anymore, Paul." She kissed the corner of his mouth as she held his face. "Would you like to go upstairs with me?"

He gave her that sexy grin that had a way of melting her. "I would like that very much."

sh

The sound of Dianna closing the bedroom door behind them seemed to confirm what Paul already knew, that they were there for more than mere comfort this time. The light streaming in through her window was enough to make out her silhouette as she led him to her bed. A storm of emotions brewed inside him —excitement and nervousness mixed with peace and a warmth that was on the verge of consuming him.

Paul slowly wrapped his arms around her waist and pulled her against him. With her back pressed into his chest, she let her head drop back on this shoulder. He lifted his left hand to her face and lightly trailed his fingers from her cheek, down her neck, and along the low neckline of her dress as he put his lips to her ear.

He slid the tips of his fingers into her neckline but didn't touch any of her intimate parts—he simply traced the border of her dress. She sighed and melted against him. He brushed his other hand over the material of her dress. She gasped and pressed her chest out as he gently moved his hand over her breast. He was moving slowly—so slowly it was torturous—and he wondered if the anticipation was killing her as much as it was killing him. He suspected it was when she sighed again.

"This dress is so sexy," he breathed in her ear, "but it needs to go."

She lifted her head and stood upright so he could reach for the zipper that ran along her spine. He found the metal clasp and eased it down. When it was free, he put a kiss to the back of her neck and then one on each shoulder as he exposed her. He pushed the material slowly away from her skin, and it fell to the floor around her feet.

He slid his palms over her stomach and then, as he had when she was dressed, pulled her back against him. This time when he brushed his hand over her breast, all that stood between him and her flesh was a thin layer of satin. She pushed her breast into his palm as he teased her, squeezing and rubbing over her taut nipple. He continued with the soft touch until she put her hand over his and encouraged him to grip harder. He tightened his hold, eliciting a mewed sound from her.

She turned and faced him, and he lowered his gaze over her.

"You're beautiful." He lightly swept his knuckles over her black bra. "Perfect."

He put a soft kiss on her lips, gently pushed her to sit on the bed, and then kneeled before her. He pushed her legs apart and moved between them. On his knees in front of her, he was eye-to-eye with her as he lifted her hand and kissed the inside of her palm.

She stroked her other hand over his hair until she was holding his face in both her hands. She kissed him, sweetly at first, but then her tongue caressed his lips and his passion exploded. He was determined to be gentle and slow, to show her how much she meant to him, but damned if his body wasn't demanding to have what he'd been fantasizing about for months.

He didn't break the kiss until he was breathless, and then he stood and removed his suit coat, tossing it carelessly to the floor. He tugged the knot in his tie loose, undid the buttons at his cuffs, and started on the buttons along the front of his shirt. Dianna watched him release his belt, button, and zipper. He pushed his shoes off and then dropped his pants. He tossed his socks aside and moved back to her. She rolled her head back to look up at him and slid her hands up the outsides of his legs until her palms were on his hips as he brushed his fingers through her hair.

"Lie down," he instructed.

She held his gaze as she slowly scooted farther onto the bed and leaned back. He pushed her legs apart as he crawled up the bed, tracing his fingertips along her thighs as he went. She gasped when he was practically lying on top of her, enough so that he could press his erection against her. He covered the cup of her lacy bra with his mouth, and she fisted his hair. He teased, taunting her nipple as he deftly unhooked her bra.

Dianna laughed softly. "You're very good at that."

"I'm quite motivated at the moment."

He pushed the material aside and suckled her unhindered nipple. She breathed his name as she lifted her hips up to meet him as he gyrated again. She fisted his hair as he pressed into her again. With his weight on his elbows, he started pressing lingering kisses, which he occasionally traded for a gentle bite, to her neck and shoulders.

"I want to kiss every inch of you. I want to savor you." He licked her nipple and then softly tugged it with his teeth. "Devour you."

"Jesus, Paul, I'm going to scream if you don't stop."

"I'm not opposed to screaming." He licked her other breast. "Or moaning." His fingers grazed over her stomach. "Or sighing. You've been doing a lot of that."

"Please."

"Please what?"

A sound, a mixture of pleasure and frustration, left her. "I want you."

"I want you, too."

She tried to pull him over her. "Then take me."

"I will. When I'm ready."

Despite her protest, the moment his mouth moved to her navel, she cried out softly. She tangled her hands in his hair and writhed beneath him. She tugged at his hair even as she pushed his head closer to her, gasping and jerking when he exhaled a heated breath against the front of her panties.

"Paul...please..."

He brushed his nose along her waistband. "I love hearing you say my name like that."

She gasped as he pressed his mouth to her center through

her underwear. He moved his hand to her thigh, over the lace top of her thigh-high. "Do you always wear these, or was this for me?"

"For you."

"I like them." He slid his finger between the lace and her skin. "Remind me to buy you more of these. I want to come home to you, slip my hand under the hem, and feel your skin." He pushed one down as he spoke, dragging it all the way down her leg and over her toes, and then did the same with the other. He returned his attention to the last bit of clothing she was wearing, the black satin panties. "I like these, too. These are lovely." He ran his hand over the front and then between her legs, making her groan. "These are *very* lovely." But that didn't stop him from tugging them free, as he had the rest of her clothing.

He took his time removing them, running his hands over her calves. "You have the sexiest legs I've ever seen. I've dreamed of having these legs around me for so long."

He got to his knees between hers and pushed his boxer shorts over his erection and down his thighs. He kicked his underwear off and then nestled between her thighs, hovering over her. He brushed her hair back and smiled. She smiled back and lifted her head to catch his mouth. The kiss was gentle, loving rather than teasing. He pressed himself against her, and her body opened to him. He broke the kiss and leaned back.

"Look at me," he whispered when she closed her eyes. "Dianna. Look at me."

She stared into his eyes as he moved his hips forward. He

filled her, and her muscles tightened around him, making him moan. The movement between their bodies was perfect, and as he slid deep, her body stretched to accept him but then clenched around him, making the fit tight. He stroked her face, silently demanding her attention as he pumped slowly in and out. She felt better than he'd ever imagined, and as she moved her hips in time with his, he kissed her softly.

She arched up and moaned his name. She started to quiver around him, crying out, as he thrust faster and harder. She wrapped herself around him, squeezing him tightly with her arms and legs as her body spasmed over and over, milking his erection as he released deep inside her.

As soon as the tension that was rolling through him started to ease and he could finally breathe, he kissed her lazily. He leaned back and stroked her hair, smiling as she looked up at him. He rotated his hips slowly, and she moaned as they both came down from their climaxes. He kissed her one more time before he eased back and rolled over. She turned onto her side and curled against him, wrapping her arm around him and putting her head on his chest.

He stroked his fingers along her back. "This is all I've wanted for so long."

"Sex with me?" she teased.

He chuckled. "Yes. And this contentment I'm feeling right now. Like everything is how it should be."

"I feel that way, too. Things are finally going right."

"Yes," he whispered. "Yes, they are."

CHAPTER TWENTY-FOUR

*E*verything was set. The yard was filled with balloons and tables for Sam's graduation party. Dianna sighed as she looked around. So many memories had been made in her backyard, and in just a week's time, she'd no longer be able to stand there and recall them. Someone else would be there, making new memories.

She swallowed hard as the weight in her chest started to form a knot.

Paul walked up behind her. "Di?"

She blinked rapidly, hoping to mask her tears, but he sighed and wrapped his arm around her shoulders as he kissed her head. She'd been an emotional roller coaster all day. Of all the proud parents at the ceremony, she had no doubt cried the hardest. It wasn't just Sam growing up and moving on. It was everything that had transpired over the last year. All the changes, good and bad, had bubbled up as she sat looking out over the sea of black caps and gowns.

Paul had held her hand and passed her tissues while Kara sat on her other side, patting her knee. She'd been embarrassed, but she hadn't been able to stop her tears. She was just glad that they'd taken all their family photos before they left for the ceremony.

"Okay?" he asked.

She exhaled loudly. "Yeah."

"Really?"

"Mm-hmm." She leaned back into him, smiling as he slid his arms around her and pulled her back to his chest. "It was nice of Annie and Donna to come over and decorate."

"They were happy to do it. They know you've been busy packing and getting ready to move."

She rolled her head back onto his shoulder. "Remind me again."

He hugged her closer. "You're doing the right thing. The new house is going to be much better for your budget. Life is going to be much simpler once you get moved." He pressed his lips to her ear. "And you will have so much less stress that, when I rub your back, it won't be to release the tension."

She grinned. "As if it isn't already."

His quiet laugh sent a thrill through her. Turning, she wrapped her arms around his neck and pressed her lips to his. Their kisses had a way of deepening, and this one was no different. She couldn't help the way she got lost in him. His arms never failed to offer her an escape from whatever was happening around her. Today, that just so happened to be the misery of knowing she would be leaving her home in exactly one week, mixed with the joy of Sam successfully graduating high school without getting suspended or becoming a father. But all that faded as Paul's lips worked over hers. She moaned quietly, content to let him kiss her as she dug her fingers into his hair.

"Hey, Di," Mitch said, "do you want me to…"

Dianna pulled from Paul as if caught doing something wrong. Guilt hit her like a sledgehammer to her gut, but she wasn't sure if it was the frustration on Paul's face or the hurt in Mitch's eyes that caused it. She held her breath as she licked her lips, removing Paul's kiss as Mitch looked away.

"Sorry," Mitch said after an incredibly uncomfortable stretch of silence. He started to turn, but Dianna stepped around Paul.

"Did you need something?"

"I was just going to see if you needed any help setting up." He looked past her to Paul. "Looks like you've got it under control."

"Kara and Annie were going to start getting food out. I'm sure they could use help."

He laughed softly. "Uh, actually, I'm a little scared to be alone with Kara and Annie."

Dianna grinned. "There are more chairs in the garage. You could bring those out."

He nodded and disappeared back into the house, and she

exhaled. Turning, she gnawed at her lip and waited for Paul to face her.

When he did, she offered him a slight smile. "So that was awkward."

"A little."

"I'm sorry."

He put his hands in his pockets. "It's important to you that you and Mitch move past the divorce so you can be a family for your kids."

"Yes, it is."

"So don't apologize. Not to me, not to anyone. You're doing this for your kids, and you're right to do so. I missed out on half of my kids' lives because their mother can't stand the sight of me. I think it's great that you and Mitch are working past this."

"You do?"

"Yes, and it doesn't matter how anyone else feels about Mitch being here. Today is about Sam, and his father should be here."

The weight of her guilt eased as she smiled at him. Stepping forward, she slipped her arms around his neck. "I love you. So much."

"Yeah?"

"Yeah."

"Well, it just so happens that I love you, too."

"Thank you for understanding and for supporting me. I know Kara is irritated that I invited Mitch. I imagine Annie is, too. I'm glad you aren't."

"I will always support you." He leaned down and kissed her. "Now. I'm going to take the high road and go see if your ex-husband needs help with the chairs."

Dianna lifted her brows. "Paul, you don't have to—"

"Hey, I plan on sticking around for a long time. I don't want every family event to be uncomfortable because there is tension between Mitch and me. Might as well settle things now. Besides..." He gripped her hips and pulled her to him. "I should thank him. If he weren't such a bastard, I wouldn't have you."

She giggled as he walked off.

Within an hour, the backyard was filled with family and friends coming to congratulate Sam. Dianna was in the kitchen fighting to remove the plastic top when Mitch walked in behind her. She glanced back, and her heart tripped a bit. She'd caught him watching her more than once throughout the afternoon and was anticipating a lecture from him about showing Paul affection in front of Sam. Just because Mitch had always been frigid didn't mean she had to continue the trend now that he was gone. Paul wasn't too embarrassed to hold her hand or give her a quick kiss in front of other people, and she wasn't too embarrassed to accept. Mitch be damned.

Defenses up, she took a breath and braced herself, more than ready to tell him to go straight to hell.

"Let me," he said.

She stepped aside, giving him plenty of room to pry the top off the container. "Thanks."

He removed the lid with ease. "Need anything else?"

"Can you grab another case of soda from the garage?"

"Yeah," he said but made no move to do so. "I've been waiting for a chance to get you alone."

"Oh?"

He leaned back on the counter. "Up until today, until seeing you with Paul, part of me thought you were punishing me. That you told me you didn't want to get back together and were dating him because you were angry. But seeing you with him... I was right when I said you were in love with him, wasn't I?"

"I didn't realize it at the time, but yes, you were right."

He lowered his gaze for a moment before looking at her again. "Well, he seems to love you, too. While we were getting chairs, he told me he'd like to leave everything that happened in the past so that we can move forward for you and the boys. He said that's important to you."

"It is. I'd like if we can do this type of thing without it being uncomfortable for everyone."

"I'd like that, too. I mean, you were right when you said that we still have to be parents, and eventually we'll be grandparents. I don't want the boys to feel like they always have to split their time. We can still be a family for them."

Relief rolled through her, easing her defensive posture, and her shoulders relaxed. "Well, today is a good start."

He nodded. "I can't remember the last time I saw you look so happy, Di."

"I can't remember the last time I *was* so happy."

"You deserve it. I know I didn't say it enough, but you deserve all the happiness you can get. I'm just sorry I didn't realize sooner that I wasn't giving it to you."

"I wasn't giving it to you either, Mitch. We're both to blame for not seeing how far we'd fallen."

"All the pain I caused you—"

"Is over. It's done. I have to forgive you so I can move on."

"Can you forgive me?"

"You know what? I already have. As soon as I accepted things were over between us, I let it go. I just want to move forward."

He laughed softly. "Karma really is a bitch, huh? I tore you both apart, and now you're together, and I'm the one sitting on the sidelines watching the one I love be happy with someone else."

"I don't want to hurt you."

"I know that. This is my comeuppance. I hurt you. I betrayed you. And now you have someone who will appreciate you. I'm just so sorry that I put us here." He looked down, but not before Dianna saw a shimmer of tears in his eyes.

She put her hand to his cheek and waited for him to look at her. When he did, she let her hand fall. "You know, I started working on this healing process a lot sooner than you did. It takes a while. You'll get there, and you'll find a way to be happy. Happier than we had been for a long time."

"I miss you, Di. I miss the life we had. I was wrong. What we had *was* enough. I want you to know that."

"Thank you. That means a lot."

"I wanted to, um… With you working on commission, you need to be mindful of your finances. I can help with that. If you want. I can help you figure out where to invest so you have a cushion."

"I'd really appreciate that."

"Okay. So, we'll talk about that once you get settled into the new house."

"Sure."

"I'll grab the soda. Anything else?"

"Nope. That's all. Thank you."

She watched him head for the garage door before grabbing the potato salad and heading back outside. She put the container on the food table and sat back down beside Paul.

"What did I miss?" she asked as laughter erupted from Paul, Matt, and Donna.

"Nothing," Annie stated firmly.

"She slipped," Paul said. "Annie slipped."

"What do you mean?"

"Apparently big sister hasn't been spending as much time alone as she's let on."

"That is *not* what I said." Annie narrowed her eyes at Dianna. "You just stay out of this one."

Dianna grinned slowly. "Wait. You mean Marcus?"

Annie looked across the table and tried to glare, but her lips curved up into a smile and she shook her head. "It's your fault." She tossed a potato chip at Paul.

"Me? What did I do?"

"All the flowers and candies you send to the office, all your gushing over Dianna. It made me feel lonely."

Dianna ran her hand over Paul's back. "You are kinda gushy."

"I thought you liked that."

She crinkled her nose as she kissed him lightly. "I *love* that."

sh

Dianna stood in her living room, bare of any traces of her life there. No, that wasn't true. There was still a stain in the carpet, barely noticeable to anyone except those who knew she spilled a glass of wine there while celebrating the start of 2008. And there was the dent in the wall from one of Sam and Jason's wrestling sessions. But the photos were gone. The books and mementos had been packed away. Her furniture had been carried out and the paintings on the walls removed. As she prepared to leave this house for the last time, it felt like she was losing a part of her soul.

Mitch stepped beside her. "You okay?"

She swallowed before looking up at him. "No." She sighed and looked to the big window, the one where they'd set up their Christmas tree for the last twenty years. "How are you?"

"I just spent the last fifteen minutes staring up at the tree where I built their tree house. There are still nails sticking out."

Her lip trembled as memories of her boys climbing up the tree to the few pieces of wood that Mitch had put there. It hadn't been fancy, but they'd used it until she had finally insisted it was too old and dangerous and Mitch took it down. By then they'd pretty much outgrown climbing trees and he didn't build another one.

"I bet the new owners will put one up," she said. "They have two boys, too. Four and eight."

Mitch smiled. "Good ages."

"We spent so much time in this room. So many good times."

She swallowed as Sam and Jason stepped into the doorway. They glanced around the bare living room, looking as sad as Dianna felt. Jason lowered his head and stuffed his hands into his pockets, as he often did when he was feeling emotional. Sam's face was tight. Mitch was quiet, hands in his pockets as well, and as Dianna looked at the three men who had made this house her home, she choked out a sob.

Mitch put his hand on her shoulder. Jason kicked at the floor, and Sam looked away and sniffed.

"Come here, guys." Mitch gestured toward his sons. They crossed the room, and he put one arm around Dianna's shoulders and the other around Jason's. Jason did the same—an arm around Mitch and one around Sam—while Dianna put hers around Sam's and Mitch's waists.

"A lot has happened in this house," Mitch said. "Good and bad. I was sitting in this room when Mom told me she was pregnant with you, Sammy. Jason, you lost your first tooth here. Di, you got drunk and spilled a glass of wine and never let me live down the fact that I didn't clean it up well enough."

She laughed.

"A lot of bad things, too. We were sitting in this room when we found out Dad died. We lost family and friends and pets. But the good times always outweighed the bad. I know Mom and I are divorced now, but we're still family, and we still have each other. And that's what's important."

Jason sniffed and Sam let out a muffled sound, but Dianna let her tears run down her face. She pulled away and hugged Sam and then Jason and then Mitch—for the first time in a very long time, and she was glad it wasn't as awkward as it could have been. A few minutes later, they left, the three of them huddled close together. She watched them, and when they were gone, she looked around the room again. Taking one more deep breath, she put her fingers to her lips and blew a kiss into the room before she headed for the front door for the last time.

She was the last one to arrive at her new house, and by the time she did, it was already filled with furniture and people were unpacking her belongings.

"Don't mind if you don't like where we put things," Donna said as soon as Dianna walked in. "You can always move it, but at least it will be clean, unpacked, and out of the way."

Kara shut a drawer and tossed a box aside. "We put everything as close to how it was at the other house as we could."

Paul and Jason shifted her sofa one way and then the other. She was surrounded by insanity. She'd spent most of the day mourning at the old house, only to walk in to the best kind of crazy at her new house. The place was cramped, loud, and everyone was stepping over each other trying to move around.

Her heart filled with love for all the people there, each and every one of them. Paul, Matt, and Harry, Kara's husband, debating which piece of furniture to bring in next, and Kara, Annie, and Donna debating over where her pans should go. Sam and Jason bickering over who got the loft and who got the second downstairs bedroom. Even Mitch, who was carrying in boxes and setting them out of the way.

The moment was madness. Sheer and utter and perfect madness.

sh

Paul opened his eyes as he drifted from sleep. It took a few seconds to register the strange room he was in. He and Dianna had been exhausted after moving boxes and furniture and unpacking all day. He'd stayed later than anyone, and when they'd finally stopped, it was late and he was tired. She'd pulled him with her into her new bedroom, and without a word of protest he'd curled up into her bed.

They'd fallen asleep within minutes, and now he was wrapped around her, surrounded by her warmth and sweet scent.

The day—hell, the last month—had been so hectic they hadn't had time to breathe. But this morning, in her new house with her sleeping next to him, he inhaled and exhaled slowly as he let life sink in. Everything was perfect. As perfect as he could expect anyway.

He kissed her head before slipping from her bed. As a pot of coffee brewed, he looked out the back door at the yard. It was the beginning of June and the air was still cool in the mornings, but he opened the door and stepped out onto the patio. He smiled as he imagined the life they were going to have there. Thoughts of family barbeques and mornings of sipping coffee at the table filled his mind and brought peace to his heart.

He startled when a cup was slid in front of his face. He didn't know how long he'd been standing there making plans in his mind, but it was long enough that Dianna had poured him a cup of coffee.

He took the mug from her. "Thank you."

Her arm went around his waist, and she rested her head to his chest. "What are you thinking?"

"I'm happy," he whispered so he didn't jinx it.

"Yeah?"

"Yeah."

"Me, too."

He kissed her head. "I was watching you sleep last night."

"Was I drooling?"

He chuckled. "No. You looked beautiful and so peaceful. It made me think about something."

"Hmm. You do a lot of thinking while I sleep."

"I get my best thinking done when you aren't nervously rambling about something."

She gasped, causing him to laugh.

"I'm teasing." He hugged her gently and pressed his lips to her head. "You know how I like to jump into things feet first?"

"I do."

"Well, I was thinking that I really love this house, and I'm probably going to be spending an awful lot of time here."

She grinned. "That's my plan."

He was quiet for a moment, debating just how much he wanted to say in that moment. "I know this is your house, but I feel like this is our place, our fresh start, *our* new beginning. So, I was thinking, maybe we should sell my house and look into investing the money in a vacation home. Something lakefront. Then we could have a romantic getaway whenever we wanted. I think we've earned some time away, don't you?"

A smile slowly spread across her face. "Yes, I think we have."

"We would each have our own house, but we'd only visit mine for long weekends and vacations."

Excitement lit her eyes. "I like your new house already."

"We should get something with at least three bedrooms, don't you think? Something big enough for our friends and family to visit us sometimes." He laughed softly as the idea warmed his soul. "Can you imagine us and all our boys crammed into a three-bedroom house on the beach? It would be insanity."

Her smile widened. "It would be the best kind of insanity. And I would love it. I would love it so much."

"But first things first," he said.

She lifted her brows.

"We can't even consider living together until I've heard you play that piano."

Dianna laughed but then took his hand and led him into her new living room. She set her coffee on the end table and sat at the piano. He squeezed onto the bench next to her. She looked over at him and smiled.

And then she played for him.

CONTINUE STONEHILL SERIES WITH
THE FORGOTTEN PATH

STONEHILL BOOK THREE

AVAILABLE NOW.

Keep reading for an excerpt.

STONEHILL SERIES BOOK THREE

THE FORGOTTEN PATH

"*So*," Mallory drawled as she stepped next to her mother, "still mad I invited Marcus to my graduation?"

Annie cocked a brow, silently telling her daughter where she could go. She'd called before she'd even gotten home the night before, wanting to know why Mallory had invited Marcus—or more to the point, why she hadn't told Annie about it. Mallory had casually said about the same thing Marcus had—besides her uncles, he was the closest thing she had to a father figure. He was the only man who had been steady in her life. Marcus Callison had worked for Annie for five years, and from day one he and Mallory had hit it off.

Sure, Annie had developed a good friendship with Marcus, and because of that he and Mallory had spent some time together, but a father figure? That seemed over the top.

"I ask," Mallory said lightly, "because you've barely stopped staring at him all afternoon. I wasn't sure if that was because you were offended by his presence or because he looks so darned cute in that suit."

Before she actually could tell Mallory to go to hell, her daughter laughed and walked off.

"Why do I get the impression she just bested you?" a deep timbre asked from behind Annie.

She closed her eyes as Marcus's voice rolled through her. Heat burned up from low in her gut and settled in her face. She had no doubt that her cheeks were deep red, but short of being rude, she had no choice other than to face Marcus.

Mallory was right. He did look darned cute in his suit. The business casual dress code at the office meant they didn't dress to the nines often. Marcus's red tie and perfectly tailored black pants and coat had caught her attention. His salt-and-pepper hair was combed to the side, a perfect cut and style for his strong jawline and blue eyes.

Damn it. She was staring at him.

She tilted her head, pursed her lips, and narrowed her eyes in an attempt to get him to back off...and to get her mind off how good he looked.

Instead of slinking away, he laughed with the same enjoyment at her expense that Mallory just had. "Damn. Whatever she said must have been good. I'm sorry I missed it."

Annie started to brush past him, but he put his hand to her upper arm and stopped her retreat. She jolted a bit—not from his touch, but from the way she felt the skin-on-skin contact all the way down to her toes. What the hell?

"Come on," he pleaded, "you have to share."

"She thinks she's smart."

"Well, she did just graduate college *cum laude*."

Annie's irritation faded and pride filled her. She couldn't help but smile. "Yes, she did."

He toasted her. "Congratulations."

"Oh, I can't take credit for that. She did it all on her own."

"She has your brains."

Annie shook her head. "I didn't even go to college, remember?"

His face softened, and he looked at her in that way that made her breath catch. "You would have if you hadn't been saddled with other obligations."

She didn't open up about her past often, but something about Marcus made her drop her defenses. She hadn't intended to, but she'd opened her mouth and spewed her emotional mess all over him. Who cared if she hadn't gone to college? Who cared if she'd had a rough go of it? Paul and Matt were grown and successful, and Mallory had just taken one more step along that path. But that hadn't stopped Annie from dwelling on things she shouldn't, and leave it to Marcus to dig in and make her feel all those...*feelings*.

She shrugged just the slightest bit. "It all worked out."

"Yes, it did," he said with quiet sincerity. "You've done amazingly well for yourself. And your family."

He tightened his fingers on her arm and ran this thumb over her bicep, as if to reassure her. Instead, it set her on edge, and she felt as if she were about to fall over. Damn it. What kind of voodoo was this man doing to her?

Annie's focus shifted to her daughter in an attempt to undo whatever it was that had made breathing nearly impossible. Her smile returned as Mallory squealed and hugged a friend who had just arrived at the party.

"I can't believe it," he said. "Our girl just graduated college."

Annie's attention snapped back to him. "*Our* girl?"

"I know I didn't have any part in raising her, but we've gotten close over the years. Like I said last night, she's the closest thing I'll ever have to a daughter."

Marcus smiled and, as tended to happen these days, her chest tightened and warmth spread through her. His gaze softened as he stared at her, and she sighed.

She actually freaking *sighed*.

His deep blue eyes were like an abyss that she fell into every time he looked at her like that. *Like that* meant with a tenderness he shouldn't have for his boss.

She didn't need anyone to tell her how inappropriate that was. She'd told herself a thousand times. That didn't stop her breath from catching whenever he touched her or their gazes stayed locked a few seconds too long—like they were right now.

Thankfully, an obnoxious round of laughter pulled her from his gaze. Annie glanced at her brothers. "I was, um, on my way to the kitchen. Excuse me."

She forced her feet to move her away from the tall drink of temptation in her living room. Alone in the kitchen, she shook her head and leaned against the island, where the extra chips and platters were piled. She closed her eyes and let her head drop forward like it weighed a hundred pounds.

"Get a grip," she muttered.

The door behind her opened, and she nearly laughed. She didn't have to turn around to know Marcus had followed her.

"Need help with anything?" he asked.

"No. I was just…"

Her words faded when he moved to her side, much too close, and she couldn't stop herself from looking at his clean-shaven face. She was tempted to run her fingers along his oval jaw to see if his skin was as soft as it looked. Her self-control was fading quickly. She'd used up damn near all her resolve during the graduation ceremony. He'd sat next to her, his arm resting along the back of her chair during most of the commencement. For nearly two hours, she'd sat stiffly, her hands clutched as she silently reminded herself not to lean into him. Not to put her hand on his knee. Not to smile up at him. Not to rest her head on his shoulder. And to breathe—just breathe, damn it.

Now he was that close again, and the urge to lean into him was nearly irresistible.

His smile faded, easing the deep lines around his eyes, and she did that stupid sighing thing *again*. Clearing her throat —*again*—she focused on the food.

"Chips," she said. "I was…getting more chips."

"Let me help—"

"No," she snapped, but then tried to cover by softly laughing. "Go back out there. Enjoy the party."

"This is Mallory's party. *You* go enjoy it. You deserve to celebrate along with her."

Her cheeks heated. That affectionate tone struck a chord it shouldn't, and her heart picked up its pace.

She lifted the chips. "I'll just take these out and then enjoy the party."

"Wait," he said.

The warmth of his hand gently grabbing her elbow spread like wildfire through her. She'd barely gotten control after his touch a minutes ago. Was he *trying* to kill her?

"Annie, I think we should—"

The swinging door to the kitchen opened. Annie's sister-in-law, Donna, stopped in her tracks and looked from Marcus to Annie, then back to Marcus.

Donna smirked a bit. "Sorry. I, um, I thought this was the bathroom."

Annie drew her eyebrows together. "That's the best you can do?"

Donna giggled and disappeared, probably to run off and tell their family all about whatever she thought she'd just walked in on.

Marcus laughed quietly as the door swung closed. "Uh-oh. The gossip wheels are turning."

Annie heaved a sigh—this time with frustration instead of whatever it was that made her exhale heavily when Marcus looked at her. "If Donna weren't gossiping, I'd be worried something was wrong with her."

"I'm sorry."

She wasn't. Okay, maybe a little, but only because she didn't want to deal with her family questioning her about her relationship with Marcus. They were convinced that just because they were all happily paired off, she should be, too. Worse, none of them saw anything wrong with Annie dating Marcus. Not that they *were* dating. Not even close. They were just co-workers—friends—who shared dinner a few nights a week. And lunch a few times a week. And attended events such as Mallory's graduation together.

And who shared a habit of staring awkwardly at each other.

She really wished her siblings hadn't started dropping not-so-subtle hints about Marcus liking her. She hadn't been this bumbling mess around him until the first time Donna and Dianna teased her about how Marcus looked at her. Hell, she hadn't even noticed he looked at her at all. Then Paul and Matt got on board, telling her what a great guy Marcus was. As if she needed them to tell her that. She knew Marcus was great. That was why she had hired him.

That, and his stupid smile that made her stomach twist around itself.

She lowered her face and closed her eyes for a moment.

"Better refill the chip bowl," he said.

Annie lifted her face. "Hmm?"

He jerked his head toward the living room. "The chip bowl."

She looked at the bag in her hand for a second. "Oh. Right. Chip bowl." A strange half-laugh sound left her. "Right." She left Marcus and pushed the door open as she went back to the party. She ignored Donna and Dianna and frowned at the chip bowl that didn't need to be filled.

ALSO BY MARCI BOLDEN

STONEHILL SERIES:

The Road Leads Back

Friends Without Benefits

The Forgotten Path

Jessica's Wish

This Old Cafe

Forever Yours (coming soon)

OTHER TITLES:

Unforgettable You (coming soon)

A Life Without Water (coming soon)

ABOUT THE AUTHOR

As a teen, Marci Bolden skipped over young adult books and jumped right into reading romance novels. She never left.

Marci lives in the Midwest with her husband, kiddos, and numerous rescue pets. If she had an ounce of willpower, Marci would embrace healthy living, but until cupcakes and wine are no longer available at the local market, she will appease her guilt by reading self-help books and promising to join a gym "soon."

Visit her here:
www.marcibolden.com

 facebook.com/MarciBoldenAuthor

 twitter.com/BoldenMarci

 instagram.com/marciboldenauthor

CPSIA information can be obtained
at www.ICGtesting.com
Printed in the USA
BVHW081127040321
601713BV00001B/66

9 781950 348039